PRAISE FOR

MW00331231

"Chiavaroli delights with this homage to Louisa May Alcott's *Little Women*, featuring a time-slip narrative of two women connected across centuries."

PUBLISHERS WEEKLY on *The Orchard House*

"As a longtime fan of Louisa May Alcott's *Little Women*, I was eager to read *The Orchard House*.... [It] invited me in, served me tea, and held me enthralled with its compelling tale."

LORI BENTON, Christy Award-winning author of *The King's Mercy*

"Captivating from the first page....Steeped in timeless truths and served with skill, *The Tea Chest* is sure to be savored by all who read it."

JOCELYN GREEN, Christy Award-winning author of *Between Two Shores*

"*The Hidden Side* is a beautiful tale that captures the timeless struggles of the human heart."

JULIE CANTRELL, *New York Times* Bestselling author of *Perennials*

"First novelist Chiavaroli's historical tapestry will provide a satisfying summer read for fans of Kristy Cambron and Lisa Wingate."

LIBRARY JOURNAL on *Freedom's Ring*

"*The Edge of Mercy* is most definitely one for the keeper shelf. "

LINDSAY HARREL, author of *The Secrets of Paper and Ink*

i

WHERE HOPE BEGINS

HEIDI CHIAVAROLI

With Hope,

Heidi Chiavaroli

Hope Creek Publishers

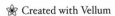 Created with Vellum

ALSO BY HEIDI CHIAVAROLI

The Orchard House

The Tea Chest

The Hidden Side

Freedom's Ring

The Edge of Mercy

The Orchard House Bed and Breakfast Series

Where Grace Appears

Where Hope Begins

Where Love Grows

Where Memories Await (November, 2021)

To Journi,
and all of the young people who are bravely walking a road that includes
type one diabetes

appy endings, and even happy beginnings for that matter, were a lot of work.

I craned my neck to look past where my sister Josie walked up the makeshift aisle of the Camden Library amphitheater. She wore a simple ivory lace dress. Her face glowed as she locked eyes with her soon-to-be husband at the end of the aisle.

If only *my* husband would make an appearance, this day would be perfect.

Where was Josh? He wouldn't miss Josie and Tripp's wedding day. He wouldn't.

I bit my lip, moved my focus to my younger sister. Josie was stunning. While she hadn't lost all of her baby weight from giving birth to Amos last month, the extra pounds suited her. The sun shone through the near naked branches above, splashing off her shoulders and giving warmth to those in attendance. And Tripp stood at the end of the aisle all handsome and tall, his gaze caught up in his bride's.

The wedding was a simple affair, just Josie and Tripp before Pastor Greg, surrounded by no more than fifty guests. No wedding party. No fancy reception hall. Nothing but a whole lot of family and love and the beautiful blessing of an unseasonably warm day.

I twisted in my seat again, willing my own handsome blessing to appear. This not-showing-up thing was becoming a frustrating habit.

Six-year-old Isaac squirmed beside me. "Mommy, I have to go to the bathroom."

I pressed my lips together. Ceremonies were tough for little boys to sit through, but this one had just started. I leaned down to whisper. "Are you sure? You went before we got here."

"I *really* have to go. Bad."

I glanced at Isaac's twin, Davey, who seemed preoccupied with a loose thread on the cuff of his button-down shirt. "Okay." I leaned around the boys to get my sister Lizzie's attention. "Would you watch Davey?" I whispered.

"Sure thing." Lizzie bounced Josie's seven-week-old son, Amos, gently in her arms.

My brother Bronson tapped me on the back from where he sat behind us. "You want me to take him, Maggie?"

I looked longingly at Josie walking up the aisle with unusual grace, but shook my head. Isaac was my son. Inconvenient bathroom duty was part of being a good mom. "It's okay, I got it. Thanks."

When Josie reached the birch arbor at the end of the aisle, I led Isaac toward the library. Familiar faces smiled at us as we passed up the aisle, and I returned the gesture to family and friends in attendance—most who genuinely cared for the bride and the groom, a few who came for the sake of gossip.

I scrambled over the manicured grass in my high heels, trying to keep up with Isaac and praying he wouldn't have an accident in his new dress pants. He'd always had a good bladder, but lately he had to go at every turn. Two nights ago, he'd even wet the bed—something he'd never done.

We slid into the library bathroom and I tapped my foot as Isaac released his bladder for an interminably long time. When he finished, I helped him tuck in his shirt. Hmm, strange. "Are these Davey's pants? They're a bit loose on you." I checked the size on the tag.

He yawned. "I don't think so."

He was right. They weren't. "Feel better?"

"I'm real thirsty."

"I have a water bottle in my bag." If I'd learned one thing in the fifteen months I'd been a mother, it was to be prepared. Snacks and wipes and extra clothes and drinks always came in handy. I clutched Isaac's hand and pulled him back outside.

He'd fought a small stomach bug the entire week—a little nausea and dizziness. A bit cranky and emotional. Maybe I should have taken up my mother-in-law on her offer to watch the boys today. But I'd wanted the twins here. They *belonged* here. While I wasn't certain Josh's mother always thought so, I wanted to cement that truth in the boys' heads—when I'd married Josh, I'd married the twins as well. I couldn't love a child from my own womb any more than I loved these boys.

There truly was nothing better than motherhood.

Even if I *did* feel like a single mother much of the time.

A wolf whistle sounded from behind, and I turned. Josh jogged toward us, his muscular torso filling out the suit he'd worn on our wedding day. My heart softened at his bright smile and off-kilter tie.

He pulled me in for a kiss, enveloping me in the scent of after-shave and Gucci cologne. For a moment, I sank into it.

"You look gorgeous, Mags." He ruffled Isaac's dirty blond hair, a mirror image of his own. "Hey, little man. How'd the soccer game go this morning?"

I didn't let Isaac respond. Instead, I pulled them both toward the ceremony. "Where have you been?" I walked toward the courtyard amphitheater, the sight of my husband all handsome and charming dissuading me from any anger.

"I was working on something important and lost track of time. I'm so sorry, honey. I know Josie's wedding's important to you. It's important to me, too."

I opened my mouth to tell him if it was that important, he would have been here. *On time.* But before the words poured forth, I snapped my lips together, a habit I'd adopted from Mom in our growing up years.

Josh was here now. That's what mattered. When it came down to it, there was nothing in all the world I wanted more than this life, this husband, these two sons.

Josh grasped for my hand as we walked. "You think we can take a quick ride together later? Maybe Lizzie or Amie could keep an eye on the kids?"

"Um...yeah, sure," I said as I led us back to our seats.

The wedding was simple and sweet, but not without tears, especially when the bride and groom said their vows.

"This is boring," Davey whispered, oblivious that his voice was loud enough to reach the ears of all in attendance. A few giggles rippled through the group, and Josh ducked down to whisper to him.

I watched the pair, my heart overflowing. If only Josh had been at the field today to see Davey score twice. He would have been so proud. Video clips sent via text weren't the same.

I leaned back in my seat, taking in the lacy train of Josie's gown beside an arrangement of sunflowers and eucalyptus. She'd had quite a year, but this happy ending couldn't have been more perfect.

My gaze landed back on the flowers beside the arbor. They needed to be transported to the reception barn after the cere-mony. I needed to remind Amie to get some good pictures of the Orchard House barn after we set up the flowers—we'd trans-formed it into a rustic yet elegant reception area. I would put the pictures on the B&B website after creating a new page advertising our availability to host events.

I blinked to attention as the crowd clapped. I stood to join them when Tripp kissed Josie.

Celebratory bubbles floated through the air, and the triumphant wedding march sounded out over the harbor. Josh squeezed my hand and winked at me. I wondered if he'd been reminiscing about our special day just over a year ago—the happiest day of my life. No doubt he hadn't been ruminating about his to-do list.

As soon as the newlyweds cleared the aisle, I scooted forward to grab up floral arrangements alongside my sister Lizzie. Planning the wedding on short notice meant we all pitched in. Having the reception at the bed and breakfast meant our family was in charge of both the decorating and the transporting of said decorations.

Josh untied a bold arrangement of sunflowers from a chair in the front, where my mother had sat during the ceremony. "So, ride later, right? I want to show you something."

"Yeah, sounds good." I shook my head. "Josh, I'm sorry, I can't think of anything else right now until this is all broken down. Fifty guests may be small, but we have tons of food to put out once we get back. Can we talk about a ride later?"

He clapped his hands together, as if ready to coach his high school track team. "Yeah, absolutely. Whatever you need, Mags."

I blew out a breath. "Thank you."

"Mommy, I'm thirsty."

I peered from behind a large arrangement of sunflowers, eucalyptus, and baby's breath. "You finished all the water I gave you already, honey?"

He nodded.

Josh held a hand up. "I got this." He scooped Isaac up and threw him over his shoulder. "I have a cooler full of water in the back of my truck. Let's go, kiddo."

Josh took the boys in his truck and I took the flowers in the SUV, making the short ride across the street to the Orchard House barn. I pressed the gas pedal of my Honda Pilot harder up the slight incline of the driveway of the bed and breakfast.

Merry mums embraced the walkway and porch. Hanging planters of begonias and trailing vines clung to their last weeks of life on the large winding veranda of the old Victorian. Historic turrets and gables spoke of bygone times that guests found irresistible. And off to the side and the back of the property, for acres and acres, an apple orchard rolled up a gradual hill, the trees' branches naked of leaves for their upcoming winter hibernation.

I still couldn't believe we'd pulled off the renovation and the start of a successful business in such a short amount of time. Not only had Aunt Pris allowed Mom and my siblings to move into the old home, but she'd let us turn it into a thriving inn. A bed and breakfast on the coast of Maine—Mom's long-held dream come true.

I parked beside the patio of the bookshop. Through the large windows, I glimpsed strings of lights alongside bookshelves. Josie still got googly-eyed over the bookshop Tripp had built. I couldn't blame her. Together, they'd breathed life into the place.

Josh and my siblings helped me set up the flowers on the tables in the barn while Josie and Tripp took pictures at Curtis Island Overlook.

Aunt Pris's old orchard barn had been transformed into a fairytale. Light draped along the rafters. We'd decorated the tables with Lizzie's flowers alongside centerpieces of books—both classic literature and classic comics in honor of the bride and groom's preferences.

It was rustic and romantic and done on a whim. Perfect for my untraditional sister.

The sun hovered over the horizon, giving way to the arrival of the bride and groom, toasting and eating, dancing and celebrating. I wiped away tears when Mom danced the mother-son dance with Tripp. Ed Colton, Tripp's grandfather, danced the father-daughter dance with Josie. At one point, Tripp took a spin on the floor with baby Amos. That's how it was in this group. Family, even if not by blood. Family, filling in the places where others had fallen away.

The twins fell asleep on a row of empty chairs pushed against one side of the wall and Josh pulled me close for *Wonderful Tonight*. I relaxed into the warmth of my husband's arms, the tune and words of the music swirling within me. The scent of spiced candles filled the room, strings of lights on the rafters above created romance and elegance. Even Aunt Pris and Ed Colton took a turn around the dance floor.

"I've missed you." I snuggled into Josh's embrace, the ambience of the night and the glass of champagne we'd toasted with wrapping me in contentment.

"I've missed you, too." Josh pressed his lips to the top of my head and pulled me against the length of his body. A stir of desire started deep in my belly. It had been too long. We'd missed one another for weeks on end. I'd been so involved in the opening of the B&B and keeping up with the boys' schedules that on the rare occasions Josh was home, I collapsed into bed at night, sleep trumping any desire for intimacy.

What happened to the heat and passion of those first weeks of marriage? We hadn't been able to keep our hands off each other, had savored those long sweet moments when the boys slept and nothing but the entire night lay between us. When had that stopped? We'd only been married fifteen months. How had the passion cooled so quickly?

"You want to get out of here?" Josh whispered in my ear, a slight tease in his tone.

I giggled. "I'm not leaving my sister's reception to go have sex."

"Not sex. Though I'm not saying I'm against that." He wiggled his eyebrows. "Seriously, Mags, I have something I want you to see. Something I've been working on for months. Just a quick drive."

"Is it something you built with Tripp, because I could see it tomorrow." Hopefully, I didn't sound tired of his building obsession. I wanted to be supportive, but Josh's summer job working for Colton Contractors had turned into a permanent part-time job. With school back in session, not only did he work as a history teacher and cross-country coach, he ran himself ragged on the evenings and weekends with Colton Contractors.

Maybe if he wasn't always working so much, I'd stand a chance at getting pregnant.

I cleared my throat. The truth was, as much as having a baby excited me, it terrified me all the more.

"It's not something for Colton. This...it's for us. Please?"

My lips inched upward at the adorable plea on his puppy dog face. "Okay." I looked around the room, spotted Amie dancing in the arms of August Colton, Tripp's younger brother. "Let me ask Amie if she'll keep an eye on the boys. We'll be back before the sendoff, right?"

"Absolutely."

I pinched Amie lightly on the arm. She lifted her blonde head off August's shoulder. "Hey, can you watch the boys for a half hour? Josh wants to show me something."

August grinned wickedly. "I'll bet he does."

Josh punched him in the arm. The two worked with one another enough at Colton Contractors to be comfortable. Clearly. "Get your mind out of the gutter, kid. The *surprise*."

August sobered up. "Oh, the surprise..." He winked at Amie. "I'll help you watch the little guys if you want."

Amie shrugged. "Sure. They don't look like they're making much mischief right now."

I looked at the sweet faces of our boys puckered in sleep, pressed to the cloth-covered seats of chairs we'd borrowed from the church hall. "I think you'll be safe."

"Great." Josh grabbed my hand and led me out into the chill of the night towards his truck, the lights of the bed and breakfast playing with shadows on patches of green lawn and herb gardens.

I rubbed off the cold climbing my arms. "So August knows about this, too?"

Josh held the door of his truck open for me and offered his hand to help me up. "I've been working on the idea since summer. August and I worked together almost every day back then, so I did mention it a time or two." He went around to the other side and started the truck.

"Since summer? Now I'm curious."

I didn't miss his grin, and it stirred something like hope within me. Maybe all the magic hadn't been lost after all. Maybe I needed to be more understanding. Patient. Maybe here, now, could be a new beginning for us.

⚜

JOSH GRIPPED THE STEERING WHEEL TIGHT WITH HIS LEFT hand, the slight sweat of his other palm dampening the skin of his wife's small fingers. He'd waited so long for this moment, had dreamed about it for months now. He hoped she liked it. He hoped she loved it.

He drove into town, past the closed shops and restaurants where the harbor shone beneath moonlight on his left. Once on Bay View Street, the denseness of the buildings gave way to sparse, tasteful inns and homes nestled within woods. He turned right on Limerock then left on Chestnut, his heart pounding out a steady beat against his chest. Maybe he should have waited until tomorrow morning. Better to see it all in the light. Then again, with the amount of work needing to be done, dark might be better.

"Where are we going?" Uneasiness coated Maggie's voice.

"You'll see." He drove for a couple of minutes before turning right onto a gravel driveway. Divots caused the truck to lurch back and forth. He pointed his headlights toward his destination.

There. The moonlight helped as well. He imagined the rundown farmhouse restored to its former glory, the boys running around in the massive yard, he and Maggie sitting on the front porch to capture the amazing sunsets.

Josh turned to his wife, who squinted past the headlights.

"I—what is it?"

"It's a house. Our house, actually."

He studied the hazy outline of her profile in the dim light, willed her to say something.

She cleared her throat. "Our—but we have a house."

"Not *our* house. Not really." He'd purchased the small house they now lived in with his previous wife. A wife who chose a fierce addiction over him and their two sons. A wife who, by the time she'd given birth to the twins, had been a small fraction of the woman he'd married.

He thanked God every day for sending him his second chance at family and life by sending him Maggie. By saving his boys in the accident. He refused to mess any of it up again.

"Our house now is small. The yard's no bigger than a pocket handkerchief. You deserve better, Maggie. So much better."

She slid her hand up his arm. "Josh, I have everything I could possibly want. I don't need a bigger house or yard. I only need you."

"I want to do this for you, Maggie. For us. For the boys. Let me, please?"

She shook her head, her earrings glittering off the moonlight. "I don't see how it can work financially. Despite the obvious work it needs, I'm cringing imagining the asking price."

"I made an offer. They accepted it today."

Her hand froze on his arm. "An offer? What did you offer them—a plate of cookies? Because that's about all we have that's of any value. Even if we sold the house, we don't have enough equity in it to make a dent."

He gritted his teeth. She didn't understand. She didn't believe in his ability to provide for her and the boys. "I've been working like a madman saving, Mags. For this. I—I thought you'd be happy."

"Honey, I'm happy with the house we have now. I'm happy when you come home in time for supper. I'm happy with being a family with you and the boys. I don't need to live anywhere else, not now. Isn't that okay?"

On the surface, he supposed it was, but just beneath the surface, just an inch deeper, it wasn't. It wasn't at all.

He dragged in a deep breath. "When we got married, I told myself it didn't matter that we were in the same house as...you know."

"You and Trisha."

"Yeah. Me and Trisha." He rubbed the back of his neck. This topic of conversation was foreign soil. Maybe it shouldn't be. "I mean, it's only wood and sheetrock, right? Some plaster and paint. It shouldn't matter. But I've been struggling with it. Like a part of me is tied down there. I want to break free of it." He lifted a hand, let it fall on the steering wheel. "I know I sound crazy right now."

A sigh from the passenger seat. "No. No, not at all, Josh."

She leaned her head back on the seat, and he studied her petite profile, her pert little nose and striking lashes and lips. Her hair fell in dark waves just past her shoulders, and he stopped himself from reaching out to touch the softness of it. His wife was beautiful. Not just on the outside, but on the inside. He wondered what a child of theirs would look like. God only knew she deserved a child from her own womb. But in some ways, he felt the house he'd shared with Trisha—the house where she'd shot up numerous times and hid her hard liquor inside the back of the toilet, the house where they'd argued and loved and cried and hated—had kept that happiness from them.

More than anything, he wanted to build a future with his own hands. Provide a place of safety and shelter for his boys, for Maggie, for whatever children God had in mind for them. One where he could come home and truly rest.

He bit his lip hard, looked out the side window into the dark. Maybe he was losing it. Where was his faith? His assurance in God to help him through his struggles with a strength not of this world?

Yet, even as he wrestled with such questions, a nagging prick of something bitter stirred within. He tried to brush it aside. Did God expect him to forgive his long dead wife for all she'd put them through?

Maggie inhaled a quivering breath, the only sound other than the idle of the truck engine. "Okay, then."

"Okay?"

"We buy the house."

"Wait, really?"

"Yes. If it means that much to you, then I'm behind it. But honey, please tell me we can change how things are. You're never home. I feel like a single mother most of the time. I miss you. The boys miss you. I'm not sure a new house with no husband in it is the answer we're looking for."

He dove across the seat to kiss her. "Things will change, I promise, Mags. I already saved a good amount. Once we sell our house, we'll be in good shape. I'll give my notice to Tripp. And with the B&B booming, in no time you'll be getting a raise for all the great work you're doing."

"Mom did say we're booked into spring."

He tapped her chin with his knuckles. "See? Everything's going to work out. And we can redo the floor plan if you want. You can pick out kitchen cabinets and countertop, plumbing fixtures and all that jazz."

"And we're going to see you every night for supper?"

"Every night."

Her smile warmed his insides. He didn't deserve this woman— her love and understanding for not only him, but his sons. *Their* sons.

He leaned closer, caught the subtle scent of the lavender shampoo she used. "I love you, Maggie Acker. With every fiber of my being. Every day I'm more and more amazed by you."

"I love you." She reached for him and he drew closer, dropped his mouth to hers, gave her bottom lip a tease of a kiss. Her arms came up to the back of his neck and their bodies sank deep and slow into one another, needing, aching.

"We have to get back to the kids," she murmured between kisses.

"I'm not thinking this will take too long."

She laughed, kissing him harder and deeper, running her hands over his chest and neck, driving him to distraction.

From the dashboard of the truck, his phone lit up. For a second, he ignored it.

"Josh..."

From her handbag, Maggie's phone let out a loud ring. A coincidence?

He grabbed up his phone at the same time Maggie answered hers.

"Hello?"

It was Tripp. He almost didn't recognize the panic in his friend's voice. "Josh, you got to get back here. Now, man. Isaac— we were having trouble waking him up. His color looked off. Then he started throwing up, a lot. He said he couldn't breathe. Hannah's calling 911."

Suddenly, nothing else mattered. Not the land they sat on, not the house he intended to build them. He had to get back to his son.

He didn't remember hanging up the phone, was only

conscious of Maggie panicked in the front seat, talking on speakerphone to Amie who assured her Isaac was in fact breathing, though his heart was racing and he was struggling to talk.

Josh pushed the gas pedal harder, peeling out of the gravel driveway. He squeezed his wife's arm, wanting to comfort. "It's going to be okay, Maggie. He's going to be okay."

He hoped God didn't prove him a liar.

2

I never knew fear—real fear—until I saw Isaac being loaded
into an ambulance on a stretcher. The sight of him, gray and
sunken, caused something deep within me to shatter. I
pushed open the door of Josh's truck before it came to a stop and
barreled toward the flashing lights while grabbing up my dress to
keep from tripping. My knees wobbled, my throat threatened to
clamp closed.

"Is he okay? I'm his mother." I placed my hand on Isaac's arm,
his breaths labored and shallow. Beside me, I sensed Josh's presence. "What's wrong with him?"

An EMT spoke as he pierced the back of Isaac's hand with a
needle. "We're starting an IV line now. He's in good hands. Are
you his parents?"

"We are," Josh said.

"Do one of you want to ride to the hospital with us?"

"I will." Josh had one foot on the back of the ambulance,
ready to hop up. "Why don't you ride with your mom or one of
your sisters, Mags?"

I nodded dumbly, though I didn't want to be anywhere but in
that ambulance.

Josh kissed my head. "I'll see you there." He cupped my face in his hands. "He's going to be okay."

Then he was gone, following the stretcher. The ambulance doors shut.

Warm hands ushered me away. "Come on, honey. I'll drive. It's going to be all right."

I allowed Mom to lead me to her sedan and open the passenger door for me.

"He looked horrible. I should have been here."

"They're going to take good care of him." This from Amie.

I sank into the passenger's seat, closed my eyes. "God, take care of him." I sat up at my sudden thought. "Where's Davey?"

"Aunt Pris and Lizzie are setting him up in the house."

"Is he okay? Was he scared?"

"He was shaken up a bit, but Lizzie will keep him busy. She mentioned making a prayer box for the bed and breakfast and putting Isaac's name in first thing."

I ran a hand over my eyes. "I thought it was a small stomach bug. Maybe he's dehydrated. After they get some fluids into him he'll be fine, right?"

"They're going to take good care of him, honey," Mom said.

The car ride dragged on forever. Once in the emergency room, I left Mom and Amie in the waiting room. A nurse led me behind heavy double doors and then behind a privacy curtain where Isaac lay, still so sickly and pale. Josh sat beside him, holding his hand, head bent over our son.

I laid one hand on Josh's arm, the other on Isaac's. "How's he doing?"

Josh wrapped his arm around my waist, brought me close. "They asked me to help him pee in a cup. His blood sugar's crazy high."

I stared at my husband, the words not quite registering. I shook my head. "High?"

"One of the doctors mentioned diabetes."

I lowered myself to the foot of Isaac's bed. "What? How is that possible? He's a healthy kid." We didn't load him up with soda and candy. He even liked his vegetables.

Josh shook his head. "I'm out of my scope here. The doctor said he'd be back in a bit."

We sat in silence. Isaac complained he was thirsty and Josh fed him ice chips. A nurse came in and changed the television to the Disney channel for Isaac, but he fell asleep in the first five minutes of *Mulan*.

Finally, the doctor came in and shook our hands. His olive skin and friendly face put me at ease. "I'm Doctor Green. How's the little guy feeling?"

"He's thirsty."

"Unfortunately, we need to keep his liquids to a minimum right now and strictly monitor the foods he's given. We'll do additional tests in the morning, but from the urine and blood tests we performed, it seems your son has diabetes."

Josh lifted a hand off his thigh. "Doc, we don't let him go crazy on sugar." He glanced at me, and with guilt I remembered a conversation we'd had early in our marriage. I'd been making cookies nearly every day for the boys to have after school, letting them have some after supper, too. I'd been trying so hard to be a good mother. To earn their way into their broken hearts with love and yes, cookies.

I remembered Josh kissing the top of my head after I pulled yet another batch out of the oven. "You sure are spoiling us, honey, but you know, we don't need desserts every night. My mom never fed the boys all those sweets, and they've never complained. They love you without the cookies, Mags."

I'd been careful to back off the sweets after that. I hadn't meant to do anything that would endanger them. And while I knew I'd never measure up to Josh's mom, I had a responsibility to do my best by these precious boys.

I turned my attention back to Josh, who spoke to the doctor.

"I guess he might have had too much wedding cake today, but not more than any other kid. And he gets plenty of exercise. He's even lost some weight recently."

The doctor nodded. "That's a sign of type 1 diabetes, I'm afraid." He took out a clipboard. "I'm going to ask you some questions, okay?"

"Of course," we said in unison.

"Do either you or your parents have a history of diabetes?"

"No, not..." I started to answer before I realized my mistake.

"No," Josh said.

The doctor looked at me, and I shook my head. "I'm not his birth mother," I whispered. I'd never felt so helpless. These are questions I should be able to answer. What if Josh hadn't been with us? What if he was an hour away at a track meet?

Doctor Green turned to Josh.

"His birth mother had gestational diabetes."

I stared at my husband. It wasn't a big deal. Not really. But it would have been helpful to know.

The doctor continued directing his questions to Josh, and I blinked fast. This wasn't about me. What mattered was that we got to the bottom of what was wrong with Isaac.

"Has he been urinating often? Excessive thirst? Extreme fatigue?"

Josh's face reddened. "I haven't been around much..."

I cleared my throat. "Yes, all of those. He wet the bed the other night which he's never done. I thought he was fighting a virus. He's been cranky the last few days as well."

"How about blurred vision? Dizziness?"

"Some dizziness. He hasn't mentioned vision problems."

Dr. Green continued down the list, and I answered each of his questions as I stared at Isaac, still deep in sleep.

The doctor made more notes, nodded his head. "We're going to start him on some insulin through the IV. We'll do more extensive blood tests in the morning. Unfortunately, he'll be here for a few more days. We'll set him up with a pediatric endocrinologist who will work with you on how to handle his blood sugar. There's a diabetes educator here tomorrow who will stop by and talk to you both. For now, we'll take good care of him."

Josh swallowed, his Adam's apple bobbing up and down his smooth throat. "Is he—can he get better?"

A look of pity from the doctor foreshadowed an answer we didn't want to hear. "Type 1 diabetes doesn't have a cure. That doesn't mean he can't learn to live with it and live a completely normal, long life. It just means there's a lot of learning ahead. Many children and parents walk this road and walk it well. I'd be lying if I said it'd be easy. It won't be. But it is doable."

I listened as he told us that Isaac had gone into DKA, or diabetic ketoacidosis. I tried to concentrate on the words *pancreas* and *ketones* and *blood acidity* and *high sugar*, but my mind kept stalling on one word. *Diabetes.*

Dr. Green straightened. "But now we know what the problem is and we can help him. We're lucky we caught it now..." His sentence trailed off, morphing into another. "Do you have any more questions? I'd be happy to answer them the best I can."

I worked my tongue around in my mouth. Yes, yes I had questions. A hundred of them. Like why was this happening to our child? Why hadn't I realized the warning signs sooner? A lifetime illness with no hope of a cure—when Isaac had already gone through an immeasurable amount of pain surrounding Trisha's addictions. It was too much to comprehend.

"What can we do? I feel so helpless," Josh said from his seat. His tie had been loosened hours ago. A questionable stain marred the sleeve of his white shirt.

The doctor smiled kindly, looked at both of us. "Isaac's safe now. Try to get some rest for tomorrow, when the hard work begins. Diabetes is a challenge, but it is manageable. If you're up for the task, your son is in good hands."

"We are." I reached for Josh's hand.

"A nurse will be in shortly to adjust his IV. I'll touch base with you both tomorrow. Get some rest if you can."

We thanked him. Once the curtain was back in place, Josh pulled me onto his lap.

I leaned against his solidness, laid my head on his shoulder. "I'm so sorry."

He pushed me back from him, met my gaze with those blue-green eyes, a near mirror to Isaac's. "What on God's green earth do you have to be sorry for?"

I shrugged, my bottom lip trembling. "He wasn't feeling great this week. I should have taken it more seriously. I was busy with the wedding planning and the B&B...I should have at least called the doctor."

He clutched me to him. "I'm the one who's sorry. If I was around more to help you and spend time with the boys, maybe I would have seen it. You've only been a mother for a little over a year, it's not as if—"

"I'm competent." I cut in. Another memory of my early days as a mom sliced deep. A terrible miscommunication. The boys forgotten, Josh's mom left to step in. My husband had every right to doubt my ability as a mother.

"Maggie, no." He reached for my hand and I allowed him to hold it, but couldn't bring myself to clench it back.

"I'm not *trying* to be a bad mother." My breaths came in fast, hiccuping sobs, fatigue and fear and helplessness piling one on top of the other until I thought I'd drop into a heap on the hospital linoleum. But no. I needed to be strong for Isaac. If he woke and saw me hysterical, what help would that be?

Josh reached for me. "Mags, you're a great mother. I couldn't have picked a better mother for my boys. You know that."

"Our boys," I said quietly.

"Our boys," he corrected, folding me in his warm, solid arms as I peered over my shoulder at Isaac.

I thought of the precious moments and milestones of the past year—bedtime stories after baths, the scent of soap fresh on little boy skin, endeavors in the kitchen to make the perfect fudgy brownie, the first time Davey had called me Mommy and the first time Isaac had hugged me. Could Josh see what those boys meant to me, the place I hoped I'd earned in their own sweet hearts?

I sniffed at the sight of Isaac, so very small against the white hospital sheets. I remembered Lizzie in a similar hospital bed nine years earlier, how scared we'd all been at that horrible diagnosis of thyroid cancer, but how we'd gotten past it.

But not all such diagnoses had happy endings. And yet Doctor Green said diabetes was controllable.

A firm resolve stirred deep in my spirit. If Dr. Green's assessment was correct and Isaac did have diabetes, and if it was indeed controllable, then there was only one thing left for me to do—do everything humanly possible to control it.

I may have only been the twins' mother for fifteen months, but that was all the time I'd been given to make mistakes. From here on out, the cost of my mistakes were simply too high to bear.

3

Josh trotted up the steps of his parents' sweeping waterfront home and opened the door without invitation. "It's me! You guys inside?"

He walked into the foyer and past the winding staircase and pristine kitchen. Massive French doors and windows lined the back wall of the living room. He spotted his mom sitting beneath the pergola watching his father push Davey on the tire swing of the massive old oak. Beyond them was lush green grass unfolding to miles of endless sea.

Though he hadn't fully appreciated the beauty of the home during his growing up years, as an adult he saw how blessed he'd been. He'd come here often the past few years, found himself comparing what his father had provided to what he could barely provide to his own family.

And now, Isaac sick. With what appeared to be a lifelong and life-threatening disease. Josh bit the inside of his cheek. If he had to work three jobs, teach summers, and work at Colton Contractors, he'd do everything within his power to get Isaac the best.

He walked across the living room, doubts nagging at him. Had he been wrong to pursue teaching instead of the law career his father had wanted him to follow?

He'd been away from Maggie and the boys so much since July, trying to get ahead on the bills, trying to save for a home for his family. If he'd been around, would things have turned out differently?

He opened the door to the back patio while commanding all such thoughts from his head. They wouldn't do any good. He'd meant what he'd said at the hospital yesterday—he couldn't imagine a better mother for Isaac and Davey than Maggie. If there was any lack, it would be found in him.

His mother spotted him, her round face lighting up. "Hey, honey." She stood to kiss his cheek. "How's Isaac?"

"He's doing better today, thank God." He sat beside his mother, exhaustion fast overtaking. Beside Maggie and Isaac all night and morning, he made sure to be strong, but here, away from it all, his resolve waned. "He could have died, Mom." His voice broke. "If he'd gone into a coma or become unresponsive...I don't know what I would have done."

His mother patted his hand. He steadied himself by studying the new lines and wrinkles upon her skin. When had those appeared? Life did go by fast—only now, after the loss of his first wife and well into his thirties could he see the truth of it.

His mother's bottom lip trembled, and for the first time he realized how hard this must be on her, too. For all intents and purposes, she'd been the closest thing the boys had to a mother before Maggie. After Trisha died, his mom had quit her job as a nurse to take care of the boys while Josh worked. Yesterday, she'd wanted to come to the hospital, but Maggie insisted more family would only exhaust them all. She'd been right, of course, but Josh hadn't missed the hurt in his mother's voice over the phone.

"He's going to be okay, honey."

Josh drew in a deep breath, nodded. "We've been learning a lot about diabetes. Maggie's been researching on her phone all night.

The diabetes educator is coming in this afternoon, but I thought it'd be good for both boys to have a visit."

"He's missed his brother." His mother's gaze settled on Davey, who Hannah had brought over earlier that morning. "It's been nice having him, though. I've missed them both so much. And with everything happening now...well honey, it's important you know we're here. We want to help."

His mother's words addressed something he hadn't given much thought to the past year—their lack of time with his parents. They lived only a town apart—there really wasn't an excuse for how little they'd gotten together.

His mom, especially, deserved more time with the boys. Sometimes, in the weeks and months after Trisha died, wracked with grief and anger, Josh wouldn't even bother picking the boys up after track practice let out. He would simply let them stay with his parents to avoid the hassle of transporting two toddlers back and forth for a single night only to return them to his parents' in the morning. He'd allowed so much to fall on his mother during that time—not only their care but their infant confusion over not having Trisha anymore. True, it didn't manifest itself in words, young as they were, but rather tears and sometimes temper tantrums. Now, neither of the boys remembered much about Trisha.

He was never sure if that was a blessing or a curse.

After he and Maggie married, he'd been glad to ease his parents of the burden of the boys' care, but his mother's words brought to light a different problem. At the beginning of the marriage, his mom had offered to continue watching the boys a few days a week, but he and Maggie thought it better to keep them with Maggie on their days off from preschool. They had a family to grow, and it seemed time was the best way to do it.

Only he hadn't taken into account how that must have hurt his parents, particularly his mom.

He sniffed hard, weighing his words carefully. "Thanks, Mom.

I know you miss the boys. Tell you what, once Maggie and I get some of this stuff figured out and Isaac settled, we'll reevaluate our schedules. It's important you guys see the boys more."

Her eyes shone. "Your father and I would love that. Maybe you could all come for dinner more often, too? Do you think Maggie would appreciate a night off?"

He blew out a breath. "I'm sure she would." And he *had* promised his wife he'd be home for supper every night. "Thanks, Mom."

"Daddy!" Davey barreled across the lawn toward Josh and threw himself in his arms.

Josh held him tight for a long moment, found something inside of him threatening to come loose at the feel of his son in his arms. "Hey, buddy. You having fun?"

"The best! Grampy hung a tire swing, see?" He pointed to the old oak, where his father now walked toward them. Davey suddenly sobered. "Is Isaac okay?"

"He's feeling a lot better and wants to see you. He's getting sick of watching TV in the hospital and could use a brother."

"Sick of TV? No way."

They laughed. Josh's father joined them, clasping Josh in a brief, firm hug. He had more silver in his hair, but it suited him in a Richard Gere type of way. "How's it going, son?"

He gave his dad a short rundown on the latest on Isaac before turning back to Davey. "You ready, kid?"

Davey tugged on his grandmother's hand. "Can I bring Isaac one of the Hot Wheels upstairs, Grammy? Please?"

She smiled. "Of course. Why don't we go up together?" She looked at Josh's rumpled wedding attire from the night before. "If you want to take a shower, honey, or a quick nap, I can wake you in a little. Don't run yourself ragged."

"Thanks, Mom. I won't. After I bring Davey back, I might take you up on that offer. I'm going to stay with Isaac tonight so Maggie can go home and get some rest."

Her gaze lingered on him again, as if she would insist he rest. "Okay."

The two departed, leaving Josh alone with his dad. He sat down, elbows on his thighs. "Maggie thought Isaac'd been fighting a small virus. That's it. We never would have guessed something like this."

"Trisha had diabetes when she was pregnant, didn't she?"

"Yeah." Josh raked a hand through his hair. "That wasn't on my radar. And it certainly wasn't on Maggie's. Honestly, I'm not even sure there's a definite connection. They're talking type 1 diabetes with Isaac."

They sat silent for a moment. "You know, son, we all only want the best for Isaac. If you want a second opinion, maybe get him over to Barbara Bush Children's Hospital. We don't want money to be an object. We'll help however we can."

Something in Josh recoiled. He tried to be grateful, but all he could summon was resentment—not at his father so much, but at himself. "We have insurance, Dad. We're not going to let bills stop us from doing what's best for him."

"How's your insurance? How much do they cover for things like this? And what about his testing supplies and all that?"

Josh stood, panic finding a way into the crevices of his spirit. He didn't have answers to those questions. He'd never had to pay attention to such things. Well check-ups had been the extent of the boys' needs so far.

"I'll figure it out, Dad."

"Don't take offense, son. I just want you to know you're not alone. You have us and, of course, you have Maggie."

A tic started in his eye, and he nodded, hard. He needed some sleep. So did Maggie. But maybe his dad was right. Maybe they shouldn't simply go with whatever pediatric endocrinologist Dr. Green recommended. They could certainly search around, make sure they started this journey on the right track.

"Thank you," he finally said. "I know I'm not alone." But he still hated being vulnerable like this. His own fault, really. If he'd followed in his father's footsteps and gone into the law profession, at least some of his financial problems wouldn't exist. He dragged in a long breath, looked at the neat rows of cobbles at his feet. "I want to get this thing under control as quick as possible, you know? Dad, if anything ever happened to either of the boys, I don't know what I'd do."

He'd known intimately the experience of death, and though Trisha had brought about her own demise in a very tangible way, it still didn't take the sting out of it. If he had done more, said more, *been* more, would it have changed the course of things? Yet, she'd almost killed their boys. He was still angry at her. Did the call to forgive include those who were no longer present in this life?

His father clasped his shoulder. "Being a parent is fun stuff, isn't it?" They shared a laugh.

"It's almost how it feels to run a race—moments of pain with glimpses of victory."

"Maybe the races *you* ran. Mine were all pain."

Josh grinned. The back door slid open and his mother and Davey stepped out. Davey clutched a deep red miniature sport's car in his hand. "You ready, kiddo?"

"Yeah. I think this will make Isaac feel a whole lot better."

He shared bittersweet smiles with his parents. If only making his son well was as easy as handing him a bright red Hot Wheels car.

❧ 4 ❧

Exhaustion pulled at the corners of my brain like a sumo-wrestler tug-of-war match. I tried to ignore the pounding in my head to focus on the information on my phone.

I'd slept little the night before, instead, surfing the web for information on type 1 diabetes. Counting carbs, checking blood sugar, giving insulin. I'd joined a Facebook group of parents with children who suffered the same fate as Isaac, read posts upon posts which made me feel less alone, but also entirely over-whelmed.

Isaac's pancreas had stopped working. His little, six-year-old pancreas had betrayed him. He would have to be on insulin for the rest of his life. Checking blood sugars and counting carbs would need to become a regular part of his everyday life. In a very real sense, Josh and I would have to be Isaac's pancreas. If we didn't regulate, he could be back in the hospital, could end up in a diabetic coma, or could even die.

My bottom lip trembled, and I ducked into the hall so I wouldn't wake Isaac with any unbidden sobs. I needed to be strong. My mother and Amie had left after dropping off Isaac's stuffed puppy and for me, a change of clothes. An intense longing for Josh surged through my veins, and I couldn't wait to put my arms around both him and Davey.

I leaned my forehead against the cool wall, inhaling deep breaths, longing for fresh air. The scents of astringents and latex and Lysol and medicines, along with looking down at my phone for hours, began to make me sick.

I breathed deep, tried to imagine cool, clean air. At the tired creases of my mind, though, came a memory of fresh air and sunshine. Of taking deep breaths for an altogether different reason during a camping trip we'd taken with the boys at the beginning of the summer. *Tent* camping in the White Mountains.

I'd originally thought the idea a novel one. What better way to bond with the boys than something as endearing as camping? I could prove myself the cool boy-mom. Josh would love my ability to fry up eggs over an open campfire, to hike the mountains with all the gusto of my sister Lizzie, and to snuggle up beneath the open stars.

Yeah, right.

It rained the first night, and Josh strung a tarp above our tent. With nothing but a dinky, battery-operated lantern, I'd navigated dark, forest-laden paths to the bathhouse but slipped in some mud. I'd washed the dirt off as best I could in the public shower before realizing I didn't have a towel.

Public showers. Gross.

I'd been cold and wet and miserable and tired by the next morning. And dirty. I hated dirty. Hated finding granules of sand and dirt in my sleeping bag. Hated stepping out of the shower to balance on flip-flops while drying my feet to put on socks. I longed for my own bed, my own shower, my own home. When I burnt the eggs the following morning, I'd abruptly left the campsite and found an out-of-the-way nook with a beautiful mountain view overlooking the Saco River. I'd dragged in deep, cleansing breaths to ground myself and face the fact that, no, I was not a super cool boy-mom.

Now, I pressed my forehead against the hospital wall and imagined that beautiful mountain view. I'd thought I had it tough, then. Huh. How pitiful and spoiled I'd been. How naïve toward the real troubles of the world. Sick children, helpless mothers. *Real* suffering. So much more than a few days of dirt and inconvenience. A lifelong diagnosis, a lifelong journey. What would I give to go back to that moment, to throw myself fully into it and soak up every ounce of blessing it contained? Life without diabetes.

"Maggie?"

I looked up at the baritone voice and blinked away my vision of the White Mountains. A white lab coat replaced it.

I pushed myself away from the wall. "Hey, Nate."

Nathan Mabbott, my friend Susie's husband. We'd practically grown up together. I could still remember him chasing me around at recess when we were Davey and Isaac's age.

"You okay there, Mags? Susie told me about Isaac. I was in the hospital, so I thought I'd stop by and check on things."

Gratitude bubbled inside of me. "Thanks, Nate. You caught me at a bad time. I apologize. I'm...overwhelmed."

"You have every right to be." He smiled, lighting up a dimple on his right cheek.

While we'd dated a few times in high school, it had never gotten serious. Despite how well he'd done for himself being the youngest family physician in the area with a growing clientele, I'd never seen much depth behind those tantalizing green eyes. In truth, I'd always considered him a bore. Now though, I appreciated his consideration.

"It's a lot to take in all at once, Mags. But you're not alone. I can introduce you to some parents I know who have gone through the same thing. It might help to talk things out."

Maybe I'd been wrong about his depth. "Thanks. I'd appreciate that." As much as I might benefit from a Facebook group, there was nothing like real, person-to-person relationships.

"Is it okay if I check in on him?"

"Sure, absolutely. Truth is, I'm scared to death to have to go home with him, to be without people who know what they're doing." Tears burned the corners of my eyes. I forced them away, prepared myself to see my son.

Nate placed a friendly arm around me. "Mags, you are one of the smartest people I know. If anyone can handle blood sugar levels, it's you."

"Then why didn't I see the warning signs?"

"A lot of parents mistake those signs for the flu. Now you know. And knowledge is power."

I smiled. "Did you have to pay for that cheeziness with your medical degree, or did they add it on for free?"

He laughed, gestured toward the room. "That was all free."

"Mommy!"

I turned to see Davey running down the hall with enough energy to knock out ten bowling pins. The sight of him caused more emotion to climb my throat. More emotion I pushed aside.

I knelt down, burrowed my nose in his neck. "Hey, sweetie." I squeezed him tight, inhaling the scent of little boy—outside air and salty sweat. If only I could stay in this moment long enough to believe the last day was nothing more than a simple nightmare.

All too soon, he wriggled out of my arms and into Isaac's room.

Josh cleared his throat, held out his hand to Nate. "I'm Josh, Maggie's husband."

"Honey, this is Susie's husband, Nate. We kept meaning to have a double date this summer but it never materialized."

"Nice to meet you," Nate said. "We were just about to check on Isaac."

"Are you an endocrinologist?"

Nate glanced at Maggie. "No, only a friend trying to help."

"Well, I'm not sure we need any more opinions right now."

I shook my head at Josh. What was he talking about? "He was in the area, Josh. Isaac hasn't been seen by a doctor all afternoon. I don't see how it will hurt anything."

Josh rubbed a hand down his face. "Yeah, you're right. Of course. Sorry. Too little sleep, too many emotions right now."

"I understand," Nate said. "I'm sure this news is the last thing you would have expected."

We followed Nate into the room but stopped short at the sight of Davey lying next to his brother on his bed, showing him a red Hot Wheels car. Isaac held out his hands and sat up, his color almost rosy.

I shared a smile with Josh, and for the first time since getting that horrible call last night, I felt that maybe, just maybe, all would be okay.

❧

"EXCUSE ME? MRS. ACKER?"

I startled awake from my spot on the chair and swiped at the corner of my mouth.

"Yes, that's me." I unwound myself to a sitting position, my shoulder stiffer than the Play-Doh creations the boys sometimes left out to bake in the sun.

The woman before me appeared to be in her early fifties with beautiful brown skin and a plethora of bracelets on her left hand. "I'm Gabrielle Jackson, one of the area's diabetes specialists. I'm here to work with you and Isaac today."

I turned to Isaac, sleeping but so much healthier than when we'd brought him in the night before. "Yes, thank you. My husband was supposed to be back by now. He went to drop off our other son at his mom's." I glanced at my phone. Three o'clock. Josh definitely should have been back by now.

I pressed buttons on my phone, gave Gabrielle a sheepish

look. "I'm sorry, let me call him to see where he is." I clamped the phone to my ear, listened to the echoing rings.

Nothing.

I let the phone drop in my lap. "He's not answering."

Gabrielle sat in the seat beside me. "Perhaps we could get started together now, and we can fill him in later."

I nodded dumbly, my bottom lip trembling. I willed my husband to walk through the door, but it remained empty. I was alone. What if I missed something? Failed to remember a vital piece of information? This was enormous, monumental. I wasn't superwoman. That horrible time when I'd forgotten to pick up the boys from school the first month of our marriage proved it.

Dreaded tears came to my eyes as Gabrielle dug out alcohol prep pads and needles and insulin bottles.

"You'll be administering Humalog every time Isaac has a meal. At night, you'll give Levemir, which is a long-lasting insulin. These insulins will help do the job his pancreas isn't doing. I'm going to show you how to count carbs so you'll know how much to give him."

The needles and insulin bottles blurred before my eyes. My breaths came fast and hard. "I need my husband. I can't do this alone."

Gabrielle's warm brown hand reached out to me. "Mrs. Acker. Maggie—can I call you that?"

I dared to look up into her hazel-flecked gaze, nodded.

"You are *not* alone. And you *can* do this."

I sniffed, not fully convinced.

"Diabetes is a disease there's no getting away from. But it is manageable. Do you know some parents come into the ER with their children to get a cancer diagnosis? Or that some parents come in here to walk out without their children? Honey, that's not you and Isaac. You're going to walk out of here with your son armed with a whole boatful of education and tools to live with this thing. Isaac will go on to live a relatively normal life. We have the technology, and every day it's increasing, making diabetes more and more manageable."

She sat back, pinned me with a stern, but compassionate look. "You're his mom. This thing is never going away and handling it correctly is a matter of life and death. Now, you can decide whether you're going to wallow in self-pity and self-doubt, or whether you're going to choose to step it up and get a hold of this for the sake of your son."

You're his mom.

Matter of life and death.

Step it up.

I blinked. She was right. Hadn't I decided to do everything possible to manage this? To be the heroine for the sake of my son? There were only two choices here—waffle and whimper and abandon Isaac, or be strong and determined and do what needed to be done for the sake of my son.

And I wasn't alone.

God, help me, I prayed. Perhaps He already had by sending me this woman. I needed to hear what she said. I needed this tough love.

I blinked, sniffed back the last of my emotion, and straightened my spine. "You're right. You're absolutely right. I choose to step it up. Tell me what I have to do."

5

Three Weeks Later

"T he Orchard House Bed & Breakfast. How can I help you?" I cradled the phone between my ear and shoulder and opened my laptop. Soft music played in the background of the downstairs living quarters of Orchard House, something that always calmed me while I sat working at my desk. I appreciated the soothing tones more than ever on this, my first day back since Isaac's diagnosis.

"Yes, dear. We're looking to see if you have any rooms available New Year's Eve?"

I opened up the online software I used for bookings. "Let me see...I think we have one room left. Yes, yes we do. The Hawthorne Room. Are you looking to book just one night?"

"We'd love to make it two."

"Absolutely. And just to let you know, we're offering guests their third night half off. Is that something you'd be interested in?"

"Oh my, that is quite a deal. Can I book the two nights now and talk it over with my husband?"

"Of course." I typed in the woman's name, address, and deposit information. When I hung up, I opened a new tab and pulled up the bed and breakfast website. I still hadn't uploaded the pictures of the barn from Josie and Tripp's wedding.

I glanced at my cell phone, then back to the computer. Isaac had been in school for two days now, a huge step on our journey. While I'd wanted to keep him home another week and had even brought up the possibility of homeschooling for the rest of the year, Josh thought it best for Isaac if we eased back into our normal routines.

In the end, I'd agreed.

The last few weeks had been a blur of sleep deprivation, carb counting, blood-testing, and insulin shots. Nightly checks every two hours, sometimes more, where I snuck into Isaac's bedroom with my headlamp set on low to prick his finger for the umpteenth time that day. Praying he didn't wake up. Coaxing him to take a few sips of juice from the straw I stuck in his mouth. Knowing I couldn't fall asleep. I mustn't fall asleep.

I'd sit in the most uncomfortable chair I could find to test his blood every fifteen minutes in order to coax a particularly stubborn low. To go back to bed and fall asleep was the difference between life and death. How many times had I woken frantic in the morning, so scared I had missed a dose or missed my alarm, so terrified that I'd find Isaac in his bed, never to wake again?

And that was only nights.

Just thinking about counting carbs made me want to crawl up to one of the unused guest rooms and take a nap. A banana unfinished, two French fries too many. No breaks, ever. Ever. It all served to throw me for a loop when it came to dosing out his insulin. So much to remember to get his insulin doses perfect.

Isaac hated the shots, and one particularly trying day last week I'd had to pin him down to give him yet another. I'd held back my own tears as I did it. He needed this. And he needed me to be strong. For him. All for him. I couldn't think of a better motivation.

I'd probably burned a hole in Gabrielle's phone with all the calls and questions, but she was nothing short of patient, instilling confidence in me that I could do this. I could take care of my son.

And now the test of school. I so wanted to keep Isaac home, yet I didn't want to stifle him, either. He missed going to school, had waited on the bottom steps of the bed and breakfast each day for the bus to drop Davey off, had pumped his brother for information about what he'd missed.

Josh was adamant that Isaac own the disease and not let it define him. He sounded a lot like Gabrielle in that regard. If we stopped our son from participating in normal activities while his twin brother continued on with life, it would only cement the idea in Isaac's mind that he was abnormal because of his sickness. It could create resentment, something we miraculously had not observed in our son—even as he balked at the many shots and blood draws each day, even as we emptied our food cabinets of any excessively sugary snacks, even as both Josh and I struggled with the feeling ourselves.

We'd visited with the school nurse last week to go over Isaac's DMMP, Diabetes Medical Management Plan, and to coordinate a time to discuss his 504 Plan, which would help all of us—including the school nurse, principal, Isaac's teachers, and the head cook of the cafeteria—get on the same page in the handling of Isaac's care. Yesterday, I'd spoken to the school nurse, Stacia, on and off throughout the day. She had texted me Isaac's blood sugar reading and insulin dosage amount.

But today, nothing. Isaac should be at lunch now. What if he forgot to go down to the nurse to have his sugar checked? Little boys got distracted, after all. And nurses were only human. What if Stacia had been busy with another sick student?

I scooped up my phone and tapped out a message, pushed send, and drummed my fingers on the desk, waiting.

Footsteps sounded above and a young couple celebrating their one-year wedding anniversary, Brad and Mackenzie, appeared in full hiking attire.

I smiled, attempting to push my worries aside. "Are you enjoying your stay?"

"Oh, so much!" Mackenzie beamed, her smile lighting up the room. "That breakfast was amazing. We won't have to eat until dinner."

I glanced at my phone. "Did you have the French toast or the burrito?"

"Brad did the burrito and I had the French toast. But we shared. Both so good. I don't know what your mom used to season that burrito, but I think it came straight from heaven."

Lizzie pushed through the door of the butler's pantry carrying several bags into the foyer. Her straight brown hair was tied back in a ponytail. She spotted our guests, her eyes lighting up at their packs, her normally timid smile bright. "Hey, you guys hiking today?"

Brad nodded. "We were thinking Mount Megunticook."

Lizzie nodded. "Great choice. Pretty view, no matter what time of year."

"Do you guys hike a lot?" Mackenzie asked.

I tore my gaze from my phone to converse with our guests. "Not me, but Lizzie's out there almost every day."

"We would be, too, if we lived here," Mackenzie said. "We'd better get started if we want to finish before dark."

"Have fun. And make sure to grab a slice of cake when you come back." Lizzie placed her bags at the foot of the stairs.

"Oh, you don't have to remind us about the afternoon dessert." Brad winked at his wife. "It's one of the highlights of being here."

We said goodbye and left the house, Lizzie looking after the couple with something akin to longing in her eyes.

"You okay, Liz?"

My sister blinked, erasing the look I'd seen. "Yeah, great. They seem happy."

I stared after the younger couple. "They do." I wondered if Lizzie longed for what Brad and Mackenzie appeared to have. So much more than a hiking partner, but a life partner. My shy sister had always seemed content to be in the garden or in the woods or in her music. She told me once that dating terrified her. But I wondered if she was beginning to think differently.

"Well, if you ever need to talk..." I blew out a long breath, and tapped into the text I'd sent, making sure I hadn't missed a response.

"Thanks, Mags, but I'm okay." Lizzie put her hands on her hips, looked at the pile of bags at her feet. "Mom's given me the go-ahead to start Christmas decorating, so I'm on it."

"Before Thanksgiving?"

"Right? She's breaking her own rules this year. I think it will make the B&B festive and pretty, though."

"I suppose." I tapped my fingers some more and looked at my phone again, inwardly demanding a text to come through. Nothing.

And Christmas decorating? I hadn't yet thought of Thanksgiving, which was only a week away. With all the goodies and treats around, the normally happy family holiday would prove an extra challenge. I glanced at my phone, then tapped the first number under recent calls, holding the phone to my ear and giving an apologetic look to my sister. "Sorry, Lizzie, I have to make a quick call."

"Oh, no problem. I'll give you some privacy. I can visit Josie at the bookshop."

"No need to leave. I'm checking on Isaac."

The automated school machine picked up, and I dialed the nurse's extension, memorized in preparation for Isaac's return to school. I pressed the phone to my ear and paced in front of the desk, concentrating on the swirling patterns of the area rug, the classical music playing over the speakers. It all failed to calm. The ringing echoed back hollow in my ears.

Then finally, "Camden-Rockport Elementary, this is the nurse."

"Stacia, it's Maggie Acker. Just wondering if Isaac remembered to come down before lunch?"

"Maggie, hey. He did. I meant to text you, but right after he left the office, I had a small emergency in the third-grade class."

I exhaled, my shoulders and chest loosening. "Oh good. Thank you. His levels were okay?"

"They weren't terrible. We injected half a unit and he was good to go. I made a note in his log book. He has gym this afternoon, so I'll check him before he gets on the bus."

"Thank you so much, Stacia. I'm sorry to be a pain, but it's torture over here."

"You're not a pain. You're a concerned mother. Never hesitate to call. I mean that. But if it makes you feel any better, we have other students with type one. We've got this down pat. We'll be checking on Isaac when we check our other diabetic kiddos. In fact, Isaac will probably meet them since they'll be in our office together."

For what must have been the hundredth time that month, emotion welled in my throat. Fortunately, I'd gotten used to pushing it back. I was almost proud of the fact that I hadn't yet let loose in a show of tears. "Thank you."

"I'll text you the results of his next reading this afternoon. I promise."

I thanked her and hung up the phone.

"He okay?" Lizzie straightened from picking up a long strand of artificial greens entwined with lights.

"He's okay." I placed my phone on the desk. "I guess it's going to take some getting used to being apart and depending on other people to monitor him."

"Of course it is. I remember a girl I used to go to school with

—Daisy was her name. She had an insulin pump. I guess it monitored her all the time and gave her insulin when she needed it. Do you think that might be an option for Isaac eventually?"

I tightened my mouth. "I sure hope so. At least after we've gotten a hold of handling it manually and after we do more research on the glucose monitors and pumps. I'm not sure our insurance will cover it, though. The costs are crazy as it is." Hours on the phone with the insurance company had peeled back the reality of the massive cost of this disease.

We'd already had to push our insurance about seeing an out-of-network doctor based out of the children's hospital. In the end, Isaac's primary care doctor had been able to refer us to the doctor of our choice, and the insurance had covered it, but that still didn't take care of our high deductible, not to mention the hefty prescription copays for Isaac's meter, lancets, and testing strips.

Lizzie flung an arm around me. "The important thing is that he's okay. You guys are doing great handling everything."

"I'm glad it looks that way from a distance." I laughed to lighten the mood.

"We missed you at Bible study yesterday. Nora does a great job, but it's nothing like how you teach, sis. You have a gift."

I smiled. "I love doing it." If only I could put all those lessons on faith I'd taught into better practice. "I'll try to be back after Thanksgiving. I'm pulled in a few different directions right now, you know? The PTO cookie fundraisers are coming in tomorrow so those need to be delivered. And I'm still behind on updating the website for Orchard House." Not to mention doctor's appointments and Christmas decorating and Elf on the Shelf plans. If I didn't need sleep—even the pitiful one or two hour snatches I did get—maybe I'd have enough time to accomplish everything that needed to be done.

"No pressure, okay? And let me know if I can be of any help with the fundraiser. They cut my hours at the school again, so I have nothing but time."

"Oh no, Lizzie. Please tell me they didn't do that to you." I studied my younger sister. In the prime of life, Lizzie should be going out with friends, enjoying her music. But she'd been working hard for her students, and for the business, too, without complaint.

She plugged one of the strands of lights into the wall. It lit up, signaling the start to the season of lights. "It's okay. I enjoy working around here. And it frees up some time for my own music."

"Written any good songs lately?"

Her face reddened. "One...but I'm not ready to share it yet."

"Well, when you are, you know your biggest fan will be waiting."

"Thanks, Mags." Her phone dinged, signaling a text. "Oops. I told Josie I'd watch the bookshop for a bit so she could feed Amos and put him down for a nap. Will you be around a little longer?"

I nodded. "Until the boys get off the bus."

"Okay, I'll see you later, then."

I turned back to my computer, updating photographs on the website, sending emails to guests to confirm upcoming bookings. I kept an eye on my phone, half expecting Stacia to call with some sort of catastrophe, but no such call came.

Determined to focus on the B&B instead of nurturing my fears, I soon became absorbed in the website. I blinked to attention when the side door beside the desk opened. I straightened, put on a smile for whoever entered.

When Josh rounded the corner, his broad shoulders filling up the foyer, my heart lifted.

"Isn't this a sweet surprise?" I walked around the desk and circled my arms around his neck. When was the last time he showed up in the middle of the day on a whim like this? Not since the first couple months of our marriage, at least.

He wrapped his arms around me and kissed me softly on the

lips. I inhaled the scent of him, all woodsy spice. "I just came from the closing and thought I might be able to steal you away for an hour or so. You up for a late lunch?"

My mind snagged on one word. "C-closing?"

The smile stayed on his face, but confusion clouded his eyes. "Yeah. You know, the closing on our new home. I mentioned it to you last night?"

I pulled away from him, tried to shake my head clear. "Was I awake?" I vaguely remembered him talking to me before bed after I'd given Isaac his long-acting dose of insulin and gotten the boys settled, but I'd been exhausted. In truth, I'd been half listening, making a mental note of the extra things I needed to pack Isaac for school the next day.

"Yes." The word was drawn out, his tone defensive around the edges.

I bristled. "Am I going crazy? Seriously, Josh. We haven't talked about the new house since everything happened with Isaac. And you closed on it...without me?"

"I knew you had a lot on your mind. I didn't want to give you more to think about. I thought if I took care of it all, it would make things easier."

I pressed my fingers to my temples. "So, let me get this straight. You closed on a property without discussing it with me—"

"Whoa, whoa. We discussed it. You told me to go ahead on it."

"Before! Before everything happened. Don't you think what we've gone through the last few weeks would warrant a deeper discussion on this? Don't you think our son facing a life-threatening disease should come before another house? I mean, two mortgages? How are we going to manage all this, especially now with all the medical bills?"

He reached a hand out. "We've got to keep it down, Maggie. The guests. Why don't we go for a car ride?"

I wanted to yell at him that I'd get as good and loud as I wanted. What right had he to close on a house without me, then come into my family's bed and breakfast and tell me to be quiet?

I inhaled a deep breath, releasing it slowly. "I can't talk to you right now, okay? I'm too mad. Go, please."

He looked at me dumbly. "Mags, come on. We'll talk this out. I made sure your name was on the deed."

This wasn't about my ownership on some property. It was about my husband's lack of consideration in making decisions that involved both of us. "Not now, Josh. Please." My voice stood firm. "The boys will be off the bus soon. I have to be ready for them."

He raked a hand through his hair. "Fine, then. Whatever you want. I'll meet you at home later."

Then he was gone.

I released a frustrated groan and sank over the desk, laying my head in my arms. How could this be happening? How could we be on such entirely different pages on such vitally important topics?

Light humming sounded from around the corner, and I raised my head in time to see my mother carrying a platter of pumpkin cheesecake covered in a glass dish. "You okay, honey?" She placed the cake on the counter beneath the stairs, above a small refrigerator we kept well stocked with water for our guests.

"Not even a little."

She arranged plates and forks beside the platter. "I think we need some cake, then."

I laughed, but it came out pitiful. "I don't know if cake will fix this mess."

"But it might give us something to do while we talk. Come on, honey. Coffee and cake in the kitchen. Aunt Pris is watching *The Price is Right* in her room, so we have at least another forty-five minutes to ourselves. The guests can ring the bell."

"Okay." I closed my laptop and followed my mother into the butler's pantry that connected the guests' living area to the private living quarters of the home. In the back of the Victorian, afternoon light splashed onto cream-colored kitchen cabinets, the scent of baked goods permeated the room.

"This is a special cake I made for the family." She cut into the moist cheesecake, placed two small slices on plates. We settled at the breakfast nook near the bay window that overlooked the naked herb gardens and cozy bookshop. Through the large windows of the shop, I glimpsed Lizzie dusting bookshelves.

I sipped my coffee, allowing it to warm my insides. I looked at the pumpkin cheesecake, covered in dabs of whipped cream. "You know I feel guilty whenever I eat something like this now."

"Because Isaac shouldn't eat it."

I looked at my mother, her kind green eyes below blond bangs. She'd stopped coloring her hair two years ago, but the slight grays appeared like tasteful highlights. "Yes."

Mom pushed the plate toward me. "Try it."

I lifted a bite to my mouth, savoring the sweet creaminess. Hints of pumpkin danced with bursts of cinnamon on my tongue. "It's delicious, Mom."

Mom leaned toward me, as if sharing a secret. "It's sugar-free. You think Isaac will like it for Thanksgiving?"

I placed my fork on my plate, familiar emotion climbing my throat. "Mom...thank you."

"It's my pleasure. I think we could all stand a little less sugar in our desserts."

"It tastes amazing." I took another bite, allowing the simple goodness to soothe the worries of the day. I glanced out the windows. A man from Dad's mission raked leaves into neat piles. Without warning, a terrible ache for my father lodged itself in my ribcage. "I miss Dad." Only I didn't just miss him. In some ways, I was grieving a simpler time. A time when I wasn't responsible for so much. A time when all of life appeared bright and beautiful and saturated with promise.

Mom put her hand on my arm. "I do too, honey. Do you want to talk?"

I pressed my lips together. I didn't like sharing arguments between me and Josh with my family, especially Mom. I never wanted to diminish him in my mother's eyes. Yet, the need to talk to someone trumped my desire to make my husband look good. Susie probably would have been a better choice, really. But my best friend had been busy of late preparing for her newborn. I sighed. "Josh and I had a miscommunication, I guess. A big one. I wasn't listening when he thought I was, but it's only because I have so much on my mind."

Mom sipped her own coffee. "You've all been through a lot. Remember when Lizzie was sick? I forgot to pick your father up from the airport. He was officiating a wedding that night, too."

I smiled. "I don't remember that. Was he mad?"

"Mad as hornets. And I was mad that he expected me to remember everything on his personal calendar with a child fighting cancer."

I vaguely remembered, though in truth I remembered my own experience during that time a whole lot more. With Lizzie's illness, I'd felt how rich we'd all been in the truest and most beautiful things—the things more precious than any luxuries money could buy. We were rich in love, protection, peace, health, faith. The real blessings of life.

I'd grown up a lot during that time, but perhaps my parents had, too.

"How'd you work through it?"

"We talked. A lot. I was so involved with Lizzie and all you kids that I realized I'd neglected our relationship. He was worried, too, but he dealt with it in a different way, burying himself in his books and in his work. Once we pulled apart the root of our problems and tried to understand one another, we could start putting things back together. It took a lot of talking, a lot of praying. And it was never perfect. But after that, we always tried to understand one another before jumping to conclusions. Almost always, anyway."

I pushed my plate aside and rubbed my eyes. "I'm not sure I'll ever understand my husband."

"Marriage is work, that's for sure. It's not easy, but it's worth it. Love is worth it, Maggie. Josh loves you and those boys so much."

"I know," I whispered. "I wish we could understand each other better. Seems we think differently on every aspect of life, lately. I wanted to keep an endocrinologist closer to home—the one the hospital recommended. Nate Mabbott said he was great. But Josh insists on traveling ninety minutes away to the children's hospital. I wanted to keep Isaac home longer, let him adjust to everything. Josh wants him back to normal activities as soon as possible." I inhaled deep, my breaths coming out on a tremble. "I want to stay in our little home. Josh wants to overextend our finances by buying a fixer-upper to build us a new house. We can't seem to agree on anything, lately."

Mom inched out a hand and squeezed my arm. "You *will* get through this. Both of you. Together."

I tried to gather strength from Mom's surety. She'd always been the sunshine-maker in our family, and I wanted to emulate that so very badly. If only making sunshine came easier these days.

"Thanks, Mom. For everything. I should get back to work. And the boys will be off the bus soon. Can't start the work of fixing things by hiding away here all the time."

I thought of Brad and Mackenzie, and the glow of their new marriage, a little younger than me and Josh's but still so fresh and apparent.

For the first time, I wondered if we had rushed into things for the sake of the boys. We'd had a whirlwind courtship—one of the reasons Josie had taken my marriage so hard. One of the reasons Aunt Pris hadn't supported the union at first. They'd both claimed it came out of nowhere. Had it? Had Josh wanted a mother so badly for Davey and Isaac that he hadn't stopped to see me for who I truly was? Had I been so enraptured by the handsome teacher I'd had a secret crush on during high school—a man ten years my elder, who seemed the perfect father, the perfect family man—that I hadn't stopped to see his own insecurities and faults as well?

And the real question: would we make it through this trying time stronger than before, or would it tear us to shreds?

6

J osh clapped his hands together in front of the twelve teenage boys standing before him. The chill in the air had caused winter hats and gloves to come out and a couple of the boys jumped lightly up-and-down in place to keep warm while awaiting instructions.

"Okay, guys. Last meet tomorrow. No matter what happens, I want each and every one of you to know how proud I am of the work you've done this season. Not one of you slacked, and it shows with your PRs." He sought out one of his freshmen who ran with asthma. His gaze moved to Will, his captain who'd come late into the season because of a broken ankle but had been at every practice, cheering on his teammates. Man, he loved coaching these kids. They wanted to be here. They put in the work every day, they listened to his advice and implemented it with enthusiasm.

And with cross-country, there was always plenty of advice. In a sport that required as much mental resilience as physical, he considered what he taught to have implications for the rest of these boys' lives.

"Now, I know more than anyone that winning isn't everything, but there's something special about ending the season on a high note, isn't there? I'm confident if you get out on the course tomorrow, ready to work, you'll see the results we want. We're looking for an easy two miles and a good stretch today."

Sometimes he ran with the group, but not today. Today he'd told Maggie he'd pick the boys up off the bus. They could all use a little family time. And maybe he could earn his way back into her good graces after their disagreement at the bed and breakfast the day before.

He scolded himself for that thought. He'd done nothing wrong, after all. She'd agreed to the house. He had it all under control—she'd see it in the end when they had their own place. He could hardly wait to dig in and start the work.

Will led the boys toward the paths behind the football field but one kid, a sophomore named Pete, hung back. The boy stood before Josh, shifting from one foot to the other, his eyes downcast above freckled cheeks.

"Hey, Pete. What's up?"

"I—uh, don't think I did so good on that test today."

He'd given a unit test to his sophomores on World War I. "I haven't had a chance to look at it yet, but you normally do okay."

"Yeah, but this time..." The boy shook his head. "Never mind. But maybe I could do some extra credit to try to get my grade up?"

Josh studied the kid. His race on Saturday had been less than stellar. Now an unusual flopped test grade? "Something going on you want to tell me about, Pete?"

He didn't like to pry into the lives of his students. He was a firm believer in keeping a healthy barrier. Not to mention he'd gotten too close for comfort one time when Maggie walked the halls as a student and he was fresh out of college. But some of these kids needed an extra listening ear.

"It's some personal junk." Pete shrugged, and Josh was going to leave it at that. Maybe he could come up with an extra credit project to try to help him out. If the kid didn't want to spill his guts, who could blame him?

But then, without warning, Pete half-turned away from Josh. "My mom left us last weekend. Like, just up and left."

Josh took a step forward. "Aw, man. That sucks, Pete. Big time."

The teenager stared at the ground. "She hasn't even called. I mean, how can you do that to your family, to your kids?"

Josh sighed, rubbed the back of his neck. How many times had he asked that question regarding Trisha?

"Man, I wish I could say something to make you feel better. I know it hurts—believe me, I know." He swallowed. This went against everything he believed in regarding boundaries, but the kid was standing there, heartbroken, his eyes watery as he tried to hold back emotion. Josh didn't think—he dove in.

"You know, my first wife left me and our two sons. Not exactly like your mom did, but she still chose something else over us each and every day. She loved her drugs so much she almost killed our kids in a car accident."

Josh shook out his hand, remembering the piece of glass the doctors had removed from the back of little Davey's hand after the accident. "The pain never goes away, unfortunately, but it does dull over time. I've had to face the fact that I couldn't change my wife. I couldn't make her decisions for her, as much as I wanted to. I couldn't make her love me and my boys how I thought she should. I had to make peace with the fact that it wasn't my fault. Pete." He waited until the kid lifted his head. "Your mom leaving is *not* your fault."

The poor kid shed a silent tear, and Josh lay a heavy grip on his shoulders. "You will get through this. You're strong—I've seen it on the course and I'm confident I'll see it in the days to come. You're not alone. Come and talk to me anytime, okay? And I'll look into some extra credit for you this time around."

The boy sniffed. "Thanks, Coach. I guess I better catch up with the guys."

Josh nodded, and watched the kid turn. At the last second, he cocked his head to the side and looked back in Josh's direction. "Hey, Coach."

"Yeah."

"You think it's horrible that I hate her right now? That I don't think I'll ever be able to forgive her?"

The simple question held so much punch it could have sent Josh reeling five feet backward. Instead, he stood his ground, unwavering and firm, which belied his stance on the topic Pete asked him to address.

He'd have to answer carefully. The last thing he wanted to be was a hypocrite. But then again, maybe claiming a faith in a forgiving God and then not forgiving his dead wife made him one in the first place.

He dragged in a long breath before releasing it good and slow. "Forgiveness can take time. I don't think anyone expects it to happen right away. It isn't easy, but it's the right thing to do. Maybe more of a choice than a feeling. It doesn't mean you forget. It means you let it go."

Pete's mouth flattened into a grim line. He nodded. "Thanks, Coach."

"Anytime." Josh's solemn response echoed after the teenager. He rubbed the back of his neck and turned toward the building.

It means you let it go.

So much for being a hypocrite. Yet, he'd tried to forgive Trisha. He thought he had after he'd married Maggie. He was happy. He didn't wish for things to be different or miss his first wife.

When it came down to it, the thing that tore him up inside wasn't what Trisha had done so much as what Josh hadn't been able to do.

In the end, he hadn't been able to save her.

And now he owned this strange urge to redeem himself *through* his second marriage. Maybe if and when he succeeded he'd be able to forgive himself for the part he'd played in Trisha's demise.

⬥

JOSH GLANCED IN HIS REARVIEW MIRROR AT THE BOYS PLAYING with their *Avengers* Happy Meal toys. Their look of pleasant surprise at seeing him when they'd gotten off the bus had caused deep satisfaction swirling inside him. His boys. They needed him, wanted him.

He'd taken them to the playground, watched Isaac carefully for signs that his blood sugar was dropping—dizziness, irritability, and confusion. He'd even gone over the signs of being low with Isaac—telling him he would probably feel weak. He instructed Isaac to tell him right away if he felt tired.

Yet, his son seemed fine. Josh had ran around the playground with his sons, making up various obstacles that included the big tunnel slide and the swings. He couldn't remember the last time the boys had laughed so hard.

Afterward, Josh had checked Isaac's blood sugar and had administered his shot of insulin before they'd gone to McDonald's —the first time he'd performed such responsibilities without his wife. And when the boys had begged for soda, he'd made sure to order diet sodas for both of them.

Truth be told, he was feeling proud of himself by the time they pulled into their driveway. He hadn't spent enough quality time with his sons these past few months. He'd let work and goals take over his life and get in the way of his family. But if anything, the last few weeks had reminded him what mattered—Maggie, his boys. Going forward, he refused to take them for granted.

Josh parked at the end of their small driveway and the boys ran into the house. Someday soon he'd come home to a house he could be proud of—one he'd built with his own hands, one that didn't haunt him with sad memories the way this one did.

Without warning, an image came to his mind of Trisha sitting on the back stairs, her hair greasy and unkempt. He groaned and tried to push away the picture but it was no use—he could remember the day all too well.

He had gotten out of his truck to the cries of his infant sons through one of the open windows. Trisha sat slumped against the back door, staring vacantly at him, a used needle on the ground beside her.

He'd never been so angry in his life. He dragged her to her feet, shook her, asked what in the name of all that was good did she think she was doing? She'd started crying then, right along with his sons. He berated himself for leaving her alone that day. She'd been having trouble adjusting to motherhood. The death of her sister the month before had driven her over the edge. At first, she'd never wanted him to leave, then she appeared anxious for him to be gone.

He soon understood why.

That was the day he realized the depth of her problems. The depth of *their* problems. That was the day he reached out for help.

The recovery program had aided Trish immensely. And thank the Lord for his mom stepping in to assist with the boys. When Trisha came out of the program, it was like he had his wife back.

If only it had lasted more than two months.

He blinked away the memories before they found the power to tunnel into others.

That was no longer his life. No more living in the past. No more blaming himself, wondering why he hadn't been enough. Hadn't he told Pete his mom leaving wasn't his fault? Did he believe that or not?

He opened the door to excited yells. A couple of cardboard boxes labeled *Christmas* sat on the kitchen table. Davey barreled out of the living room, stocking in hand. "Mommy started Christmas decorating!"

Maggie appeared around the corner, her face flushed and pretty. "Hope it's okay. Lizzie started decorating the bed and breakfast yesterday and it got me in the holiday spirit."

Though he didn't consider himself a guy with many opinions on domestic affairs, decorating for Christmas before Thanksgiving was definitely something he had an opinion on.

As in, you don't do it.

But with his track record with Maggie the day before and the boys already excited about the holiday decorations, he figured this was one battle he didn't need to wage. Besides, Maggie was clearly trying to get past their disagreement yesterday. The least he could do was get on board.

"This house could use a little Christmas joy." He glimpsed the Nativity set up on an end table in the living room and briefly thought of Trisha once more. She'd lovingly set up the pieces every year. The last Christmas she'd been with them, heavily chained to her addictions yet struggling to find freedom, she'd cried as she placed baby Jesus in the spot between Mary and Joseph.

He hadn't asked Trisha about the tears. Knowing her parents had given her the Nativity set when she was a girl, he'd assumed his wife was simply sentimental about setting up the old gift. Now, he wondered if there'd been more to her tender touch of the small Jesus. Had she been thinking of their boys, a little under a year old? Why had she allowed the death of her sister to swallow her up to the extent she neglected her own babies?

Josh squeezed his eyes shut, forced the memories away, feeling failure with each and every one that poked at the tender flesh of his conscience. He couldn't *wait* to get out of this house.

He turned his attention to Maggie who was bent over, whispering to the boys about their Elf on the Shelf.

"I think I saw Buddy sneaking around here somewhere, too...I don't know if he'll come before Thanksgiving, but I bet it won't be long before he starts getting into mischief." Her sparkling gaze went from the boys' expectant faces to the small kitchen table, where it landed on a Happy Meal toy, a half empty paper cup beside it, droplets of dark brown soda on the plastic straw.

If there was any holiday magic in his wife, it disappeared in that moment.

She straightened. "Soda?" Her hands began to shake as she fumbled past boxes toward the counter. "Where's his extra meter? We need to test him right now."

Josh put out a hand to calm his wife, but it fell short of touching her. "Give me some credit, Mags. I made sure to ask for diet. For both of the boys, so no chance of mix-ups."

His words didn't stop her frantic search. Finally, she practically pounced on the pouch and unzipped it, drawing out Isaac's lancing device and alcohol swab. She popped the lancet into the device.

Isaac whined. "Daddy just checked me."

Maggie knelt by their son. "Sorry, honey, but we have to."

"Maggie. Did you hear me? It was diet soda."

She ignored him, putting a test strip into the meter before swiping a swab over Isaac's ring finger and poking the side of it. She gently touched the test strip to a drop of their son's blood. More whining from Isaac. Maggie stared at the meter, her shoulder's visibly relaxing. "One-twenty. He's fine."

Frustration welled in Josh. "Of course he's fine. Have you been listening to anything I've been saying? You think I'd go and feed our diabetic kid regular soda?"

"Don't call him that." Maggie scribbled the results of the reading into Isaac's log book.

"What?"

She grit her teeth, glanced at the boys. "Why don't you two wash up and go outside? Try to find some pinecones to decorate the tree, okay?"

"Let's bring our toys." Davey scooped up Ant-Man, pushing past his brother.

Isaac looked first at Maggie, then at Josh, his eyes a bit wider than usual. He grabbed his Hulk toy. "Okay."

Josh heard the water run, then the back door shut, rattling the house.

"Our *diabetic* kid? Really, Josh?"

He rubbed his face. "You're right, that was careless."

"Do you know how hard I've tried to make Isaac realize this disease does not define him, that it's not a label? How do you think it makes him feel when his own father slaps it on him like it's no big deal?"

She was right. But that didn't make her any less at fault than him. "And how do you think it makes him feel when his mother dives across the kitchen for his meter at the sight of a Happy Meal toy? I mean, do you trust me or not, Maggie? He's my kid. I wouldn't do anything to hurt him."

"*Your* kid, huh? *Your* kid?"

He lifted his hands in the air, nearly ready to surrender. She was impossible. "That's not how I meant it, and you know it."

"Well, it sure feels like it half the time. I suppose this is your house too, to sell whenever you please?"

He dragged in a breath, forcing himself to stay calm. It *was* his house. His and Trisha's. Couldn't she understand that was the problem?

But how did they make their way around to that? They'd been talking about Happy Meals. "It was diet soda. That's all I'm saying."

"And we're going to put our son's life in the hands of some distracted teenager getting paid minimum wage to not screw up a drink order? Do you want to know how many diabetics have gotten a wrong order? He could have gone into DKA, ended up back in the hospital or in a coma. There's some things we can't afford to mess around with, Josh, and I vote that fast-food soda is one of them."

"What about my vote? I thought we were supposed to be a team."

She looked at him hard, her snapping brown eyes on fire. Then they dropped to the meter, where Isaac's dried blood browned the test strip. "I thought so, too."

She turned and went upstairs, leaving him still boiling. He was only trying to be a good father, a good husband. Where had he gone wrong?

He'd thought this time around would be different. Maggie and him, they weren't anything like his first marriage. But if things had already spiraled out of control after one year, if they couldn't handle a major life complication together, he had to assume that the problem was not Trisha and not Maggie.

It was the common denominator in both equations—him.

7

I readjusted my grip on the box of cookie dough and pressed the Mabbotts' doorbell with my elbow. My purse slid off my shoulder to the crook of my arm and when Susie opened the elegant wooden door of her massive colonial, I was practically crouched with the box of cookie dough at the top of my thighs.

"Maggie! I didn't expect you. Come on in, girl. I'd take that box for you but the doctor said nothing over five pounds." She patted the small mound that was her baby.

I shuffled in the door, placing the box on an elegant bench in the foyer that looked like an old, straight-backed church pew.

"You look great." I gestured to Susie, who'd announced she was pregnant a week before Josie married. Nate and Susie had been trying to conceive for about two seconds before they found out their happy news. "How do you feel?"

"A little nauseous in the morning but nothing I can't handle. What do you have there?"

"Your cookie dough. The PTO fundraiser for school you ordered a few weeks back?"

"Oh, yes! Nate's been looking forward to that. Would you mind bringing it into the kitchen?"

"Sure." I walked into Susie's massive kitchen. A grand island with a sink and hanging farmhouse lights dominated the space. Above the counter on the far end stood a bay window that looked out over the cove. "I can never get over how beautiful this place is."

Susie grinned. "Nate works hard for it, believe me. Stay for coffee, won't you?"

"I'd love to." I said the words, although I wasn't quite sure of their truth.

Susie and I had been close at one time, but I couldn't deny we'd been growing farther and farther apart. Only natural, I supposed. My friend had little to worry over other than when the housecleaner and lawn care services arrived, what time her doting parents expected her for afternoon tea. And now she would have a baby.

A tickle of emotion stuck in my throat and I tried to clear it. Susie and I hadn't hung out for months, and I wasn't sure I could stand sipping coffee in her perfect kitchen, in her perfect house, with the bump of her perfect baby across from me...pictures of her and her perfect husband all over the walls framed in perfect matching frames. Perfect, perfect, perfect.

"You know what, Susie? I'm so sorry, but on second thought I can't. I have so much to do. I just wanted to drop off the dough and thank you for supporting the boys' school."

Susie stuck out her bottom lip. "Please, Mags? It's lonely around here and we haven't caught up in eons. How's Isaac doing?"

I blinked back unwelcome tears at the remembrance of my fight with Josh last night. He'd come into the bedroom late, had touched my shoulder tentatively, but I couldn't summon the energy to turn toward him, to cross the divide between us. He'd given up and turned on his back, sighing deep and speaking softly. "I just want us to be us again, Mags."

But that was the problem, wasn't it? What was *us*? How it was during the brief time we'd been dating, when the boys weren't around as much? How it was those first few months of marriage? Maybe the problem wasn't that we needed to be who we'd been, but that we needed to grow with one another *now*. Discover who *us* was.

If only we could grow in the same direction, instead of pulling and twisting away from each other.

"Awww, honey. You're upset. Come and talk." Susie grabbed my hand and pulled me toward her bright dining room. "You want coffee or tea?"

I shrugged. "Whatever you're having."

She brought over a tray of herbal teas and a steaming pot of water. "Now, tell me what's going on. Is Isaac not doing well?"

"No, all things considered, he's doing great."

"It's you, then. Maggie, I know you'll get pregnant sooner or later. I know it."

My smile tightened. Better to let Susie think my inability to conceive was the sole cause of my problems. In truth, with each passing day, the thought of a baby terrified me more and more. I could barely keep my head above water now. A baby would mean more stress, more expenses, more sleep-deprivation, and less time working at the B&B. A baby would make everything more complicated.

And admitting that to myself only proved I wasn't the mother a baby would need. I wasn't even confident I was the mother Davey and Isaac needed.

"Thanks, Susie. And please know I *am* happy for you."

My friend grinned. "I couldn't stand it if you weren't, Maggie. And you'll get pregnant soon and our kids will be the best of friends." Her pretty blue eyes grew wide, and she clutched my arm. "Or maybe they'll get married someday and we'll be family. How fun would that be?"

I laughed. "We must be getting old if we're planning betrothals."

Susie sat back, sipped her peppermint tea. "High school is feeling farther and farther away, isn't it? Remember when Nate and I first got together? He was the last person I expected to be with, especially with him moping after you all the time. It was at the Small party—hey, didn't you meet Josh that night, too?"

My face reddened at the memory. Wow, I'd almost forgotten that night. Probably because remembering was too painful. Josh and I had a sort of unspoken agreement not to mention it.

"That was a horrible night," I said.

Susie started with a dreamy smile on her face. "Not the way I remember it."

"I should have never let you talk me into going to that party."

"But you did."

I shrugged. "I was caught up in the shine of it all, I guess. Seems silly now."

Susie sat up straighter. "Well, you should thank me then. If it wasn't for that night, you never would have met Josh Acker." She wiggled her eyebrows. "Mr. Acker."

A smile found its way to my face. Maybe there was something healing about remembering. Even if that wasn't truly the start of me and Josh. Even if I was only seventeen and Josh hadn't married Trisha yet. Even if that night hadn't been so much as a blip on his radar, it would be one I could never truly forget, no matter how hard I tried.

Logan Small's parents had hosted the party of the century. At least that was the word around school. I still remembered Susie practically jumping up and down in front of her locker at the invitation from the captain of the football team.

"He said you could come, too." Susie clutched her biology book to her chest, clear blue eyes bright.

I closed my locker, started walking toward the science hall. "I don't know...it's his parents' party, right? I'm nobody to him. Why should I go?"

"Oh come on, Mags, it's a super fancy event. Caterers and romantic lights and music and dancing and champagne."

I raised an eyebrow. "Champagne?"

Susie rolled her eyes. "It's classy. No one's going to get rip-roaring drunk. All of the football players will be there, Nate Mabbott and his friends. Maybe you can finally talk to him."

I felt myself wavering. Not because of the mention of Nate, who was a year older and had been adamant in asking me on many dates which I'd always declined, but because no matter how I denied it, I couldn't help wanting to be part of that crowd. The crowd where easy confidence was the norm. Where elegance and affluence weren't scoffed at, but admired. I'd always felt on the fringe, while Susie had entered the sacred inner circle—not hard for her, considering her parents owned the nearby country club.

What would it be like to feel a part of things for just one night? To not play the role of responsible, oldest sister to five siblings with a father who was rarely home? With a mother who ran herself ragged trying to keep up with the needs of a large household while also opening up room on the couch for wayward souls?

Just that morning, I'd woken to see Harry Thorton on our couch. The quiet boy in Josie's grade held an unkempt way about him. His mother had left a few years back, his father spent more nights than not at a casino in the city. Harry could take care of himself, but Bronson had invited him home for supper after playing basketball one day. The boy had been a regular dinner guest, sometimes falling asleep on our couch. Mom never woke him to go home—instead grabbed a pillow and a blanket from the closet.

I didn't have anything against Harry Thorton, or any other poor soul my parents supported, but the town gossip pushed me into a box where I couldn't quite be proud. My family was poor, Dad often throwing himself wholeheartedly into various endeavors that wore out after a spell and did nothing to create stability in our family.

Just one night....

Logan Small's parents lived in a veritable mansion on the water. Was it wrong to want to feel like a princess for a few hours of my teenage life? Surely, God didn't frown upon such parties once in a while?

"I'm not sure I have anything to wear."

Susie grinned, linking arms with me. "Come over after school and raid my closet. I have a red dress that'll look amazing on you."

I couldn't contain the giddy emotion bubbling inside, and when Susie and I walked into the sparkling home of the Small mansion, I truly did feel like a princess. And while I tried not to be vain about my looks, I couldn't ignore how much I enjoyed the admiring gazes. In many ways, I did feel like Cinderella, trading my worn-out jeans for Susie's shimmering red dress. It hugged my curves without being immodest and swayed above my knees. Susie had done my makeup and curled my hair, which now lay in loose waves along my shoulders. I knew I looked older than my seventeen years. A group of seniors glanced our way and Susie tossed her hair over her shoulders in an easy show of confidence.

"I think I'm going to pass out," I whispered. "They're all looking at us."

"Isn't it great? I told you we looked hot."

Logan sauntered over, beer in hand. Warning bells went off in my head, but the thrill of it all snuffed them out.

"Hey, ladies." He grinned, his teeth white against tan skin, his dark hair slicked back with gel. He smelled amazing...like a man. Some sort of spicy, sophisticated cologne that probably cost as much as my family's grocery bill. "Glad you could make it, Suse. Your name's Maggie, right?"

He knew my name. For the love of all that was good in the world, he knew my name!

Susie practically shoved me forward. "Maggie Martin. Logan, your house is gorgeous."

Logan's gaze drifted lazily over my dress, hovering at the slight dip at the neckline. My skin heated in a way that both excited and terrified me.

"You want something to drink? We have a full bar outside."

"B-bar?" I stammered as we followed Logan. Susie had mentioned a glass of champagne, but judging from the beer in Logan's hand and the offer, it seemed like more than a celebratory glass of bubbly was offered. "What about your parents?"

Logan led us outside, where a grand white tent stood on a lush lawn. Behind it all, moonlight shone on the sea. "My parents are cool. The bartender's a friend. They said they don't mind if my friends and I have a few drinks as long as we stick around. No driving."

I supposed that made sense, but Mom would still likely kill me if she found out. Besides, something about it didn't feel right. But declining would mean embarrassing Susie.

I supposed I could get a glass of wine—my parents allowed me a small glass on holidays sometimes—and take a few sips.

"Isn't it magical?" Susie made a sweep of the patio where strings of lights lit up cozy chairs alongside the outdoor bar. "And there's Paul. Oh my goodness, I hope he comes over."

I recognized most of the kids and a good amount of the adults, mostly those active in town politics, a few who attended church. With a start, I spotted Mr. Acker talking to Logan's dad.

The new freshman history teacher had caught the attention of most of the girls in the school, and though I tried to be above it and would rather die than admit it to anyone, he'd caught mine as well. I watched him now, talking, gesturing with his hands, broad shoulders filling out his suit in a way that no high school boy's could. I shook my head, chastising myself. Silly schoolgirl fantasies.

Logan stepped away from the bar and approached me and

Susie with a fruity-looking cocktail in each hand. He handed one to me and one to Susie. "Here. These are my mom's favorite. Try it."

Susie held her glass up in a toast. Logan met it with his beer can, and after only a split-second's hesitation I followed suit, raising the glass to my lips for a dainty sip. A splash of sweet and sour flavors met my tongue. Not horrible, but foreign and forbidden, a touch of something that felt like sophistication lingering in my mouth.

From under the tent, Paul approached us. His blond hair glimmered beneath the romantic lighting. "What's up, Small? You keeping the two prettiest girls here all to yourself?"

Susie giggled. While I had to keep from rolling my eyes, I couldn't help but feel flattered. I wasn't a cheerleader or a star athlete. I wasn't super smart in school like Josie or gifted at a musical instrument or art like my other sisters. Most of the time, I hung out with Susie or helped Mom take care of my younger siblings. I tried to keep decent grades, but I wasn't anybody special. I was just Maggie. Pretty enough, kind enough, but also plain enough.

Tonight though, was entirely different. Entirely special. What if this could be my life? Fancy parties, handsome, sophisticated guys? What if I married one of these boys one day? I thought of ambitious Josie, tallying straight As like one would orders of hot dogs at a snack shack. She would gain success in a career of psychology. Probably go make a name for herself in New York or California. Maybe write books one day.

Me, on the other hand? I simply wanted a home and a family. I didn't feel the need for a fancy career or to reach any noteworthy accomplishments. And money? If it happened to come by way of association in a marriage...was that so bad? Was it horrible that I didn't want to live the rest of my life like I had the past seventeen years, always on the cusp of enough, always longing for more?

A server came by and offered us each a tray of bacon-wrapped scallops. I took one, nibbling the appetizer off the toothpick, savoring the delicacy. "Oh wow, that's delicious." I reached for another, but caught Susie shaking her head at me. I lowered my hand. "I guess I better not."

Logan laughed. "Hey, I like a girl who isn't bashful about eating." He snapped at the server, who'd started walking away. "Maggie, have as much as you'd like."

I glanced at Susie and shrugged, taking another and washing it down with another sip of my drink.

"How about a dance?"

I looked around at Logan's words, half expecting he addressed someone besides me. "Me?"

"Of course you." He took my drink from my hand and placed it on the bar. I allowed him to lead me toward the white tent where Christina Perry sang out *A Thousand Years*, only the most romantic song in all of history. And here I was, in the arms of the most handsome guy in school. Swaying back and forth, welcoming his strong hands on my waist, allowing him to pull me close, to send my nerve endings dancing and swirling in a heady cacophony of desire. Desire for him, but desire for something else as well— this moment that felt like a fairytale fantasy, this life that beckoned me with its shiny interior and elegant exterior.

The words and tune of the song, the zesty scent of Logan— the waft of beer on his breath—pulled me in. And when Logan drew me to him, the length of his body brushing against me, I didn't resist. A sense of anticipation made me feel I could fly. I wondered if this was what love felt like.

When the song ended, Logan leaned toward my ear, his bristly cheek alongside mine. "Don't go anywhere, promise? I'll be right back."

"Okay," I breathed. I watched his retreating shoulders as he walked toward the patio. Beside me, Paul and Susie stayed wrapped in one another's arms despite the upbeat change to *Hey, Soul Sister*.

"Need a dance partner?" I turned to see Nate Mabbott, lean and tall, beside me. He started some crazy robot dance move.

I searched for Logan at the edge of the patio, but he'd disappeared. I supposed dancing with Nate was better than hanging out alone with myself on the dance floor. I smiled. "Sure."

I sang along with Nate, both of us laughing, Paul and Susie joining in.

Susie leaned toward me. "Logan *likes* you."

"You think so? I probably got ditched is more like it."

"Are you kidding? He can't take his eyes off you. And can you believe me and Paul? Yummy."

I laughed, knew we were both being silly. The tune changed to *Unchained Melody* and Nate held his hand out to me while Susie turned back into Paul's arms.

"Whoa, Mabbott. Cutting in on my girl?"

Nate turned wounded eyes to me. "You guys are…together?"

Logan handed me a drink. "I was hoping we were. What do you say, Maggie?"

Something told me to take it slow. To remember reality. But one look at those deep brown eyes, ready to swallow me up, was enough to silence everything. This was it—my chance to be a part of things. I'd been trying to dissuade Nate for awhile, anyway. Maybe this was the time.

"I'd like that." I spoke the words quietly, half-buried them in my drink. Just in case I'd heard Logan wrong. Just in case this was all a dream or one big mistake.

I tried not to dwell on Nate's devastated look as he sulked away. I didn't mean to hurt him. I took another sip of my cocktail. It tasted stronger this time. "Is this the same drink?"

"Yeah. You left it on the table near the bar, right?"

"Yeah." Right. Had I? I couldn't remember.

"You want to dance?"

And then the drink was out of my hand and I sank into Logan's arms, the romance of the tune sweeping me into its embrace. Logan held me closer this time—closer than I'd ever been to any boy—and it ignited a fire inside me. His fingers tightened around my waist. He leaned down to whisper in my ear. "Every other guy here is wishing they were me right now, you know that, don't you?"

I giggled, and it didn't sound like myself. His words were preposterous. Yet, I *did* feel terribly grown up. It was nice to be admired and doted upon. And I could certainly get used to the compliments pouring out of Logan's mouth.

"You're special, Maggie. Do you know I have a picture of us at middle-school field day? We did the wheelbarrow race together. Remember?"

I did, though never in a million years would I have guessed that he remembered. "Really?"

His mouth was closer to my cheek now, the warm breath of his words pleasant on my skin. "Yeah, the picture's right on the cork board above my desk where I can see it every day."

I laughed and my head swam. I couldn't seem to get a grip on myself. At the same time, it didn't bother me as I might imagine. For one night, I would be crazy Maggie instead of prim-and-proper Maggie. Tomorrow, I'd return to my old ways and be desperately good again. "You're lying."

"I'm not. I've liked you for a long time. You just were out of my league, you know?"

What? If anything, I was out of his league. I was a Martin, after all.

"You still don't believe me, do you? Come on, I'll show you."

I let him drag me off the dance floor. I sank into the sensation that I floated above the crowd. Shimmering lights and candles, succulent foods, ladies and gentlemen in elegant dresses and suits. Logan led me through the kitchen and up the stairs. No one seemed to notice. We'd read *The Great Gatsby* in school. What had Fitzgerald said about large parties?

Oh yeah, that they were more intimate than small parties. Right now, I could certainly see the truth in that.

Logan kept a firm grip on my hand, leading me to the first door on the right. Quiet enveloped us, the bass of the music outside muffled through the windows. Logan turned on his lamp, pointed to a picture at the cork board above his desk. I squinted, could just make out part of my face. The majority of the picture was of Logan, holding up a trophy for our win.

I supposed it was still kind of sweet that he remembered. "Fun times." My voice sounded strange. Distant, far away. I swallowed. "We should get back to the party."

"So soon? I was kind of hoping we might...you know, stick around for a little."

"I don't think so, Logan."

He stepped closer, raised a hand to my face, ran a thumb over my bottom lip. "I only want to be with you, get to know you better. Don't you want that?"

My skin hummed beneath his touch, and when he dipped his mouth to mine, I gave in. He felt so good. He smelled so good. He *tasted* so good. I'd never even kissed a boy before, but Logan didn't make me feel nervous at all. He made me feel wanted. Special.

He deepened the kiss, his mouth moving over my own. At first it was pleasant, but then it turned to something hungry, alarming. His tongue turned into a warm, probing, intrusive thing. I pushed him back to catch my breath. "Let's go back downstairs."

"Why? Don't you like me, Maggie? Just one more kiss?"

I did like him. Of course I did. He took me in his arms again, and this time pulled me gently on his bed, his hands traveling slowly over my stomach, then upward. It scared me how I found myself in this position so quickly. Scared me how I'd ended up on his bed in the first place.

But when his hand slid beneath my dress and upward, I shot up to a sitting position. "I want to go back downstairs."

"Come on, Maggie, you can't kiss a guy like that and then leave him hanging. This is what you wanted, isn't it? You like me, don't you?"

"I like dancing with you," I whispered.

"But I like doing other things." And then he was on top of me, the yeasty scent of the beer heavy on his breath, his persistent hands lifting my skirt, probing and reaching for hidden places.

My body felt like lead as I tried to use my legs and arms to push him off of me. The only thing I could manage was a single, short scream.

He pressed a hand over my mouth, whispered in my ear. "That won't do, darlin'. Come on, you know you like this. Relax, sweetheart."

This couldn't be happening. He was going to rape me. But was it actually rape? I'd come to his room willingly, had kissed him willingly, had wanted to be with him. But not this. This isn't what I'd intended at all.

Without warning, overhead lights turned on, making me squint. Logan jumped off me and I yanked my dress down, breaths coming fast.

"What's going on here?" A deep voice, but I couldn't look in its direction, shame making me hide behind my hair.

"Yo, man, this is my room. Why are you here?"

"I heard the girl scream. Go downstairs, Logan."

"You can't tell me—"

"Downstairs, or Coach Stillman will hear about this and you'll be benched for the rest of the season. You can kiss your scholarship goodbye."

"Mr. Acker, you're not serious. We were just having fun."

"It didn't sound like it from where I stood."

Logan swore, but then he was gone, leaving me alone with the history teacher.

"Are you okay?" he asked.

I nodded, but my limbs trembled.

"Did he...?"

I shook my head violently.

"Who'd you come with? I can take you home."

I stood, but couldn't make it to the doorway. Mr. Acker held my arm with a strong hand and guided me down the stairs and out to the driveway. He settled me in the passenger seat of a beat-up Nissan Sentra, asked me who I'd come with.

"Susie Granier."

He shook his head. "What's she look like?"

"She's in a black dress. She was with Paul Livingston."

"I'll be right back. Don't go anywhere, okay?"

I nodded, feeling nauseous. How had I gotten myself in such a predicament?

A short time later, the back doors of the car opened. Both Susie and Nate slid into Mr. Acker's car.

"That was real stupid, Suse," Nate said. "I think he snuck something in your drink."

"I had everything under control," Susie snapped. "You're just jealous Maggie ditched you." She realized my presence for the first time. "Mags...you're here too? What's up? Are you okay?"

My bottom lip trembled, the enormity of what had almost happened—what could have happened—beginning to make itself real in my mind. "I want to go home."

Mr. Acker dropped Susie off first, then me. I remembered mumbling a thank you, wondering if he would go in and talk to my parents. But he didn't. Instead, he'd appeared at my doorstep the next morning.

I'd met him outside after Amie reported that one of my teachers was outside asking for me. Dad and Mom weren't home, which saved me the hassle of questions. I still remembered Mr. Acker, dark blonde hair neatly cropped and gelled, kicking the bottom of the step lightly with one of his scuffed shoes—an action that proved endearingly boyish. I'd been drawn to Logan because he appeared so grown-up, like a man. What a crock.

"I was trying to wait until Monday to talk to you during school, but if there's something we need to report, I thought sooner than later would be better."

I'd stared at him, his words a jumble in my brain. Report?

Mr. Acker continued to kick the bottom step. "I don't want to insert myself into a situation I don't belong, but...Maggie, I'm trying to do the right thing here, you understand?"

I cleared my throat, but no words came out. Instead, I nodded.

"Did you talk to your parents?"

My tongue loosened. My parents couldn't know. I'd been irresponsible, too. Drinking. Trying to impress a boy because he had money and dimples. I'd been so completely stupid. "Mr. Acker, please don't tell them. I—I'm super embarrassed as it is. And nothing happened, thanks to you."

He looked as if he was going to disagree with me, but decided against it. "I don't think Logan will be trying anything for a long time. With you or any other girl, for that matter."

I didn't know what that meant, exactly, or why it didn't make me feel better. "I was stupid. I shouldn't have been there, definitely shouldn't have taken that drink."

"You can say that again. But I guess you learned your lesson, huh?"

"I'd say so." I took a step forward. "Thank you, Mr. Acker. I'm still humiliated, but I'm thanking God for sending you to that room last night."

He nodded his head and gave me a small smile. He walked down the stairs, and I thought that he was the type of man I should want to marry someday. No doubt a teacher's salary couldn't compare with that of a doctor or lawyer or NFL star, but what did money matter in the end? I'd let the appeal of shiny material things get in the way of what was truly important— human decency, caring, and love.

The next time I spoke to Josh Acker it was seven years later at the Camden Fall Festival. He'd been with the two cutest little boys I'd ever seen. After working up some courage, I'd approached him, feeling that a more thorough thank you for that night was long overdue. Not realizing he'd lost his wife a year-and-a-half earlier. Not realizing it would be the beginning of something extraordinary.

Now, in Susie's kitchen, I blinked, realized my tea was empty. Susie smiled at me. "A trip down memory lane is good sometimes, isn't it?"

I dragged in a breath. "I think so." I stood, grabbed my cup and saucer. "Thanks, Susie."

I'd allowed the circumstances of the last several weeks to consume me. I'd forgotten why I'd fallen in love with Josh in the first place. He always had the well-being of the underdog at heart. He was smart, caring, and he loved our boys. He was an amazing dad, and I'd done him a disservice casting blame on him these last several days.

My husband was right. We were a team. But I'd tried to take the reins of control.

I could hardly wait to make it up to him.

8

After he'd ironed his clothes for the next day, Josh fell into bed, exhausted, sliding beneath the sheets and letting his shower-wet head fall onto the pillow. He'd been over to the new house after school today, the bittersweet ending of the cross-country season freeing up more of his time, making his promise to be home for supper every night more attainable.

But now that he'd closed on the house, the burden of paying two mortgages became a reality. The sooner he could make the house on Chestnut Street livable, the sooner they could sell this one.

The shower down the hall turned on and he forced his eyes open, tried to stay awake so he could talk to Maggie. She'd been docile at dinner, almost peaceful—a change he couldn't help but notice. But they still hadn't spoken since their argument yesterday afternoon. Not more than "Could you please pass the butter?" or "Could you grab Isaac more water?"

His eyelids grew heavy, sleep overtaking him. He'd wanted to make another attempt at talking to his wife, but maybe in the morning....

His dreams came without effort, stemming from another time and place—the day he'd known he was going to ask Maggie to be his wife. They'd walked along the boardwalk on the harbor a long time that night, talking, passing the restaurants and shops through town. They'd sat on a pair of abandoned chairs and watched the boaters and tourists. They'd talked of their growing up years, of their families. Then they'd walked more, the long summer night stretched before them. They'd gone all the way to Laite Memorial Beach and continued on to Curtis Island Overlook. When the night ended, he realized he never wanted Maggie to leave his side. He didn't want to ever say goodbye. That's when he knew he would ask her to marry him.

The feel of soft, bare skin against his arm stirred him from the dream-filled memory. His senses came alive as he reached his hand out to his wife. It grazed her waist and he turned onto his side, drew her toward him, soaking in the lavender scent of her, the smoothness of her bare skin.

He kissed her cheek, her neck, her collarbone, and she returned the affection, setting him on fire—both physically and emotionally. He'd missed his wife. He loved his wife. Nothing should get between them as they'd let it the last several weeks.

When they came together, he thought he could be content forever in her arms, was thoroughly convinced that there was nothing their love couldn't handle.

Afterward, he burrowed his face in her neck, surprised at the emotion clogging his throat. "I'm sorry, Mags. I'm sorry. I don't want us to argue. We are a team and those boys—those boys are just as much a part of you as they are of me. I mean that, wholly and truly."

Her arms came around him again. "I'm the one who should be sorry. I know you love Isaac—of course you do. I don't mean to make you feel incompetent. Josh, you're the smartest, most caring guy I know. I freaked out. I'm so, so sorry."

He kissed her eyelids. "We'll work through this, all of this, together. I should have talked to you more about the house, about everything. We've missed one another, Mags. I've been at work, trying to build what I think you want."

"I never wanted anything but you, Josh. You and the boys. You're enough."

He smiled. "I'm no fool. You could have had Nate Mabbott or someone like Logan Small. Big shot doctors, raking in the money. I'm almost ten years older than these guys and I still feel like I'm behind, like I'm competing." He winced at the foreign vulnerability in his voice. Would opening up to Maggie like this make her think less of him?

She slid her hand along his stubbled cheek, propped herself on one elbow. He could make out the shadow of her profile from the soft glow of the alarm clock, the waves of her dark hair falling over one bare shoulder.

"Logan Small...are you kidding me? There's no competition, Josh. None whatsoever."

He thought of Dr. Mabbott, his easy demeanor, the way he had so efficiently calmed Maggie's fears after examining Isaac in the hospital. Josh could have never done that. For goodness sake, he couldn't even give her a halfway decent house.

For the millionth time, he wondered if things would have been different with Trisha if he had done more, *been* more. Had he failed his first wife in some way he couldn't see?

Maggie tapped his face. "Are you listening to me, Mr. Acker?"

He put his arms around her. "Mr. Acker, huh?"

"You remember that party at Logan Small's house? When I was in high school?"

"How could I forget?" The memory of Maggie's muted scream, of seeing Logan on top of her still caused his body to hum with anger.

"I was thinking about that night today. Josh...the truth is I used to believe that I wanted that sort of life. You know, the elegant, the glitzy. My parents worked so hard for us with little to show for it. I didn't think I wanted that. I remember that night, dancing with Logan, thinking that was the life meant for me. But I was wrong. So wrong. That night proved it. *You* proved it."

"You were only a high-schooler to me back then, but I'm still glad I met you that night. Not glad about what almost happened, but glad because it opened up a door for us later. I remember seeing you at that fall festival and being completely bowled over by the woman you'd become. You had a light in your eyes back then, Maggie. And I still see it, but I'm scared to death I might be the cause of it dimming."

"Oh, Josh."

She curled her head against his neck, her quiet breaths taking up the space of the night.

Finally, she spoke. "Who would have thought that nine years after that party we'd be here? Together like this?"

He kissed her hair, still damp from the shower. "I certainly didn't. In fact, it makes me feel pretty old. Life's crazy, isn't it?"

"It's an adventure, that's for sure. But honey, there is no one else I want to share this adventure with. Okay?"

"Okay. Let's talk more. How can we talk more? I mean, do we need counseling or something? Maggie, I want to do whatever it takes to show you how much I love you. I will do anything."

She clutched the covers to her neck. "Counseling? Do you think we're that bad?"

He attempted to measure his words. "No, but I don't want us to get to 'that bad.' We need to talk more."

"Not at counseling."

"Fine, no counseling. What do you suggest?"

"Early-morning coffee dates?"

He winced. "Better make it an after-coffee date if you want any coherent thoughts."

She slapped him playfully and he cuddled her closer.

"I'm kidding."

"You better be. Okay, then. Tomorrow morning, 6AM?" She

rolled over to set the alarm on her phone, though he knew it wouldn't be for their morning date. She woke up every two hours —sometimes more—in order to monitor Isaac's blood sugar and treat any lows or highs.

"Won't you be tired, what with waking up so much with Isaac? Why don't you let me take a shift during the night?"

"I don't mind. Besides, I can sleep for another hour after you go to work before I have to get the boys up for school. It makes sense. So are we on? Morning coffee date?"

He couldn't help but notice how she'd brushed his help off so efficiently. A quick *no* to a counselor's help when it came to their marriage. Another easy *no* when it came to helping their son.

He wanted them to be a team. But how could that ever happen if she always pushed him away?

9

There was nothing better than Thanksgiving and family. Something about the non-commercialized holiday had always appealed to my senses. Simple gratitude, celebration, food, family, and friends.

And now, constant anxiety. Blood sugar anxiety, that is.

I watched Josh dish out a small mound of mashed potatoes on Isaac's plate after we'd said grace. We'd given him his insulin shot fifteen minutes earlier, but that didn't mean he could eat whatever he wanted. I'd already planned on coaxing the entire family to go for a walk around the orchard after our Thanksgiving feast—something that would help lower high sugar levels.

"You going to stare at that casserole all afternoon, girl?"

Josh elbowed my arm and I blinked, the green bean casserole in front of me coming into focus, oozing mushroom sauce and French's fried onions.

I tried to estimate the amount of carbs in a serving, but couldn't begin to guess.

"Sorry, Aunt Pris." I handed the casserole dish to Finn, who handed it to my aunt. I cleared my throat at Isaac placing two rolls on his plate.

Josh caught the gesture, took one of the rolls from our son's plate. "Sorry, kiddo."

"But Davey has two, Daddy."

"I know, buddy. But if you want some special dessert, we have to go easy on the rolls and mashed potatoes."

Isaac stuck out his bottom lip but didn't make a fuss.

Davey held up one of his rolls, clenched in his fist. "I'll put mine back, too."

I winked at him. We tried to keep things fair, but sometimes it simply wasn't convenient or possible. Davey's sacrifice made me smile. "It's okay, honey. You keep it this time." Davey's finger-crushed roll would probably go to waste anyway.

Josh tussled the top of Isaac's head. I breathed deep, felt the tension ease from my chest. We could do this. We had to do this if we were going to manage holidays and special occasions for the rest of Isaac's childhood years.

I caught my husband's gaze and smiled. Though we didn't make our coffee dates every morning, Josh made a real effort. He even ran to the donut shop down the street to get us muffins every now and then. He was trying so hard, and I loved and appreciated him for it.

Mom smiled down the table at us. "Maggie said your parents were enjoying a quiet Thanksgiving at home, Josh. Please let them know they're welcome anytime."

"Thanks, I'll let them know. Maybe next year."

A prick of guilt started in my breastbone. I should have thought to invite my in-laws. But Josh hadn't said anything, and I'd been preoccupied with simply trying to get Isaac through the holiday.

"You going shopping tomorrow morning, Mom?" Amie speared some white turkey meat onto her plate, then drizzled it with gravy.

Mom shook her head. "Not this year. Too much to do. I can't believe how many guests we have this weekend."

"What about you, Lizzie? You up for some Black Friday fun?"

Lizzie laughed. "Crowds and stores? You're talking to the wrong gal. You want to go for a hike instead? We could catch the sunrise at Mount Battie."

Amie wrinkled her nose. "I'm afraid I'll have to pass."

"I'll go." Josie spooned squash onto her plate.

"Hiking, you mean?" Amie asked.

"No. Shopping. It would be fun."

I tried to contain a smile. Amie and Josie had never been especially close, but ever since Amie helped deliver Amos, something had changed between them. Something for the good.

"Really?"

Tripp's mouth turned downward. "No can do, ladies. Sorry. I'm helping Josh out on the house tomorrow, remember? I won't be around to watch Amos."

"Aww, don't worry about it," Josh said. "Come when you can. Maybe they'll be done by eight. Don't most Black Friday shoppers start early anyway?"

Amie took a dainty bite of her squash. "Not *this* Black Friday shopper. Sorry."

"I could watch Amos."

The table grew silent at Finn's words, the tension palpable. Though Finn was Amos's father by birth, he'd seriously injured his back two months ago in a terrifying skydiving accident. Still in outpatient rehab, he'd recently moved into the apartment above Tripp's grandfather's garage. Josie and Tripp had committed themselves to helping Finn through this time, to embracing him into the family. Even though Finn had all but abandoned Josie when he'd found out she was pregnant. Even though having Finn close by caused a tangled mess at times.

From what Josie told me, they had no regrets so far. It was hard and crazy and completely irrational. But it was also love and grace—walking out their faith in a tangible way.

I couldn't help but admire the way Tripp and Josie handled it all. Just thinking about it now inspired me.

Josie appeared to be suddenly preoccupied with her corn kernels. My sister spoke without looking at Finn. "You think you're ready for that?"

I tried not to stare at Finn. Earlier, his movements as he left his walker to sit at the table had been stilted and awkward. The smatterings of gray at his temples had become more pronounced the last several weeks. Even now, as he took the green bean casserole dish from Tripp, his hand shook slightly. Beside my strong brother-in-law, Finn appeared small and weak. And yet there was no denying the big improvements he made each and every day.

"Come on, Josie. I can move around now, pick up Amos. I can certainly change a diaper or feed him and watch him sleep for a few hours."

Josie looked at Tripp, who nodded.

"Okay, let's give it a try. What time do you want to leave, Amie?"

They set up the details, little corners of conversations starting around the table.

Aunt Pris padded a roll with a liberal amount of butter. "I will never understand how someone thought making the day after Thanksgiving a national shopping day was a good idea. Ruining all that is still good with commercial rubbish."

"It's part of the fun, Aunt Pris," Amie said. Her large, leaf-shaped earrings shook slightly as she spoke. "Getting in the holiday spirit, planning gifts for everyone."

"Speaking of which, we should probably draw names tonight." Josie stood to check on Amos, sleeping soundly in the basinet in the next room.

Aunt Pris threw up her hands. "It looks as if we can't have Thanksgiving dinner without a conversation about Christmas. Am I the only sane person who thinks Thanksgiving should be kept sacred?"

Aunt Pris's dog, Cragen, brushed by my ankles.

"I agree with you, Aunt Pris," I said.

"You do?" The older lady raised a gray eyebrow.

"Absolutely. It's fun to know Christmas is around the corner, but Thanksgiving should be about Thanksgiving. About being thankful."

Aunt Pris smiled at me, and I returned the gesture. We hadn't been on the best of terms since I married Josh. Aunt Pris had high hopes for me, her oldest niece, and it didn't include marrying a poor, widowed high school history teacher with two sons. But Aunt Pris had come around to the boys, even sneaking Werther's caramels to them on occasion.

Speaking of which, I'd have to make sure Aunt Pris understood that even a piece of candy had to be monitored, especially if she doled out several at a time.

Mom sipped her sparkling cider. "Okay, then, what are we all thankful for?"

From the other end of the table, Bronson groaned. "Come on, Mom, it's so cheesy to go around the table saying what we're thankful for on Thanksgiving. Everyone gives the typical answers."

Amie nodded. "Yup. Family. Friends. God. Food. That about sums it up."

"Okay, then. Why don't we switch it up this year?" Mom said.

Bronson squinted, clearly suspicious. "How?"

Mom sat straighter. "By using one of my favorite things. A story."

Amie moaned. "Why does everything in this family have to do with books or *Little Women*?"

We all laughed. Mom and Dad naming us after *Little Women* characters wasn't always something the Martin children embraced. While I had never particularly minded it, Meg March was probably the easiest "little woman" to live up to. For a long time, Josie had suppressed her desire to write, knowing she could never match the likes of Jo March. Lizzie used to battle fear that her bout as a teenager with thyroid cancer hinted at a tragic end to come. And while Amie mirrored a few qualities of Amy March, she thought the entire idea ridiculous and cast aside the notion while clinging to her own individuality—never once admitting that she was probably more like her March "twin" than the rest of us.

"Oh, come on now. It sounds like it might be fun. What'd you have in mind, Mom?" Josie stuffed a bite of turkey into her mouth.

"I thought it might be fun if we took turns sharing stories about a time when we were thankful for someone around this table."

Amie slapped Bronson's arm playfully. "You should have kept your trap shut. That's way harder than saying what we're thankful for."

"I think it's a great idea." Finn shifted in his seat, wincing slightly. "I'll go first. Just last night, I managed to lock myself out of the apartment. I couldn't find my keys to save my life. Ed and August weren't around, so this guy"—he jerked his thumb at Tripp—"came over to let me in."

Tripp shrugged. "No big deal. Did you end up finding your keys?"

"I left them at rehab. One of the nurses called this morning."

Mom smiled at Tripp and Finn. "That's a great way to start. Thank you, Finn."

"Okay, I have one," Lizzie piped up. "Remember the time I had the solo in the school play? I was petrified. But Josie helped me get over my stage fright by researching every trick in the book. From picturing the crowd in their underwear to belly breathing, she wouldn't give up even when I wanted to. Remember, Josie?"

Josie smiled. "You ended up killing it."

"Because you sat front and center, told me to pretend you were the only one there. It worked."

"And now look at you. You're practically a pro. Oh, you should play that song you wrote for us after dinner. It's amazing."

Lizzie's face reddened. While she had conquered her stage fright, getting her *up* on stage was still often a battle. "We'll see. Who else has a story?"

I studied Isaac, drawing circles in his mashed potatoes with his fork. If he didn't eat everything on his plate, we'd have to figure out something to adjust his levels. Maybe I'd be asking Aunt Pris for some of those caramels.

"Okay, I'll go." Amie said. "I was in eighth grade. I decided to paint my bedroom this awful teal color—do you remember? I hated cutting in with the brush, so I decided to roll right over the door. I didn't think about propping it open at all. By the time I was finished I was locked in my bedroom. I panicked—you know how I hate being locked in places, right? Maggie was the only one home and she managed to calm me down. She ended up wrapping a kitchen knife in bubble wrap and throwing it up to my window so I could cut myself out."

I joined the others in laughing at the memory. "That door was hideous. You were scraping paint for hours."

We went around the table, Bronson sharing how Josh had taken him out for a game of basketball when he felt overwhelmed with all the women in the house. Aunt Pris sharing about how Josie had gifted her a sheep figurine at the open house of the bed and breakfast.

Josie drummed her fingers on the table. "Someday I'm going to find out why you like sheep so much, Aunt Pris."

Aunt Pris rolled her eyes and shook her head, though a slight smile pulled at the edges of her mouth.

"Okay, me next," I said. "But it's not about someone who's physically here. It's about Dad."

Mom's expression softened. She nodded her encouragement.

"I was seven. We all went for a hike in the State Park. I remember Dad carrying Bronson on his back. Amie wasn't even born yet. I brought my Cabbage Patch doll, and somehow, I lost her. I didn't realize it until we got home. I remember crying and Dad sitting me on his knee. I thought he might try to comfort me by reminding me that a Cabbage Patch doll wasn't real, that I shouldn't put so much emphasis on worldly objects. But he didn't."

Emotion climbed my throat at the memory. I pushed it down. I definitely needed more sleep. "Dad went back with me to look for her. We spent hours retracing our steps and still we couldn't find her. But the next day, Dad took a day off to search for her while I was at school. I got off the bus and she was sitting right on our front steps. I couldn't believe he'd done that, but I will always remember it."

Lizzie sniffed. "He had such a big heart."

The table grew silent. Mom cleared her throat. "I think that's a fine story to end on."

We shared a smile and Josh squeezed my hand.

The conversation turned to the guests we expected that weekend, the song Josie wanted Lizzie to perform for us, the art class Amie felt stifled in, Bronson's side job tutoring, Tripp's construction jobs, and finally our new house.

I looked at Isaac, who shoveled in a mouthful of mashed potatoes. Maybe holidays would be okay, after all.

"So what are you hoping to get done tomorrow, Josh?" Tripp asked after the dishes were cleared.

Josie held a content Amos out to Finn, who cradled his son with care. I watched Tripp witness the exchange. It must be crazy to have to share a son with another man. Though Trisha had been gone for years now, in many ways I still felt like a second-choice mom. I wondered if Tripp could relate.

That thought only lasted a minute as I studied Tripp leaning back in his chair, waiting for Josh's answer, unfazed by Finn holding Amos. The guy exuded confidence. It didn't seem as if anything fazed him. I could only wish I was wired that way.

"Everything needs to be gutted. The structure's good, roof is decent, but the entire thing's a total renovation. I want to get it livable. I don't mind doing cheap for now. Linoleum, some basic wooden shelves instead of cabinets. I just want to get in there. I'll do the rest how we want over time."

I raised my eyebrows. "Won't that be more money and aggravation in the long run? Why not make it the way we want from the get-go?"

Josh's mouth tightened. "I thought we could, but I don't want to overextend ourselves. Unless you want to put the house on the market now..."

This was not a discussion we needed to have in front of my entire family, in front of Tripp. "Why don't we talk about this later?"

Josh leaned forward. "I'd like to get Tripp's opinion, actually. It's a seller's market now, right? Might as well make good on it and put it up for sale. Am I wrong in my thinking?"

Tripp looked between me and Josh before answering slowly. "Makes sense if it works for you guys. But I've seen the Chestnut Street house. You're not living there anytime soon."

"Can we slow down, please?" I wrung my hands on my cloth napkin—a fancy detail Mom insisted on for the holidays. "This is happening so fast, and I'm not ready to camp in a half-finished house for months on end." I could practically feel my blood pressure rising.

Josh squeezed my knee. "We're not making any decisions, honey. I only want to talk it through with a guy who knows the business."

I stood. "Okay, then. I think I'll ask my mom and sisters if they want to go for a walk with the kids." Isaac could certainly benefit from a walk after all those carbs. We all could.

I walked past Finn and Bronson, who were talking about the

struggles Bronson had with one of the students he tutored, and into the spacious kitchen of the bed and breakfast.

Mom stood over the sink, dish gloves on, hair pulled back. Lizzie separated leftovers into plates and containers. Amie washed the counters and Josie lightly bounced Amos, who had started squirming in Finn's arms.

Sunshine streamed through the back windows of the bed and breakfast onto the floor where Davey and Isaac played with their LEGOs. Aunt Pris had gone in her bedroom to rest.

"How about a walk around the orchard to aid in a little digestion?" I asked.

"That sounds marvelous." Lizzie sealed a giant container of turkey.

Mom slid off her dish gloves. "Dishes can wait. Let's get the food stored away, then head out."

I spooned leftover squash into three sets of containers—one for my family, one for Josie and Tripp, and another big one for Aunt Pris, Mom, and the rest of my siblings. I opened the fridge. "This huge refrigerator comes in handy, doesn't it? No having to store leftovers on the back patio this year."

Josie patted the counter. "You can put my stuff right here. I'll run it up to the apartment before we walk. I need to grab a warmer blanket for Amos anyway."

I held my arms out. "Let me take him? He's so sweet."

Josie handed off her babe and I closed my eyes, relishing the sweet weight of him in my arms, trying to imagine how my own babe might feel in that space.

A cool breeze swept through the room when Josie returned. She rubbed her hands together to ward off the chill.

I turned, shielding Amos from the cold. "That was fast."

"I ran. Feels good to get back at it."

"How's the apartment with the three of you living in there now? I'm surprised Tripp isn't planning a crazy beautiful house on the water somewhere."

Josie smiled. The gesture gave her a glow she hadn't possessed this past summer. Marriage agreed with her, softening the bristly outside burr of her, wearing it away to reveal the softness within. "I'm not thinking we'll live above the bookshop forever, of course, but right now we're content. It's good to be close to everyone and to work. Tripp and Amos and I don't need much."

I helped Josie slide Amos into a soft, warm onesie before grabbing the boys' coats. "Come on, guys. You can bring a LEGO guy with you if you want."

Davey held up a man with a red baseball cap. "This one! He's a builder like Uncle Tripp."

Isaac grabbed a knight figure and held his arms out so I could slide his coat on.

"You feeling okay, kiddo?"

He nodded. "A little tired."

Amie came up behind Isaac and tickled his sides. "It's all that turkey. What does it have in it that makes you sleepy?"

"It starts with a T, doesn't it?" Lizzie pulled a knit hat over her ears.

"Tryptophan," Josie said. "It's an amino acid that increases serotonin in the brain." We stared at her. She shrugged. "I read it in one of the new cookbooks we got for the bookshop the other day. Oh, Mom, that reminds me, what do you think of doing a holiday sale tomorrow? I can put it out on social media, put a sign at the end of the driveway, try to get new customers up here. Who knows, someone could end up booking a room for next year. And what with The Red Velvet Inn stealing your five-course breakfast idea, we need all the help we can get." Josie stuck out her bottom lip, for she was still sour over the recent news that another inn in the area offered such an elaborate breakfast.

Amie clenched her fists at her side. "I can't believe Jolene Andover had the audacity to do that. Weren't you friends back in high school, Mom?"

Hannah's mouth tightened into a line. "More like acquaintances. Jolene never cared for me, unfortunately. And she had a terrible crush on your father. One he didn't return."

Josie raised her eyebrows. "I can't picture Dad ever interested in someone as shallow and cold-hearted...sorry. I just don't see why she has to go and steal our idea. That was the one unique thing we had going for us."

"You mean a bookshop and author-themed guest rooms aren't cutting it?" I joked.

Lizzie pinched Davey's cheeks after helping him zip his coat. "I wouldn't sweat it. Jolene can call it gourmet and five-course, but the end result is nowhere near comparable to Mom's. Ashley visited her aunt for brunch there one day, and she said the French toast was soggy and the presentation awful. I say we keep doing what we're doing and not get sidetracked."

Mom nodded. "I'd say that's sound advice."

"As far as tomorrow, I could make some cookies. We could advertise free treats. Food always draws people in." Lizzie tugged Davey's hat over his ears.

I bit the inside of my cheek. "Sounds like a great idea. But tomorrow? We should have been planning this a month ago." I loved my sisters' spontaneity, but it didn't jive well with my plan-and-prepare personality.

Mom nodded. "Maggie's right, girls. Better to take things slow this year. Though I do hate to miss out on gathering people in for the holidays. And the bookshop's a great opportunity to do that, especially with all the gift ideas and Christmas product we ordered."

Josie had partnered with an organization called Narratology that provided beautiful handmade products such as jewelry, hand-bags, soaps, and candles and supported ethical buying habits. All of the money was given back to charities that supported family preservation and marginalized communities. Skilled artisans and refugees, the more vulnerable of society. The products were so uniquely captivating that they brought in new customers each day, many who purchased additional books and book-inspired apparel.

My head spun. It was a shame to miss out on the promotion. Especially with everything we'd done to capitalize on the unique appeal of the bed and breakfast tied into the gift shop. "Why don't we do it next Saturday? Give me time to get the word out? Maybe reach out to the newspapers. It would be great if they highlighted the products we receive from Narratology. People can feel good about purchasing products with money that will go to actively loving their neighbor. We'll support the non-profit and get some business of our own."

Mom tapped her chin. "I *do* like that idea. And Amie, don't you have a few of your handmade nightlights? This might be a perfect time to try them out before a crowd." Amie was experimenting with a different form of art, crafting leaves in between lampshades to create beautiful, nature-inspired light fixtures. I'd already placed an order on her ebay store, which was in full swing. But the time it took to make them was no small sacrifice.

"Yeah, that'd be great if I can find the time to get a few more made." Amie opened the door for us, and we headed out. The cool breeze met our cheeks. The sun warmed our backs.

Lizzie tapped Josie's arm excitedly. "Oooh, do you think Santa might come for a story time?"

Josie scrunched up her eyebrows at her sister. Beside them, Davey jumped up and down. "Santa's going to come?"

"No, honey. It was just an idea." I took long strides toward the orchard. In the distance, the harbor glimmered to our right. In front of us lay acres and acres of bare apple trees, hibernating until next spring when their white blossoms would adorn the landscape with a beauty only God could orchestrate. I breathed it all in.

Lizzie gave Josie a pinch. "Well, *couldn't* he come?"

Josie's eyes widened, catching Lizzie's intended meaning. "Oh! Um, I suppose I could speak to him, see if he's not too busy."

Davey watched my sisters' exchange with the most tender of care. "Aunt Josie, you know *Santa?*"

I hid a smile, for I couldn't think of anyone better suited to the role of Santa than Tripp. With a lot of stuffing, it might work.

Josie shrugged, Amos cuddled against her in a sling. "I've seen him around." She wagged her finger at Davey. "But don't get too excited, okay? He's super busy this time of year."

"It would be a great help to get him for some promotion. What's more perfect than Story Time with Santa at The Orchard House Bed and Breakfast?"

"Santa's coming!" Davey looked around for his brother, who was several feet behind. He ran to Isaac. "We're going to see Santa!"

Isaac smiled, but stopped walking, then swayed. My blood grew cold, then ran hot within me.

When my son fell, I couldn't make my limbs move fast enough to get to him.

❧ 10 ❧

I pushed my legs, weighted with fear, forward. Rushing, racing to my son. Shouting for someone to get Josh, get Isaac's supplies. How had I been foolish enough to leave the house without his kit?

I fell at Isaac's side. He stared blankly toward the sky. "Honey, are you okay?" I forced calm into my tone as I ran a hand over his face, studying his dazed look. As if he saw me through a thick screen of fog.

"Isaac, answer me."

"Okay..." he slurred.

"Dear Lord, why is this happening?" I spoke the words loud and in frustration as I scooped Isaac up, swaying beneath his weight. I took quick steps toward the house.

"You don't have his kit with you?" Amie was by my side, along with the rest of my family, but they probably had trouble keeping up as I ran fast, a rush of adrenaline pushing me forward.

"No." The one word stank of despair. I'd screwed up, again. I'd thought we'd figured out the carbs and dosing correctly. Passing out was a sign of low blood sugar, but I'd been so scared of him going high today. Could his body be reacting this way with a high? With this disease, and in that moment, anything seemed possible.

"Josh will be here any minute," Lizzie tried to assure me as she pressed her phone to her ear.

I looked at my other son, keeping up with us with little effort. "Davey, did Aunt Pris give you two any candy?"

He shook his head, hard. "No, Mommy. I promise, she didn't."

"He's not answering. I'll call Tripp," Lizzie said.

I spoke to Davey. "Go run and tell Daddy we need Isaac's kit, okay?" Josh had his phone on silent during the meal. He likely hadn't turned it back on.

Davey raced off through the orchard, not stopping to grab up his hat when it flew off. I continued my own frantic pace, Isaac's weight making my arms ache. Why could one twin's body run like the wind and the other's not handle a single Thanksgiving meal?

God, help.

How could I have forgotten his kit?

"You with me, honey?"

Lizzie patted my arm. "He nodded. You want me to take him?"

"No." I couldn't trust anyone, even my beloved sister with this task. I pushed myself forward, running. My foot rolled over a rotten apple, my uncoordinated movements matching those of my harried thoughts.

Then, the most welcome sight. Josh running toward us with powerful, sure movements. Without a coat, his arms pumped as fast as his legs. He ran faster than I'd ever seen, faster than his 5K finish for a race he ran for Alzheimer's last spring.

When he reached me, I gave Isaac over to his strong arms. Josh breathed heavy, laying Isaac on a patch of dry grass. I tore open the pouch, going for the insulin.

Josh pushed my hand aside. "We need to test him."

I ignored him, grabbed for a needle. "I know. I'm prepping."

He'd had too many carbs, surely. And I still wasn't entirely sure he hadn't sneaked a candy or a treat from somewhere in the house.

Josh uncapped the lancing device, prepped it with a lancet. I crept in close, prepared to dose the insulin.

"Back off, Maggie. We're testing him first." He hadn't ever spoken so firmly to me.

Yet, he was right, of course. Everything I read and studied and heard stories about told me to test first. But my mother instinct was right, too. I knew it. And time was not something we had a lot of. We certainly didn't have time to fight.

I nodded, sitting back on my heels, ready with the insulin Isaac would no doubt need.

I watched the meter hum to life, calculating my son's blood, measuring and gathering data that would instruct us how to best keep him alive and well. When a number finally lit up, I blinked. Looked at it again.

"He's low." Josh dug out the pack of glucose tabs, stuck two in Isaac's mouth.

I fell back on the grass, staring at the number 50. Low. So low. It didn't make sense. "Should we take him to the hospital?"

"I don't know. Let's see how he does." After several long minutes of everyone huddled around, squeezing my shoulders and praying between encouraging words, Isaac became more cognizant and managed to sit up on his own.

After a few more minutes, Josh tested him once more. This time, his blood sugar was at 70. Still low, but going in the right direction.

"I'm calling Nathan." I slid my phone out of my pocket.

"Maggie, don't. It's Thanksgiving. We should call his primary instead."

"And wait forever for a call back?" I held the phone between my ear and shoulder.

"He seems better. We're getting him back up. There's probably no need to bring him to the ER."

But I didn't listen, was dialing Nate's number.

"Hello? Mags? Everything okay?"

"Nate, I'm so sorry to bother you on Thanksgiving, but Isaac went low. We got him up to 70 and he seems to feel better. Do you think we should take him to the hospital?"

"Aww, poor little guy." Nate's voice held genuine sympathy. He asked a few more questions, which I answered the best I could. "Call me anytime, Mags. A trip to the hospital isn't necessary. Just give Isaac the glucose tabs and continue monitoring him."

"Okay, thank you so much, Nate." Relief filled me at the sound of his calm, knowledgeable, assuring voice. "Happy Thanksgiving."

"He's going to be okay, Mags."

"Thanks." I smiled before hanging up the phone, breathing easier than I had in the last twenty minutes. "He says he'll be fine. We should watch him for the next couple of hours. Maybe we should go back and feed him a small meal."

"More food?" Davey scrunched his nose.

"A little bit for Isaac. Maybe he'll be able to have a piece of the pumpkin cheesecake Grandma made for him."

Josh helped our son to his feet. He walked steadily toward the house alongside Mom, Lizzie, and Amie.

I watched them walk away, the gravity of what almost happened settling thick around me. I put my head in my hands, bottom lip trembling.

"Mags?" That Josh didn't simply leave me there broke my heart all the more. "You coming?" He held out his hand as the rest of my family led Isaac and Davey down the hill.

I shook my head. "I need a minute."

"He's okay, honey. Unfortunately, we're going to hit these scares more than we want to."

"I wanted to give him more." I closed my eyes. "I could have killed him."

"But we didn't. He's okay."

We. It was generous. More than generous considering what he didn't know. I wished there was a way around this, but he deserved to know the full truth. "I gave him a little more insulin than I should have before dinner."

"Maggie...what?"

"It was just a little. I thought it would help keep us on top of the extra food today. I was so scared he would go high, so certain that if it was going to happen it would be a holiday like this." Sobs choked my words. What kind of a mother was I? The kind that forgot to pick her kids up at school when they were still learning to trust me. The kind that disregarded the laws of diabetic care-giving because I thought I knew better. What a joke. "You have every right to be angry with me. I am so, so sorry. It—it kills me that we can't predict or control this thing. I hate it, Josh. I hate it, I hate it, I hate it."

It was the first time I'd said as much. I'd done so well keeping my emotions in check, particularly in front of the boys. And now, here I was, sounding like a temperamental toddler, but blast it all, I was frustrated. And mad. Mostly at myself.

Silence settled over us, and I kept my gaze fixed on the ground, frightened beyond belief to see the sight of Josh's retreating back.

Instead, I saw the palm of one work-roughened hand being held out to me. "Come on, Mags. It's okay."

Emotion climbed my throat. I took his hand, allowing him to pull me into his warm chest. My tears wet his shirt.

"I'm sorry."

"I forgive you. We're a team, remember?"

It felt so good in his arms. A small, selfish part of me wanted to stay there the rest of the afternoon, alone with my husband. We could forget about all of our problems—diabetes, houses, even the rest of the family. It could just be us.

He dipped his head to kiss me, and I sank into the incredible comfort of his affection. "I don't deserve you, but I thank God every day I have you," I said against his neck.

He hugged me, rested his chin on the top of my head. "We will get through this, Mags. What do you say we go and supervise the eating?"

"Okay."

We started back toward the house, our fingers entwined. He squeezed my hand. "It's going to get better. Easier. It will take some time, that's all."

I clutched his fingers tighter. He was right. Someday we would have a real handle on Isaac's illness. Surely, someday I would learn enough to feel capable and experienced. Maybe time and practice would wear away the troublesome mistakes like the one I'd made today.

Things would get better. The question was, would I be able to hold on tight enough to my family—and my faith—until they did?

Josh wiped thick dust off his forehead with the back of his hand. Resting his crowbar against the wall, he stood back and breathed deep through his respirator. There was something freeing about tearing down the old and decrepit, making way for the new.

And the Lord knew how much he needed a new beginning. On second thought, forget a new beginning—at this point in his life, he'd simply take a second chance.

He stepped back and looked at the dusty space, imagining in its place a bright and airy kitchen. Maggie at the sink, up to her elbows in soap suds, a bright smile on her face as he walked through the door. The boys would be running around outside, climbing trees or building forts. And maybe there'd be a little one sitting in a highchair, gumming Cheerios.

Tripp tapped his arm, dispelling the vision. He gestured outside. Josh nodded, and they both took off their respirators once they forged out into the sunshine. Josh went to his truck, grabbed a bottle of water.

Tripp took a swig of his own. "Man, you have a mess on your

hands, but this place has character and charm. Lots of potential. It's a good pick."

Josh capped his water. "Can't beat the area. Though I wish Maggie was more on board." He sat alongside Tripp on the open tailgate of his truck. "Shoot straight with me, buddy. Do you think I'm biting off more than I can chew?"

Tripp exhaled long and slow. "You have a lot of work ahead of you, but you got this. You have the skill. The time...that might be another question. How long you thinking?"

"You mean how long can I pay two mortgages? Five months, probably, and that's cutting it close."

"I'll help you when I can, you know that."

Josh's mouth tightened. "I appreciate it, but you have a new family of your own, not to mention the business. I'm happy with a day here and there, but not expecting any more."

They were silent for a moment as Tripp bit into a banana. "You give my proposition any more thought?"

Josh licked his lips. "I have, but I haven't come any closer to a decision."

"You talk to Maggie at all?"

He shook his head.

"Scared?" Tripp asked. Josh couldn't tell if he was joking.

"I'm not *scared* of my wife." Why had he kept silent then, when Tripp had come to him a week and a half ago? Josh lifted a hand, let it fall on his thigh. "She'll think it's crazy. I'm still not certain I don't think it's crazy."

"Do you want the job? And I'm talking to you as a friend now, not a potential employer."

Josh ground his teeth. "Yes, I do. I love building. But... construction? My old man will fall into an early grave."

"Hey, what's wrong with a career in construction? And I'm offering you more money. If it didn't work out, you could always go back to teaching."

Josh rubbed the back of his neck, sighed. "I like teaching. I love coaching. But truth is, I'm getting burnt out. It's not like I'm getting any younger. To start a construction career with forty on the horizon..."

Tripp nodded, and Josh knew his friend wouldn't badger him. This was a decision he needed to make on his own.

His hand tightened on the bottle of water. "I don't know, maybe it's time for a change. The satisfaction I get from building with my hands, from creating out of nothing...I used to get excited about teaching the same way. Now I'm too busy competing with social media and cell phones for attention."

"You have a gift. Not just for building, either. You're a leader, Josh. I need another foreman, and you're worth the money Grandpop and I are willing to put down. If you ever felt the need to leave, there would be no hard feelings. I guarantee it."

More silence.

"Hash it out with Maggie, at least."

Josh raked a hand through his hair. "It seems all we've been doing lately is hashing. I'm not sure how much more our marriage can take. I caught her by surprise with the house, now a career change? And what with Isaac's diabetes...the school offers decent health insurance. I can't pretend that isn't a factor, especially now. Maggie'll probably think I'm suffering a midlife crisis or something." He shrugged. "Maybe I am."

Tripp elbowed him. "Aww, come on, you're not *that* old."

Josh laughed, but the truth was, he felt old. Wherever he looked, he was at the mercy of younger, more accomplished men. Men with money. First Tripp, offering him a job and a salary that the school district couldn't touch. Then yesterday, when their son had a health scare, Maggie had rushed not to him, or even to Isaac's doctor, but to Nathan. A man who had been obsessed with his wife in high school. A man who could probably pay Josh's two mortgages without blinking an eye and still have money left over for a few fancy vacations a year. He tried to tell himself he'd have his act together if Trisha hadn't gone down such a rough road, but he wasn't sure that were true.

He couldn't afford to make any more mistakes. Not when it came to his family.

"I'll talk to her." He tore open a package of peanut-butter crackers and slid one out of the sleeve. "How about you? How's Finn living at your grandfather's place working out?"

Tripp stared at the pebbles and dirt at his feet. "I'm not going to lie. It's not all roses and rainbows. He's more mobile now, you know? When he was in rehab full-time, he was dependent on us. We made sure to make time for him. But now that he's driving again, he's more accessible. Amos is his son, I get that. And I'm trying to live behind what I said about making Finn a part of the family. Half the time I think I'm doing a good job. But the other half...well, I wouldn't mind keeping Josie and Amos all to myself."

Josh chewed carefully. "You're a better man than I am. I don't know how you do it. That doesn't mean I don't admire you for it."

"It's the grace of God, man, pure and simple. It's never been harder to love someone. Let me tell you, dropping Amos off at the apartment this morning was one of the hardest things I've ever done. That little guy has become my world. And it's gotta be my ego, but I want to be his. I have never, ever been so humbled in my life."

"That kid is going to grow up knowing what love is, and that's not a mistake. He's going to know what you've done for him—know what you continue to do every day. It's no small thing." Josh grew silent, slid another cracker from its package. "He's your son, Tripp. As much as he's Finn's. Love doesn't know blood."

Tripp smiled. "I guess you should know right? I mean, I've never seen a mother more devoted than Maggie. If anyone's proven the whole 'love doesn't know blood' thing, it's her."

"What she has with the boys is special. But we're not without our share of troubles, as I'm sure you've realized lately." They both laughed. "One day at a time, right?"

"And don't be scared of your wife."

Josh gave Tripp a hard jab in the side with his elbow. "Had to take me down a notch, huh?"

Tripp laughed. "You bet." He hopped off the tailgate and headed toward the dumpster that sat on the side of the lot. "Ready to get back to work? We got five months and this place isn't looking a whole lot better yet."

Josh surveyed the farmhouse before him, tired and sagging. How could he love it already? Much easier to be content with the house he'd bought with Trisha. But thinking of living all his years in the little brown house was enough to bring on a near panic attack—and he didn't consider himself prone to such anxiety.

He pondered Tripp's joking comment that he was scared of his wife. Crazy, of course. He wasn't scared of his wife.

Yet, maybe if he were honest, he could admit one fear: fear of opening himself up, letting himself be fully understood and known. Trisha had always shut him down when he'd tried to do that—had chosen to find release and comfort and meaning in substances that took her life, and nearly stole the lives of his boys as well.

But Maggie wasn't Trisha. She was open to talking, open to listening. Though she'd brushed off his counseling suggestion and though they'd been choosing twenty minutes extra sleep over morning coffee dates more often than not, she wasn't afraid of talking. She wasn't shy about making her opinions known, and she wasn't a wall. She loved him, supported him.

Maybe that's what he was scared of—not her, but the fear of disappointing her.

Just as he'd done with Trisha.

I shifted in my seat, looked upon the small sea of faces gathered in our church's hall. The scent of coffee mingled in the air, toasty and warm. The group of women sat in a large circle, chatting among themselves. I loved that some of my own family came. Lizzie sat on the right talking to Ashley Robinson, and Aunt Pris sat, Bible open, alongside her lifelong friend Esther, who ate a slice of coffee cake.

Mom would be here if it wasn't for the bed and breakfast. Josie on the other hand, wouldn't be caught dead spending a Wednesday morning with a bunch of ladies "who cried over Bible verses in the morning while wagging their tongues with gossip in the afternoon."

Josie and I had fought long and hard over that one day. The thing was, I knew what my sister said sometimes held a grain of truth. I knew the deadliness of hypocrisy and had fought with it on occasion. But I kept on, had to believe these women, including myself, were better off for our weekly study. If words could pierce hearts, then I'd have to leave it to scripture and the Holy Spirit to do its job.

The Lord knew I didn't have enough strength to be anyone's

keeper, let alone my own. I fought off a yawn, a reminder of the little sleep I'd gotten the night before while treating a stubbornly low blood sugar level.

As soon as I thought we'd figured out correct doses and stabilization, something would throw off Isaac's levels. We could do all the same things on two consecutive days—feed him all the same foods, ensure he received the same exercise, give him the same doses of insulin—and still he'd be off. If the disease was logical, I could handle it. If it could be reasoned with, I could figure it out. But this unwieldy, invisible, deadly disease that threatened the life of one of the people I loved most in the world? It was wearing me down and I wasn't sure I was strong enough to do battle and win over it in the long run.

I gathered a breath and looked down at my notes. It'd been weeks since I'd taught a study, but I had planned to finish it before Christmas, which left only a couple of weeks. Along with treating Isaac's low blood sugar the night before, I'd been trying to prepare the lesson. I hated leaving things for last minute, but I'd been so busy with doctor's appointments and insurance calls, not to mention planning the bed and breakfast sale for this coming weekend. I'd fallen behind. As usual these days.

I led the group in prayer, read the scripture verses, and began my talk. I'd written the lesson the night before with the help of several commentaries and books. But I hadn't let it soak in, hadn't given myself the time to do so. Now, as I taught, the words brought on new meaning and life.

"In verse 6, Peter says to 'humble yourselves under the mighty power of God, and at the right time he will lift you up in honor. Give all your worries and cares to God, for he cares about you.'" I looked at the tender faces of the women around me—different ages, different colors, different cultures. And yet united in this: our desire to seek and love God. Our measures of faith may be different, but the object of our faith was the same. "I know sometimes I look at these verses and they seem to apply to me and my life, but I confess other times I see Peter's advice and it seems too trite for my big problems. I wonder if that's how Mary felt while her brother, Lazarus, lay rotting and dead in a grave? I wonder if, when Jesus told her that her brother would rise again, if she found comfort in that? And yet, Jesus proved his words. And here, now, no matter our circumstances, He's calling us to humility"—my voice caught on something thick in my throat as the words I spoke hit home—"and trust."

I cleared my throat. I could not break down in this moment. I was the teacher, the leader. At home, I was the mother who needed to keep it together. The wife who needed to be the sunshine-maker of the family.

A wobbly sort of panic started in my chest. I was crumbling.

"I think we sometimes think—I sometimes think—that I have to be strong, but I miss the fact that being strong is depending not on ourselves for strength but depending on Him." A small sob escaped and I choked on it, scurrying out of my chair. "Excuse me."

I fled the room. All I could think of were those beautiful words, telling me God cared for me, gently calling me to an act of humility and trust.

An act so simple in thought and yet lately, so tough to implement. Why was it so hard to cast my cares on God?

But I knew. In a disease that depended so much on my ability to maintain it, the pressure was constant. And I'd been capable my entire life. Capable to take care of my younger siblings, to take care of the house when Lizzie got sick all those years ago, to battle through math problems with Amie.

I had gone into my marriage so determined that I could be the best person for Davey and Isaac, and even Josh. But early failures and small comparisons to Josh's mother cured me of those illusions fast. I found myself always striving, always straining to do better, to be better. And, I realized, I'd left God behind while I grasped for success.

I climbed the stairs to the second-floor bathroom used for nursery and Sunday school. I shut myself in and leaned my forehead against the wall.

I thought of Trisha. Of her struggles, which I could not relate. But here I was, having a nervous breakdown instead of leading a Bible study. Here I was, encouraging the women downstairs to trust in God when I couldn't summon up the faith of a mustard seed myself. Talk about being a hypocrite. If someone offered me a pill or a drink to make all this better, would I not take it? Who was I to judge, in the grand scheme of things? I'd never known desperation until now, never known what it was like to feel so helpless and incapable in every area of my life.

I turned from the wall, my gaze landing on a basket of complimentary feminine products. From somewhere far away, I realized it had been a long time since I'd had my period. My mind skidded to a stop. No. No, not now. I'd wanted a baby for so long but this couldn't be God's plan—to send me a baby in the midst of the most chaotic time in my life.

I was stressed. That had to be it. Stress could do crazy things to a woman's body.

I straightened and dragged in a deep breath, my sleep-deprived mind clearing. I wasn't pregnant, of course. Of all the months we'd been trying to conceive, surely the most anxiety-producing, sleep-lacking last two months wouldn't provide the necessary conditions for fertility.

I sucked another breath, trying to get a grip.

God, give me strength.

I settled into the prayer, my mind relaxing as I dwelled on the fact that I wasn't alone. That another cared for me and could be my strength.

Failing my family was not an option, but I didn't have to fight alone.

A knock came at the bathroom door, and I opened it.

Lizzie stood on the other side. "Are you okay?"

The sight of my sister was enough to cause my bottom lip to tremble. I shook my head and she enveloped me in a hug.

"I'm sorry, Lizzie. The entire class deserves an apology. I—I was hearing those words for the first time, realizing how much I needed them."

"Oh, Mags. We all do." She pulled back. "Maybe it's too soon for you to be teaching. You still have a lot going on."

"I hate letting the ladies down. I hate letting you down. I'm supposed to be the big sister, aren't I?"

"You are the best big sister." Lizzie squeezed my arm. "But you're not indestructible."

I sniffed, wiped my nose with the back of my hand. "I feel like a fraud, you know? Sitting up there, reminding these ladies to lean on God when I haven't been doing anything of the sort myself."

"It can be hard to live out. I think God gave us one another, too, to help us in the weak times. Like this, Mags."

I leaned against the wall. "Everything seems like it's falling apart, you know? Isaac's health. The house situation. My marriage. Josh suggested counseling the other day."

"He loves you. I can see it plain as day. I'm sure he only wants what's best for your marriage."

"I do, too," I whispered. "I'm just overwhelmed."

"Can I pray for you?"

I sniffed, nodded.

Then my sister prayed for me, right there in the bathroom. She asked that God place His strong arms around me, that I would feel them. She spoke of Him knowing the number of hairs on my head, of Him knowing every intimate detail of my struggles, of Isaac's health. She asked that the Holy Spirit come upon me.

I sank into her words, felt myself lulled by a peace that hadn't been there before. There, in the bathroom, I knew the Lord's presence.

When Lizzie finished, I clutched her tight for a long while, then finally released her. "Thank you." I searched for something to lighten the mood. "So can I tell Josie you said I was the best big sister?" I laughed through the last hiccuping sobs of my tears.

Lizzie giggled. "Only if you want to make her stark raving mad."

We left the bathroom with our arms around one another. "I'm so grateful for you. So grateful for all my siblings."

I would return to finish out the Bible study, but this time, I wouldn't pretend. I would open up to the ladies and ask them to pray for me. I would be vulnerable. I would trust that they would pray me right into the arms of God. And that He would keep me in His embrace.

❧ 13 ❧

There were moments when I wondered how I'd make it through the day—and then there were moments like these, when I wished time would slow.

I squeezed the small hands clasped in my own as I walked Davey and Isaac out of their school and toward our car. Someday, probably sooner than I'd be ready for, they wouldn't want me to hold their hands.

I breathed in the moment, the rollercoaster of emotions at that morning's Bible study easing farther and farther away with each step I took with the twins, with each precious second their fingers clutched my own.

"How was your day, boys?" I forced a little pep in my step, trying to set the mood for the afternoon. I didn't have to work at the bed and breakfast—in-person, anyway—and I planned to take the kids to the library to pick out some new books to read tonight.

"Ms. Lindrooth has the Christmas tree up. She read us *Merry Christmas, Curious George.*"

"That's a good one." I opened the back door of the car and helped Davey in while studying Isaac, searching for warning signs that his sugar was off. Though his color looked healthy and I couldn't put my finger on anything blatantly wrong, something seemed amiss. I brushed a hand over his head. "You okay, sweetie?"

He nodded and stepped up into the car.

While making the drive to the library, I asked the boys questions—how was lunch? What was their favorite part of the day? Who did they play with at recess? Davey chatted away the entire time, but Isaac remained subdued. Maybe we should skip the library. Or at the very least, I should check his blood sugar.

"Isaac, are you sure you feel okay?"

He gave an uncharacteristic, huffy sigh. "I'm good, I said."

I pressed my lips together, squelching the need to remind him about his tone. In truth, I could understand his frustration. We'd been together for twenty minutes and I'd asked him how he felt at least four times.

I parked the car, and since Isaac was the first to hop out, I decided against testing his sugar. We walked across the street, and Isaac hurried ahead into the library.

Davey tugged on my sleeve. "I think I know what's wrong with Isaac."

I bent down to look into my son's brown eyes, realized it had been too long since I'd given him my full attention. While I'd been grieving and groaning for the loss of Isaac's health, Davey had lost a part of his mom as well.

I ran the back of my fingers over his soft cheek, vowing to spend some one-on-one time with him soon. "You do?"

Davey nodded. "Matt Nordic called him a baby today."

I sucked in a breath, tried to remind myself that getting angry at a six-year-old bully would not solve any problems. "Why would he do that?"

"Isaac had to sit out of gym class again today cuz of his sugar. Matt called him a baby."

A lump formed in my throat. "Oh, poor thing." Stacia had reported that Isaac's sugar had dropped late in the morning.

"I told Matt to be quiet. I wanted to hit him, Mommy, but I knew I shouldn't."

I squeezed Davey's shoulder. "You're right. You shouldn't hit. Thank you for sticking up for your brother, though. I'm sure that meant a lot to Isaac."

Davey shrugged. "I guess." He looked after his brother, who waited for us at the library door.

I kissed him on the cheek. "Why don't you two go on ahead? I'll meet you in the children's section."

He ran off and I turned toward the harbor, breathing in the crisp air and the scent of the sea. A smattering of naked masts dotted the seascape. In the distance, a thin covering of snow from the night before illuminated Curtis Island in white. I looked at the wharf, where two Adirondack chairs now sat empty. I thought of the long-ago summer night where Josh and I had sat on those chairs talking for hours, getting to know one another, falling in love. How far away it all appeared.

I dragged in a breath around the hurt I felt for Isaac. Bitterness would do nothing for my son, but for all that was good in the world, I wanted to stop his hurt. If I could take away the pain and unfairness, I would.

I turned back to the library and met the boys downstairs. Though I desperately wanted to talk to Isaac about his day, I managed to wait until we got home. Both boys had put away their schoolbags and lunchboxes and washed their hands before having a snack—nut crackers and cheese with strawberries on the side. They talked about playing on the jungle gym at recess, how they had told their friends about Buddy, our Elf on the Shelf, wrapped up in a tube of toothpaste near the sink, a smiley face drawn in paste on the counter that morning.

When they finished, I tussled Davey's hair. "Do you think you could shovel off the back steps so they're all clear when Dad gets home?"

Davey nodded, and thrust out his chest, as that was a job Josh or I usually handled. I helped him bundle up in his coat, hat, and mittens. The door slammed behind him.

"Do I need to take a test before I play?" Isaac sat at the table, his legs swinging well above the floor, his shoulders hunched as if the weight of the world was upon him.

A test. One where a passing grade would result in relief and a smile, where a failing grade would result in an insulin shot or a glucose tab. I closed my eyes, feeling utterly defeated for the hundredth time since Isaac's diagnosis. I'd read about kids connecting their worth to their blood sugar levels—being made to feel "good" when their levels were stable and feeling as if they fell short when their levels were off. It sounded silly to me at first— for a child to blame themselves for something they couldn't control—and yet the more I learned of the disease, the more I understood the factors that aggravated it. If Isaac accepted a candy bar from a friend at lunch, it could mess with his levels. If he ate too many carbs, or if he overdid exercise.

How many times, when his blood sugar had been high, had I gone over the day carefully with him, trying to catch the reason for the levels—not to make him feel bad, but to educate. And yet the fact remained: other children didn't need to pay attention to such things. Even Isaac's classmates began to pick up on something different about my son. And now, he spoke of testing blood sugars as if it were the most daunting of math tests. Poor kid.

I knelt beside him, beseeching God to direct my words. "No. No test, honey. I wanted to talk to you about school. Davey said you had to sit gym class out and that Matt said something mean to you."

Isaac's bottom lip trembled, but he shrugged, seemed as if he would try to brush it off. "I'm *not* a baby." He clenched his fists tight as if to prove the point.

"I know you're not, but it must be tough when kids say stuff like that. They don't understand, and I'm sure that can make you feel lonely sometimes."

Isaac sniffed. "Why are you a bad mom, Mommy?"

I let out a short, surprised exhale, oxygen draining from my body. Time froze as I grappled with his question. I put my hand on Isaac's arm—more to steady and ground myself than to reassure him about anything. I lowered myself to the chair beside him. "W—what do you mean, baby? Why am I a bad mom?"

A horrible part of me felt as if someone had peeled back my exterior and found my secret, exposing all my faults and sins. I fell short in so many areas of motherhood, now here my son was confirming the truth.

"Kids at school said I have diabetes because you gave me too much sugar."

The words squeezed and twisted, wringing my spirit dry. I tried to sort them out. A misunderstanding. It was all a misunderstanding. I couldn't be mad at Isaac's classmates. They didn't understand.

And hadn't I thought the same at one time? That you only got diabetes from not eating well, from having too much sugar. Could I fault children?

"Honey, you don't have diabetes from having too much sugar. You have diabetes because your pancreas stopped working. Remember we talked about that? How there's two different types of diabetes? Your classmates don't understand."

"Why did I have to get this stupid disease?"

I placed my hand on his arm, wondering the same question myself.

He continued. "Why don't the other kids have it? Why did I get it, but Davey didn't? You and Daddy don't have it. It's stupid."

"I know, honey. I know. I wish I had answers for you, but all I can say is you are *not* alone. You have me and Daddy and Grandma and all your aunts and uncles and Grammy and Grampy. We all love you so much and are going to help you any way we can. You will never be alone." I inhaled deep. "It's not fair, and I wish I could take it from you. I would in a second if I could, Isaac, but no matter what, I am here for you. Forever and always. And so is Daddy."

His dejected demeanor caused my mind to race to think of a way I could ease his hurt. "I think there might be a way to help the kids in your class understand about your diabetes a little bit better, but it might take some work. Do you think you're up for it?"

His face brightened, those deep green eyes, so like his father's, filling with a tiny bit of hope. He nodded.

"What if I spoke to Ms. Lindrooth about you and me talking to your class about the kind of diabetes you have. Explaining about your pancreas and how we need to monitor your sugar levels, how sometimes you might have snacks when they can't, how sometimes you might have to take it easy during gym class. We could bring in snacks and maybe make a poster board explaining about type 1 diabetes." If we educated Isaac's class-mates, if everyone in his class was armed with understanding, they could be part of the team instead of a hindrance.

Isaac eyed me. "What kind of snacks would we bring?"

I laughed. "Maybe veggie sticks with yogurt—and maybe a sugar-free dessert. How's that sound?"

He nodded, satisfied. "Maybe cookies?"

I hugged him. "Cookies sound perfect." I sat back on my heels, looked into his face. "You come talk to me whenever you need, and I will drop whatever I'm doing. Nothing is more impor-tant than you and your brother. I will always be here for you, okay?"

"Unless you die like our other Mommy."

Oh gracious. I grabbed Isaac up in my arms, squeezed him tight, whispered fiercely against his hair. "I am *not* going to die. Not anytime soon, anyway."

It was perhaps too bold of a promise, for life was uncertain indeed. And yet, in that moment, determination consumed me like nothing I'd ever known.

Isaac lifted his head off my shoulder. "Am I going to die?"

"You are not going to die, either. Not until you're an old man." I tapped his nose, remembering Lizzie's prayer that morning. "Do you know that Jesus is with us, no matter what? He knows all about you. He knows about your diabetes and how hard it is to sit out of gym class when your sugars are off. He even knows the number of hairs on your head. Your Aunt Lizzie reminded me of that today."

Isaac stared straight ahead, his face serious. "That's a lot of hairs."

I laughed.

"Should we pray for Matt?" Isaac asked, and my chest ached from the tender innocence of his request.

I stared into his clear eyes, so sincere. "Do you want to know how blessed I am to be your mother?"

He wrinkled his nose. "Even though you have to be my paincrest, too?"

I tickled his side. "Yes, most definitely. There's no one else's pancreas I'd rather be."

He smiled, seeming convinced of the sincerity of my words. I hoped he was, for in that moment I realized they were one-hundred percent most definitely true.

"Okay, do you want to pray now?"

He nodded, closed his eyes and started. "God, I'm mad at Matt and want to call *him* a baby. But I won't. Help Matt and all the other kids know that Mommy's not a bad mommy. Amen."

"Amen," I echoed.

"Amen."

I jumped at the sound of Josh's voice and smiled up at him before dragging Isaac in for another squeeze. Josh walked over and enveloped us both in a hug. He smelled of outdoors and crisp air and wood. I closed my eyes against his jacket.

"Can I go outside with Davey?"

I grabbed Isaac's coat and bundled him up. "For a little."

Hopefully, Josh and I could talk while the boys were out. There was something important we needed to discuss that hadn't made it into our infrequent early-morning coffee dates.

14

There were times lately when Josh questioned everything —his desire for a new house, changing careers at this point in his life, what medical care they sought for Isaac. But entering the warm kitchen, seeing his wife and son wrapped in one another's arms in a prayer was enough to assure him that, in the end, all would be well.

A fierce inundation of love rose within him along with a desire to take care of these precious people, to keep them safe and loved, always. He was indeed blessed. He had a family who loved him, a family whom he'd give his life. What else mattered?

Isaac barreled out the back door, tugging on his mittens as he went. Josh gathered his wife in his arms, kissing her softly. She melted into him but pulled away too soon.

"Can we talk?" she asked.

"Sure." He opened his small cooler, taking out his empty travel mug. He rinsed it in the sink. "I'm listening, Mags."

She waited until he turned off the sink. "I think we should look into a CGM for Isaac."

A continuous glucose monitor. A small system that would give real-time readings of Isaac's sugar levels.

He nodded. "I've been thinking about that, too. At least try it. It could make all our jobs easier—and make him feel more normal."

Tension eased from her face and shoulders. "I didn't expect you to agree."

"Well, the doctor said it's important we have a handle on the diabetes before depending on a CGM. Do you feel like we're there? And then there's the expense. Not to mention there's something about having him hooked to a machine 24/7 that rubs me the wrong way, but if it works..."

Maggie stepped closer. "I've been doing some research. The system I'm looking at would give us constant information on his levels through our smartphones. And if we decided on a pump, there may be hours at a time that Isaac doesn't need to think about his diabetes. I think it might improve his mental state too, not to mention ours."

Josh furrowed his brow, sat at the kitchen table. "It sounds great, but how much does the insurance cover?"

"Not as much as I'd like."

"That's what I was scared of."

"Think of the benefits, though. Physically, emotionally. We're managing to redo a house—isn't Isaac worth more?"

She had to go throw in the house guilt, didn't she? But he didn't want to argue. He wanted peace. Peace and a happy, healthy family.

Josh hadn't planned on bringing up Tripp's offer. Not yet. He'd planned on this weekend. Maybe during a nice date or with a glass of wine. He wanted to have a long uninterrupted talk, spend some quality time with his wife. But maybe all that would have to wait.

He cleared his throat. "I actually have something I wanted to talk to you about that might play into this conversation."

He hated how she practically wilted against the counter, as if any more hard things *he* wanted to talk about would put her over the edge. Well, he'd put it off long enough. "I got a job offer.

One that would give me an opportunity to rake in more income."

She perked up. "Josh, that's great."

"I've been mulling it over, wondering if it's the right decision for us."

"Is it the department head? A job at another school?"

He shifted in his chair, avoided her gaze. "Not exactly." Another moment of silence. "It's for Tripp."

She blinked. "Construction?"

"Yeah."

She sat down at one of the chairs at their small table. "Didn't see that coming."

He laughed softly. "Yeah, me neither."

"What are you going to do?"

He shrugged. "I don't know. I wanted to talk to you. Get your thoughts."

"You did?"

"Of course, Mags. This is huge. I mean, it's bigger pay but probably longer hours."

"You'd have to give up coaching." She fiddled with an empty plate leftover from the boys' snack.

"Yeah, I would."

"How do you feel about that?"

"I love coaching. More than teaching, to tell you the truth. I would miss it."

"Josh, I don't want to ask you to give up your career for money. Some things aren't worth it. You're a *great* teacher."

"Yeah, but I'm kind of handy with a hammer, too. Tripp wants me to be a foreman, said he'd send me to get my license. That he has that much faith in me...well, it means a lot."

Maggie's mouth tightened. "I hope he's not trying to do us a favor. It'd be like him, you know."

"I'd like to think I've earned the offer."

"Josh—no, I'm sorry. That's not what I meant." She sighed,

fanning hair out of her face. "Why can't we have one decent conversation lately without jumping down one another's throats?"

He slumped in his chair. "You're right. I'm sorry." But her words niggled. Had Tripp offered him the job out of pity? He knew his friend and Ed Colton had gone out of their way to help Maggie's family make the B&B feasible. Was this simply another way of paying back a debt Tripp thought he owed Hannah and her children?

Maggie inched out a hand. "What do you want? Do you want to build every day?"

He tapped nervous energy out onto the table. "Yeah, I do. I don't know if I could do it forever. Even now, inching toward forty, I wonder how long my body will be able to take it. But I'm in shape. The work agrees with me. Maybe I could still help out with some Saturday and nighttime track meets."

She nodded. "I'm behind whatever you decide, okay?"

"Tripp's having his secretary put together an insurance packet for us to look over."

She nodded, mouth tight.

"Your Aunt Pris's quilting club is going to have a field day with this information. And my old man will probably try to commit me."

She smiled. "Camden High's favorite teacher turns in his textbooks for a tool belt. I can see it now. Remember how set my aunt was against me marrying you? As if I could have ever done any better."

"I don't know, Mags. Sometimes I wonder."

She stood and kissed him. "Don't."

He pushed out the chair and pulled her onto his lap. "We're going to be okay."

She grabbed up his face in her hands. "We're going to be okay," she repeated.

She dipped her mouth to his and kissed him with a tenacity he didn't expect. He sank into her, his hands traveling over her back and down her sides, the softness of her curves pressing against him. These were the moments they needed. Less conflict and stress, more getting on the same page, more showing love for one another. The love that seemed to get shuffled around and pushed to the side with all the chaos in their lives of late.

The back door opened and shut loudly. He sighed wistfully as Maggie jumped off his lap to direct the boys to take off their boots before they dragged wet snow and mud through the house.

He watched her gather up their things, hanging up coats and hats and mittens. He remembered Trisha coming in that very door and telling him she was pregnant.

It had been one of her better days and he'd taken her in his arms in the same way he'd done with Maggie a moment earlier. A twinge of guilt mixed with hurt and regret tore through him at the memory. That day with Trisha had been one of their best, but the next several months would prove trying as trust upon trust was broken, and little progress gave way to bigger failure.

He turned away from Maggie and the boys and forced the memories from his head. The memories were part of the house. That was it, right? Once they sold the place and moved, the memories wouldn't come poking around as often. He was sure.

Josh went to the boys, flung Davey over his shoulder and asked him about his day. He tried not to see Trisha in every corner, tried to push aside the old bitterness.

Soon. Soon, they'd be out of here.

❧ 15 ❧

I looked through the lens of my phone, zoomed in on Isaac and Davey sitting cross-legged on the floor of the Orchard House bookshop. Amidst a gaggle of other children, they leaned forward to look at the book Santa read to them, *The Tree That's Meant to Be*.

Tripp made his deep baritone lower and ten times more booming as he read about a tree that felt out of place in his forest home.

I snapped my picture. There. Perfect for the B&B Instagram account.

I gently elbowed Josie, who stood in the back of the room beside me, bouncing Amos on her hip. "He's good," I whispered.

Josie leaned over, whispered back. "Right? And is it just me or is that Santa costume super sexy?"

I smuggled my laughter in my sleeve, trying to contain my giggles. "I'm pretty sure it's just you."

She shrugged, sighing happily as she gazed at her husband.

When was the last time Josh and I looked at one another like that? Before he started working so much? Before Isaac's diagnosis? Yet, isn't that how marriages worked? The newness and shiny glow gave way to something more real, something more true.

If only the real and the true felt a little more like joy and a little less like super hard work. If only my husband's eyes weren't haunted with the ghosts of his past—if only I could heal and fill that place of pain inside of him. Inside of our sons. Inside of myself.

I tuned back into the story, a beautiful tale about a lonely little tree who learns what it means to be loved. A message that instilled the worth of each person—or tree—on the earth. I listened, let the story lull me with its harmonious rhythm. I glanced at Isaac. While I'd spoken to his teacher and set a date for our special presentation, and while Isaac hadn't mentioned any more run-ins with his peers, he'd been subdued the latter part of the week.

We would see his endocrinologist on Tuesday—a doctor from the children's hospital who I couldn't summon fond feelings toward. Nevertheless, I'd mention the change in mood, as well as our desire of getting a CGM and pump.

When Tripp ended the story, Josie walked to the front. "Can everyone thank Santa for reading us such a beautiful story?"

The children echoed back their thanks.

"If you'd like to speak with Santa, form a line right down the middle here. And feel free to grab some cookies and hot chocolate while you're waiting."

The children scurried to find parents or treats or Santa. I watched as Isaac went to the snack table and picked out a cookie from the tray labeled "Sugar-Free." He grabbed a bottle of water instead of hot chocolate, then held up his items to me, smiling as if to say, "See?"

I returned his sweet smile and gave him a thumb's up.

"He's doing pretty well, huh?" Josie put Amos over her shoulder and patted his back.

"We're trying to get things under control. We're looking into getting him a CGM, which will make things a lot easier, I'm hoping."

"A what?"

I shook my head. Words such as *insulin* and *glucagon* and *DKA* and *CGM*—words that were now a part of my everyday vocabulary—were not on most people's radar. I could spout them off to doctors or Josh and be understood, but there was still so much my family didn't know about Isaac's disease. Maybe I could stand to give them a presentation, too.

I gave Josie a quick explanation, barely unable to comprehend a world without finger pricks myself.

"Wow, sounds great."

"I think it would give us a bit more peace of mind. Not that any technology is fail proof, but we want to give it a try."

Josh entered from the side door wearing a large chef's hat and an apron that proclaimed *An Apron is Just a Cape on Backwards*. He held a tray of freshly-baked cookies in his hands.

I laughed. "Looks like Mom's put him to work."

"Nice apron," Josie said.

I giggled. "It's almost as sexy as Tripp's Santa suit." My laugh ended on a sigh. "I miss this. I miss you. Life's been too serious lately. I forgot how good it feels to laugh."

"We need each other, Mags. I've missed you, too. How about an impromptu sisters' night? I'll talk to Lizzie and Amie, see if they have any plans. Nachos and guacamole, maybe some cider, right here in the bookshop."

"That sounds wonderful. But I've been making a big deal about Josh being around more and not working so much. I don't know if I feel right running off on a Saturday night."

Josie wiggled her eyebrows. "Leave him to me. I'll tell him it's for the sake of my sanity, which it is. I miss my girls."

I shrugged. When Josie made up her mind about something, there was usually no getting around it. "Okay. Let me know how it goes."

"I will. Oh, looks like Rose needs help on the register." She handed Amos over to me. "How in the world did you get us on the front page this morning?"

"The angle of story time with Santa practically sells itself this time of year."

Josie wrinkled her nose. "Ick, you make it sound so strategic and commercial."

I pressed my lips into a thin line. "It is strategic and commercial. And a good thing, too. We're making a profit."

Josie worried her bottom lip between her teeth. "There was nothing strategic or commercial about that story Santa read, and you know it. We're a business, but we're a business that cares about people. The moment we make it only about profit, I'm out of here."

"The moment we stop profiting, we'll all be out of here."

"Oh, you! I have to go, but we are not through with this conversation."

I bounced Amos gently as Josie ran over to help Rose at the register. Tripp took a little girl onto his knee while Davey waited excitedly for his turn. In line, two older women showed one another macramé snowflake ornaments they'd found, crafted by Narratology. Another held one of Amie's nightlights. Behind them, Isaac took another cookie from the sugar-free plate and Josh demonstrated how his apron could in fact be turned into a cape to a small boy who stared wide-eyed at his ostentatious outfit.

I sighed, content for the moment. Of course Josie was right. This place was far from only profits and commercialism. Here, we all created a story. A story that included so much more than the Martin family, but also the lives of those we touched.

I could only do what I could when it came to marketing. The Lord would decide if the business sailed or failed—and right now, it seemed He deemed it fit to sail.

❧ 16 ❧

I reached for a potato skin and bit into it, the cheese, bacon, chives, and sour cream dancing on my tongue. Soft lights and tasteful candles placed amid the greenery of the bookshop reflected off the massive windows. My sisters gathered around the gas fireplace, and I leaned back against the couch, more relaxed than I'd been in...well, I couldn't remember the last time I'd been this relaxed.

I sighed with contentment. "This is long overdue. Thank you, Josie. I needed this."

Amie leaned her head on the back of a deep-cushioned chair. She propped her feet on the coffee table. "I'll say. I might not have kids to tire me out, but my classes have been all sorts of taxing. Sometimes I wonder why I'm in school."

Lizzie hugged her knees to her chest from where she sat on the rug by the fire. "Because an education is never a waste and can open doors to your future."

Amie released an exaggerated sigh. "All I can think about is my art, you know? Math and science are such a waste to me right now."

I put my plate on my lap. "Could you take some business

classes in the spring? Maybe you'll learn something about selling your art. You have a gift, but Lizzie's right. An education is never a waste."

"I suppose." Amie perked up. "I talked to Miss Lena the other day. She's agreed to offer my nightlights on consignment. I'm working on some table lamps as well."

"They're beyond gorgeous, Amie." I could understand my younger sister's frustration. She had a real talent, could probably earn a living from her art and grow a business without devoting so much time to classes. The lamps and shades she created from fossilized leaves created beautiful patterns in an eco-friendly package. Using an iron frame, wood, and manila rope, the lamps had an exotic but rustic feel. "Grow it slow and steady, and you won't be disappointed or burned out."

Amie studied the gentle flames in the fireplace. "I've decided to give school until the end of the year. After that, I'll make a decision."

Seemed there was no use trying to dissuade her. Maybe completing college wasn't the answer for my sister, as much as I believed it a wise move.

"You need to follow your heart." Josie picked up a squalling Amos. "No one could have told me a year ago that quitting school would be a good move for me. But I don't regret it...think I might be better for it. Life can be a sort of college, too."

Amie gave Josie a grateful smile. The two hadn't always gotten along but the last several months had cemented whatever fracture had been between them. It did me good to see my two most contentious sisters supporting one another.

"What about you, Lizzie?" Josie gave Amos a firm pat on the bottom, vibrating his entire body and soothing him instantly. "Has going to school helped you achieve your dreams?"

Lizzie blushed. "It helped me become a teacher, which I love. If only teaching could support me enough to pay off my student loans." Her voice quivered.

I slid onto the floor and placed an arm around her shoulders. "What's the matter, honey?"

From this close, I could see my tender-hearted sister's eyes glisten. "We found out earlier this week that they're doing away with art and music in the new year. I don't see that there's anything that can be done about it."

"Oh, Lizzie," Amie whispered. "It isn't right to take that away from the kids. High school art was where I could finally express myself and not feel like a dumb kid in math class." She looked at me helplessly, as if I might have an answer. The oldest sister, always solving everyone's problems. "There has to be something we can do."

My head spun as I thought not only about Lizzie and her job but all the high school kids in her private school who would be losing out. One thing Dad had instilled in us was the value of a well-rounded education. That included the arts. But what could we do? And why were each of my sisters' eyes on me as if I had the answer to all life's problems?

Because I was a fixer, that's why. A solver. When someone needed help with homework, even if I didn't understand complex math or the keys to writing a great paper, I would trudge through and help if it killed me. Anything could be fixed. Anything solved. It was simply a matter of finding the right answer.

That's why Isaac's diabetes was giving me so much trouble. Why my marriage was on shaky ground. Because I hadn't yet found the right answer. Or maybe because there wasn't only one solid, right answer to find. No clear-cut solution.

I licked my lips, searched my mind for a solution to Lizzie's problem. "What about some sort of fundraiser? We made a good amount with the cookie dough fundraiser for the boys' school, and I bet we could make more if we thought out of the box. Maybe a 5K? Josh could help organize it." On top of the million other things he had to do. "Or what about selling some of your students' art?" I grasped Lizzie's arm. "You should put on a concert, Lizzie. We could have it here. A concert in the barn. Get the kids in on it. Maybe we could make enough to support the music program at least until the end of the year."

Lizzie squeezed her knees tighter to her chest. "I hadn't thought of anything like that. I've been so upset with the news." She bit her lip. "What about a New Year's Eve thing? Though that would be a lot of organizing in only a few weeks. Bonfires and appetizers and a concert in the barn?"

"I like it," Josie said.

"I do, too." Such events and community outreach were what we'd envisioned when we'd opened the B&B. Not just a service for paying guests, but a way to help our neighbors. "I was already thinking of running a Christmas giveaway contest on our Instagram page to increase exposure. They might work nicely together. We could reveal the winner the night of the concert."

Lizzie straightened, loosened her grip on her knees. "You know, I think this could work. It's last minute and people might have plans for New Year's, but—"

"But a lot of people don't and are looking for an excuse to get out of the house and celebrate," Josie said. "We'll have to run it by Mom and Aunt Pris, of course."

"Of course." Lizzie smiled. "Maybe this will give me the motivation I need to finish one of my songs."

"Yes! Oh, I can't wait." I could hardly imagine my sister singing solo before a crowd, and yet little by little Lizzie appeared to be coming out of her shell. "You have something in mind?"

A small smile graced Lizzie's face. "I think so. It's coming slow, but there's nothing like a hike in the woods and a song in my head to inspire. Thanks, guys. I'm excited. I hope the school goes for it." She shook her head. "Now enough about me. Catch us up on married and mama life, Josie. I'm surprised Tripp didn't take Amos out with the guys tonight."

"I was too scared they might use him as a football." Josie

laughed. "I'm kidding, I think. Tripp's a great father. You know, Finn is too for that matter."

"Yeah," Amie sat forward and grabbed a nacho with a healthy serving of guacamole. "How's that all going anyway? I tell my friends I don't need to watch any soap operas. I have my sister's life."

Josie chucked a pillow at Amie, nearly upsetting her guacamole. They all giggled.

I cleared my throat. "Seriously though, you handling everything okay?"

"I am. I think Finn might be starting to get antsy with small-town life, though. He's making more and more progress and he loves Amos so much. He's good with him." She shrugged. "Who knows, I could be wrong about him wanting to take off. He talks to Tripp more than me, which has to be the weirdest relationship ever, but it's working. Only by God's grace, that's for sure."

"And you have no regrets about school?" I sipped my winter sangria—non-alcoholic, which suited me fine since my period still hadn't made an appearance. The cinnamon and cranberry flavor burst in my mouth, and I closed my eyes, savoring it.

"Maybe someday I'll go back and finish up, but I'm content where I am right now. The bookshop, the bed and breakfast, Amos, Tripp. I've never been happier. I've been writing again, too. Nothing genius, but it's creative and it's fulfilling. Wherever the winds of life take me I am ready to set sail."

Lizzie sighed, stared wistfully into the fire. "You make the unknown sound so romantic."

"If you remember correctly, I didn't always think that way. Tripp had a lot to do with changing my mind."

"I know." Lizzie stared into the crackling flames.

I contemplated the deep thoughts hidden beneath her quiet exterior. I also knew she was more likely to share them in a one-on-one setting than in a group, even of her sisters. If we went through with this concert, we'd no doubt have plenty of time together.

"That leaves you, Mags." Josie laid Amos in the bassinet that she kept in the bookshop so she could work during the day. "Catch us up, lady. I know you have a big appointment for Isaac coming up."

I rehashed what I'd told Josie at the story time event. "I'm hoping we can get him on a better schedule. And if Josh takes the job offer from Tripp, we might be able to make it work."

"Whoa," Amie held up a hand. "I missed something here."

"He hasn't made a definite decision yet, but I think he's going to quit teaching and go into construction with Tripp full-time. Maybe not forever and maybe not long-term, but temporarily. I think it will do him good, and it will give us a financial boost. CGM's and pumps aren't cheap and Josh enjoyed working with Tripp over the summer. He didn't want to give it up."

"Nothing like keeping it in the family, eh?" Amie dug into more nachos. "August says he likes working for his grandfather and brother, though it's sometimes hard getting bossed around by Tripp at home and at work."

"Tripp's a great boss," Josie said. "And August mustn't mind it if he keeps coming back for more on the weekends. You've been seeing a lot of him lately, haven't you, Amie?" Josie plopped onto an empty chair and grabbed a plate, filling it to overflowing with potato skins and nachos.

"We're talking about Maggie now, I believe." Amie scrunched up her nose.

Josie wagged a finger at our youngest sister. "I'm not forgetting this so easily, little sis." They all laughed, but she did turn back to Maggie. "And she's right. We have more to cover. Like how is the baby-making coming along?"

I slapped a hand on my forehead and shook my head. Lizzie giggled ferociously into her knees.

Amie sat forward. "Oh yes, do tell."

I leaned back into the plush chair, the fire warm at my feet. "It's not, to be honest. Josh and I are okay, but ever since Isaac's diagnosis, things have been so stressful. It's been hard to want to be intimate. It's like it's another added pressure. You know, figure out my child's health crisis and oh yeah, make sure to do everything right so I can get pregnant. I'm a mess." I opened my mouth to tell them I was late, but something stopped me. If I spoke now, there was no turning back. Josie would run out to buy a pregnancy test and demand I take it on the spot. I wasn't ready for the possibility.

I wiggled my toes in my boots. "Actually, it might be better if it doesn't happen yet. I can barely handle everything on my plate as it is."

"Mags, it's only natural to be nervous, but once you hold that sweet little babe in your arms..." Josie spoke her words through large bites of potato and sour cream.

I shook my head. "It's all for the best, anyway. We need to adjust to Isaac's new normal before adding any more additions."

"What about IVF or adoption?" Lizzie asked.

I nodded. "Both expensive, neither what I envisioned. But we'll see what this next year brings."

Maybe I *should* pick up a pregnancy test. Just to make sure.

J osh bit into a greasy slice of pizza, covered in cheese, and turned his attention to the football game on his television screen. The room erupted in cheers as the Black Bears scored a touchdown against Ball State.

"That's Kyle Andrews who made that play." Bronson tapped Tripp on the arm with the hand not holding a chicken wing. "Remember him? A year older than me. We used to play in the sandbox together. He's top of the draft this year. Maine's best chance of seeing the NFL."

Tripp nodded. "That quarterback isn't too shabby, either."

August shook his head. "Are you kidding? He was way off on that throw. Andrews being fast is all that saved them."

Josh wasn't quite sure how he'd ended up with a houseful of guys stuffing their faces with pizza and chicken wings while watching a college football game, but he was okay with it. When Josie suggested the idea and Tripp offered to bring pizza, how could he say no?

As long as they cleaned up the mess before Maggie came home, he could call the night a success. Oh...and keeping Isaac away from the junk food.

He got up from his spot on the couch and walked past Finn and Ed Colton talking about the stock market. In the kitchen, he found the boys playing on the floor, tower blocks and LEGOs splayed across the tile. "You two okay? Bedtime in ten minutes." He studied Isaac. "You didn't have any more pizza after that one slice, did you buddy?"

"No."

"Your mom left some trail mix and veggie sticks if you're still hungry."

Who was he kidding? What kid would opt for veggie sticks over a second slice of pizza and potato chips? He sighed, tried not to waver before his son. Maggie had told him one of the most destructive things to a diabetic child was one parent being the good cop, the other being the bad cop. She'd read it in some book or online somewhere. But the poor kid. Having to eat those sugar free cookies and only one dinky slice of pizza.

"Can I have another piece of pizza, Daddy?" Davey asked.

This was the hardest part. They'd done their best to empty their cabinets of any sugary, processed foods. No more pop tarts or fruit roll-ups or sweet cereals, most of which Maggie had never been a fan of in the first place. But it was the out-of-the-ordinary days that were hard. The special occasions. How could he tell Davey he couldn't have another piece of pizza because his brother couldn't? Why should Davey suffer also? They'd vowed to keep things fair. But how many slices of pizza had Josh eaten? Fair his backside.

He sighed, making a quick decision. "Tell you what, why don't you both split a slice of pizza and we'll call it a night."

Isaac's eyes lit up. "Really?"

"Yeah. We'll check your sugar before bed and make sure you're good, okay?"

They cheered, and he thought that maybe it might be worth it after all. Isaac had been stable all day. Josh would let them stay up a little later and test Isaac a half hour after he ate the pizza. If he was high, he'd give him a little extra insulin. The kid had to live once in a while.

If you wanted to call half a slice of pizza living.

He cut a slice in half and told the boys to wash up after they finished so they wouldn't get their LEGOs greasy from the pizza.

August's phone was ringing when Josh came back into the living room. Tripp's brother dug it out from his pocket, his face reddening slightly. "It's Nicole."

Tripp and Bronson made obnoxious noises as August slid out of the room to take the call.

"He serious about this young lady?" Ed asked Tripp.

"You should ask him, Grandpop. All I know is she's pretty, into architecture and football, and crazy about August. And yet, he keeps coming home for the weekends instead of staying at school to hang out with her."

Tripp's grandfather nodded. "Sometimes a girl can have everything going for her, but the stars aren't aligning."

"Wow, Mr. Colton. That's deep." Bronson popped a potato chip into his mouth. "Is that how it was for you and Mrs. Colton? Stars aligning and all that?"

"Oh, maybe. Our parents were the ones who wanted us together. I'd been seeing another girl at the time. But loving Edith wasn't hard. Family obligation meant something back then."

Tripp squinted at his grandfather. "I didn't realize you and Gram got married because of your families. I thought you married for love."

"Love came with time."

"Who was this other girl, then?" Finn asked.

Josh leaned forward.

"Oh, a little spitfire."

"Is she still alive? What's her name?"

Ed's eyes twinkled as he looked at Bronson. "She's alive, all right. And still has quite a bit of spunk. You know her quite well, in fact."

Josh slapped the arm of the couch. "Ed, you dog. You and Aunt Priscilla were a thing back in the day?"

"No…" Bronson stared at the rug, shaking his head.

"Grandpop, why didn't you ever say anything?" Tripp's jaw hung open.

"Oh, I don't know. It felt disrespectful to your grandmother's memory. It all happened some sixty years ago. It's water under the bridge to me."

"So, was Aunt Pris…nice back then?" Bronson managed.

"Young man, that woman has opened up her home to you, helped make your mother's dream come true, and has been financially generous to all of you kids at one time or another."

Bronson shrunk back. "Aww, come on, Mr. Colton. I know that. And we love her for it. But you have to admit, there's a little bit of crust around her edges."

"She had quite a time of it with her husband," Josh volunteered. "Maggie told me it was why she was so set against us marrying. I think she was scared for Maggie with the history behind me and the boys' mom."

The corners of Ed's mouth tightened. "Yes, your aunt has had a rough road, but I think, in her own way, Priscilla is the most kind-hearted soul I've ever had the privilege of knowing."

Josh exchanged a look with Tripp. If he didn't know better, it seemed Ed may still have feelings for Maggie's great-aunt. Interesting.

August walked back into the room, looked at the television. "What'd I miss?"

"Quite a lot, actually." Tripp smirked.

"No one scored," August said.

Bronson laughed. "How's your girlfriend?"

"She's not my girlfriend. And she's fine. Hey, do you know if Amie's busy tomorrow?"

Bronson shrugged. "I'm not her keeper. Why don't you ask her yourself?"

From his corner chair, Ed smiled, looked between Tripp, Josh, and Finn. "When the stars align. What'd I tell you?"

To August's frustration, they all let out good-natured chuckles.

As Josh put the boys to bed, remembering to check Isaac's blood sugar, he thought on Ed's words.

Looking back on his life, he thought of the hard times he'd had with Trisha. Strange that he didn't regret those years, for the end result had been two of the greatest gifts of his life. In some ways, Trisha's poor decisions had led him *to* Maggie. Crazy how the mess of life could sometimes lead to the most beautiful.

So why then, couldn't he let go of the mess? A nudge within his spirit told him the answer. One he didn't want to face, but one that was becoming harder and harder to ignore.

With some pain, he remembered Trisha's pale, lifeless body in that lonely casket. One of the twins had been in his arms, one in his mother's. He remembered grieving in that terrible moment, but he also remembered another feeling—hatred. For himself.

How could he get past it? How many hours of beating himself up would it take? When would the race of trying to outrun his first marriage end?

He sighed and went downstairs to see Tripp and Ed gathering their coats. He shook their hands, thanked them for coming and bringing food. Without overthinking it, he turned to Ed.

"Mr. Colton, I want you to know how appreciative I am of your job offer. To both of you. I've given it a lot of thought, and I talked it over with Maggie, and I'd like to take you up on it."

Tripp clasped his hand, a grin spreading across his face. "You're serious."

Ed chuckled, elbowing his grandson. "That's one bet I won, now, isn't it?"

Josh looked from the older man to the younger. "You didn't think I'd take the job?"

Tripp shrugged. "I didn't. But I'm happy you're ready to jump in."

Ed pumped Josh's hand. "It will be a pleasure to have a fine young man like yourself as part of the crew. When can you start?"

"I'll ask to be released from my contract on Monday. With our new medical expenses, I think they'll give it to me if I give them time to find a replacement teacher. Hopefully, I can start with you in January."

Tripp grinned. "I'll send you the materials to study for your supervisor license in the meantime. You probably know most of it already." He pumped his fist in the air. "I am stoked."

Ed crimped his brow at Tripp.

Tripp tapped his grandfather's arm. "Excited, Grandpop. I'm excited."

Mr. Colton shook his head, started for the door. "We'll talk soon, Joshua. Welcome to Colton Contractors, son."

Josh waved goodbye, confident he'd made the right decision for both his future and that of his family.

⊗⊗⊗

TOWARDS THE END OF THE NIGHT, A MYSTERIOUS TEXT FROM Tripp prompted Josie to invite Mom and Aunt Pris to join us in the bookshop.

While we waited for them, and while Josie made more nachos upstairs, I contemplated Tripp's report that Aunt Pris and Ed used to be an item. "How did we never know about this?"

"Aunt Pris isn't exactly an open book," Lizzie said.

"And Josie thinks the old girl is going to turn over a new leaf tonight?" Amie shook her head, swirled her glass so her cranberries made a little whirlpool in her drink.

"You know Josie. Always trying to figure things out. Like life's one big puzzle." She'd been the driving force behind the bed and breakfast after all, piecing together Mom's dream into reality, stitching together details and solving Aunt Pris's very practical dilemma of growing older alone and needing help.

The bells on the door jingled just as Josie returned with a warm plate of nachos. Mom opened the door for Aunt Pris who entered with her cane—a commodity none of us were convinced she needed.

"Let's get one thing straight." Aunt Pris took off her hood to expose meticulously placed curlers in her hair. "I'm here for the sangria and nachos. I'm not sure what's so urgent that you all feel you need to drag an old lady out of her warm bed on a cold December night."

"Aunt Pris, we didn't mean to bother you. We thought this might be fun." At least that's what I thought Josie had envisioned when she called Mom.

I went to my great-aunt's side and offered my arm, but the old lady shooed me away.

"I still have both feet well out of the grave, young lady. Where's the sangria?" She sat down in the comfy chair closest to the fire.

"Here you are, Aunt Pris." Lizzie ladled some sangria into a large wine glass. "It's non-alcoholic."

Aunt Pris raised her thin eyebrows. "Now I'm truly regretting getting out of my bed." But she took the drink all the same, sipping it with relish.

Mom sat down and leaned back, closing her eyes. "This place is certainly cozy at night. And today was amazing. With the event and the newspaper article, we raked in quite a few reservations."

I glanced at Josie, then back to Mom. "We want to keep the trend going and were just brainstorming some ideas."

Mom opened one eye. "I thought you girls were supposed to be relaxing and catching up. Not spending time on marketing strategies. We're off to a great start with this business. Don't overwork yourselves, especially this time of year." She gave me a pointed look.

I scooted forward in my seat, tried to ignore her unspoken

message for me. "We *were* catching up and trying to solve Lizzie's job predicament. That's when we got the idea."

Mom raised her eyebrows. "Oh?"

"A fundraiser to support the music and art programs at the high school. At least until the end of the year."

Aunt Pris grabbed a potato skin. "Not a cookie dough fundraiser, I hope. Those treats went straight to my hips."

Josie elbowed Aunt Pris and winked. "Hate to tell you, but these potato skins are apt to do the same."

Aunt Pris scowled at her outspoken niece.

I cleared my throat. "No, not cookies. Something a bit bigger. A concert. A New Year's Eve ticketed concert in the barn. What do you think?"

Mom stared at the rug, silent but nodding slowly. "It's certainly ambitious. Have you spoken to the school board?"

"Considering we came up with the idea twenty minutes ago, no. But I don't see why they would deny it. We'd be doing all the work. They wouldn't have anything to lose."

Lizzie nodded. "And I could perform some of my new songs and get the students to do a few as well. Some of them are in bands outside of school. I'll bet they'd be more than willing to pitch in, gather the talent from the surrounding areas. We could feature all sorts of music and celebrate the diversity of the art form."

Amie waved her hand in the air as if she was in one of her classes. "Oh, I have another idea! Why not get some of the art students to donate a piece of their artwork? We could frame them and auction them off. Have them displayed along the walls of the barn during the concert."

"That's perfect!" Josie went for more nachos. Where did my sister put all the food she ate? She was already back to pre-pregnancy weight.

"It definitely has potential, but it will require a lot of planning. I'm afraid my hours are tight as it is, especially with the holidays and my commitment to the mission." Mom still devoted as much time as she could to the project our father had started five years ago, volunteering to serve food, give out clothes, or offer a listening ear whenever she could.

"We'll do all the work, Mom," Josie said through a mouthful of food. "I could organize the cooking myself."

I held up my hand. "That *definitely* won't be necessary." We laughed. "But we'll do all the leg work, Mom. Nothing for you to worry over."

Mom's mouth tightened. "I'm not necessarily worried about myself. Maggie, your plate is too full and you keep taking on more. You think this is wise, honey?"

Was my mother right? There were only so many hours in the day. But something propelled me to do this. Perhaps it was the distraction—something to think about besides Isaac's health. Sitting with my sisters tonight, laughing with these people who grew with me and challenged me, I realized all I'd pushed aside the last several months while I wrung my hands first over my inability to conceive, and more recently, over Isaac's diagnosis.

I pressed my lips together before answering. "I want to do this. And we have one more idea we wanted to run by the two of you."

Mom shook her head. "More, huh? Why doesn't that surprise me?"

I placed my drink on the table. "Instagram contests are incredibly popular. If we could give away something big, like a two-night stay at Orchard House, we'd gain more attention for the B&B. We could reveal the winner the night of the concert on New Year's Eve. What do you think?"

Aunt Pris cleared her throat. "I don't know much about Insta-grammer, but I can have the quilting club spread the word about the concert and the auction. A lot of their grandkids and great grandkids are at the school and they would be more than willing to support them."

Lizzie gave our great-aunt a grateful smile. "That would be amazing. I know how committed your club is to you, and how much influence they have in the community. Thank you, Aunt Pris."

Mom lifted her hands. "Then I guess it's settled. Let me know what you need. Of course, I'll help make some appetizers for the evening. We might want to ask some of the businesses we use to donate baskets to add to the auction as well."

"I'm on it," Amie said. She had searched out organic and locally-sourced soaps, shampoos and lotions for the guest rooms and had started building a relationship with the local shop owners, including some who now carried her art products. "I could donate some of my stuff, too."

"That's sweet, Amie. I know how long it takes you to make one item." Lizzie leaned her head against Amie's knee.

Amie squeezed Lizzie's shoulder. "It's for a good cause. And I'm not going to lie—the advertisement won't kill me, either."

I sipped my sangria, let the warmth of the moment soak into my soul. "You know, I have to say that we all make a pretty great team. I'm not sure what we Martin women can't do when we all get together."

"We *cannot* improve Josie's cooking skills." Amie shielded herself behind her hands, anticipating the pillow that sailed across the room.

"We all know what I lack in the kitchen I make up for in literary taste."

I tried to catch Josie's gaze. I jerked my head toward Aunt Pris, but my sister jerked her head back at me. I shook my head fiercely. No way did I have the audacity to question our great-aunt about her long-ago love life. Josie was the far better choice.

She must have thought the same, for the next moment she cleared her throat and folded her hands over her knees, an entirely un-Josie-like gesture. "Actually, we have a question for Aunt Pris."

"Well, don't dilly-dally, girl. This drink's almost done and then I'm off to bed."

"We found out something rather interesting from Mr. Colton and wanted to ask you about it."

Aunt Pris raised her eyebrows almost high enough to reach one of the pink curlers on top of her head. "Is that so? What's that old coot spreading now?"

Not exactly the answer I'd been hoping for, but Josie licked her lips and wiggled herself to the edge of her chair, undeterred. "We don't want to be nosy, of course—"

"Too late for that, I'd say."

"But Mr. Colton said that you and him used to be a thing."

"A thing?"

Josie's cheeks reddened. "Like, you know. A pair."

"A pair of what?"

I hid a giggle in the crook of my arm. Did we expect Aunt Pris to play into our nosy questions?

Josie released an unladylike breath. "A couple, Aunt Pris. Did you and Mr. Colton used to date?"

"Court, girl. We courted. So much more tasteful than dating. And obviously, there isn't much to talk about, so I don't know why you're so intent on digging around in the past. I'd say it's a good thing for you it didn't work out between me and Ed, either. Tripp wouldn't have existed."

"Aunt Priscilla, I had no idea." Mom put her hand to her lips. "All those years Ed was our neighbor and you never said anything."

"What happened? Why didn't it work out?" Josie asked.

Aunt Pris released a long, exaggerated sigh. She sat quiet, and I wanted more than anything to know what memories Josie's question pulled to the surface. From the look on my great-aunt's face, they were memories not devoid of pain.

Finally, she drew in a deep breath and opened her mouth, spoke softer than her normally forceful tone. "Too many differences. Then there was the war. We went our separate ways after a time."

"But after you both lost your spouses, you never revisited a relationship..." I'd spoken my thoughts without monitoring them, but Aunt Pris didn't appear to mind.

"We'd changed a lot by then. I reckon Ed didn't want anything to do with an old widow like me. He was a virtual stranger to me, as well. We'd lived entire lives since we parted. For him that meant children and grandchildren. For me, you all and my old family home. What was the point of opening Pandora's box?"

"Oh, how sad," Lizzie murmured.

"Why is it sad to be without a man? My experience with men may be somewhat limited, but all I've gathered over the two relationships I've had was hurt. There's nothing wrong with paddling my own canoe. And I have to say, I've done quite well for myself. And now, I'm content to live out the last of my days with those I care for most. *Despite* their prying questions." She eyed Josie pointedly.

The topic dwindled and we drank the last of our sangria. As I hugged each member of my family goodbye and headed out into the chilly night to my car, I wondered about my aunt's words.

Yes, I supposed living alone was easier in some ways. If you were alone, you only had to worry about yourself. You didn't have to risk anguish over a fractured relationship or a child's failing health.

But as I drove home, anticipating the warmth of Josh's arms, the two little boys I loved tucked in their cozy beds, I knew I wouldn't trade the pain, or the risk of having my heart broken for the world. Love would make all the inconveniences worth it in the end.

❧ 18 ❧

Josh plugged the space heater into the extension cord and cranked it up. He laid a blanket down on the bare plywood of their future living room. He lit a candle and placed it on the center of the blanket beside a slim vase with a single rose. Next, he grabbed up the Subway bag and napkins and laid them on the corner.

He straightened and admired his work. Not bad. A little chilly. Okay, a lot chilly. But it would be nice for him and Maggie to have a picnic lunch, just the two of them. As soon as Maggie dropped the boys off at Orchard House to stay with Lizzie for a little, she'd be here.

He admired the new windows he'd installed Friday night. He'd cleaned up the debris from the demolition, and the electrician was scheduled to start the coming week. It was a lot of work, but he loved seeing the progress. He hoped Maggie would love it, too. They could start dreaming together, building new memories. Today.

He squinted down the driveway. Where was she? Probably giving last minute instructions to her sister. Well, no use standing around when there was work to be done.

He climbed the stairs and opened one of the windows that contained a chute to the dumpster. Taking his shovel, he began cleaning up bits of plaster and sheetrock and sliding it down the chute, getting lost in the work.

"Hello?"

Josh swiped a hand over his brow. The sound of his wife's voice in their new home caused a foreign sort of emotion to stir inside of him. "Be right down!"

He shut the window and trotted down the stairs in time to see her come around the corner to the living room. She gazed at the picnic he'd set up, the candle snuffed out, likely from a draft of air. "Oh, Josh."

He stepped closer, took her hands in his own. "Do you like it? I wanted to make your first experience in this house a good one."

"I love it. And I love you." She stood on her tiptoes to kiss him and he drew her close, wrapping her in a tight embrace, burying his face in her soft hair.

"Do you like the new windows?"

She nodded. "It really does look so much better. Do I get to see what you've done with the rest of the house so far?"

"Absolutely." He led her from room to room, excitement building within him at the prospect of living here with her and the boys.

He showed her what would be their bedroom, pointed out how the windows would look out over the trees until they could glimpse the harbor. "I want to put in one of those big old windows with a bench seat here, so you can read in the morning and watch the sunrise."

Her hand went to her throat, but her bottom lip quivered. "I'm sorry."

He put his hands on the sides of her arms, bent his knees so he could look directly at her. "What on earth do you have to be sorry for?"

She avoided his gaze, shrugged. "For not believing in this for us, I guess. For thinking this was some macho desire to prove something to yourself, for doubting for a second that you didn't have the very best for all of us in mind."

He closed his eyes, drew her to him until she was nestled against the crook of his neck. "Oh, Mags. I'm the one who's sorry. I do think this is what's best for us, but the truth is it's about me, too. I can't escape Trisha in that blasted house. I know it doesn't make sense. I know I should be more grown-up about it. But I can't. I'm sorry."

"Then this is what's best for all of us."

"I think so," he whispered into her hair.

They stayed wrapped in one another's arms for another minute. He was about to suggest they go downstairs to eat their sandwiches when Maggie spoke into his shirt. "Do you still love her?"

He pushed back to see his wife better. "Do I still love...?"

Those beautiful brown eyes searched his own. "You know, Trisha."

He tried to contain the groan that climbed his throat. "I wish we wouldn't talk about her here."

"You can't erase her existence simply by moving to another house. The boys deserve more than that. I deserve more than that. You deserve more than that."

She was right. He knew it and hated it.

He rubbed the back of his neck. "I loved the person I married, and I tried to love the person Trisha became. I tried to do all I could as her husband, and I failed. I failed, and I hate myself for it."

Maggie's expression softened, but she didn't speak, giving him the opportunity to purge his thoughts.

"Mags, I think the reason I'm so hard on myself about Trisha's death is because at the end, she made it extremely hard *to* love her. I struggled with the fact that I didn't love my wife a lot. I mean, what kind of a husband feels that way? What kind of a husband acknowledges that he feels that way?"

She gripped the sleeve of his shirt, rubbed it between her thumb and forefinger. "Oh, honey. You tried. It was the drugs. They stole her from you."

"For so long, I told myself I could love her out of the addiction. Love's supposed to be that powerful, isn't it? But it wasn't. At least not mine. So to answer your question, no, I don't still love Trisha. In fact, I have a hard time not hating her every single day. And that's what makes me hate myself."

He took a deep breath, stared at the dusty floor of the place he'd wanted to lay down new dreams.

He felt the soft skin of Maggie's hand upon his face. He leaned into it.

"Thank you," she whispered.

"For what?"

"For being honest with me. For not pretending like everything's fine when it's not."

He let out a soft snort. "Anytime. No perfection here."

She cuddled back up to him. "You mentioned counseling the other day for us. I have to admit, I hate the thought of going, but if you think it's something we need to do to work through all this...your mess and mine...then, I'm willing, Josh."

His heart near exploded with love for this woman. He'd told her some of the ugliest things in his soul, and she still stood by him, wanted to help him. "Thank you. Let's just keep talking, okay? We've been missing too many coffee dates."

"Life is crazy right now, isn't it?"

"Maggie Acker, there's no one else I'd rather live the crazy with." He kissed her then, tasting her sweetness and wanting to never let go, wanting to draw out this moment forever and ever. And for the first time in a long time, his world righted. For the first time in a long time, he thought that maybe there was hope of getting past the trauma of Trisha after all.

I grated the head of cauliflower, watching small white flakes pile into the shallow bowl below.

I wondered if the boys would be fooled into thinking the chicken and cauliflower rice bowl I'd prepared for dinner was *actual* rice. For that matter, I wondered if Josh would be fooled.

At the thought of my husband, I allowed a smile to soften my face. Our time at the new house yesterday had been amazing. The picnic, the conversation, the kissing...perhaps this house would be a new direction for us. Perhaps we'd climb out of the well of despair we'd fallen into the last few months.

When things got hard, I'd have to remind myself that there was no hole we couldn't climb out of, if we did it together.

I grated the head of cauliflower with more fervor, thinking about the pregnancy test I'd bought that morning, sitting beneath the bathroom sink. Sooner or later, I'd have to take it and face whatever it told me. I'd be happy if two pink lines appeared, wouldn't I? Yes, it would be a lot, and yes, I'd be scared to death, but we'd wanted this for so long....

The doorbell rang and I placed the cauliflower on the dish and wiped my hands. When I glimpsed Josh's mother through the window, I pasted on a smile and swung open the door. "Denise, how are you? What a surprise."

She stood, looking a bit unsure, a covered casserole dish in her potholder-clad hands. "I don't plan to stay, Maggie. I know you must have so much going on. I was making lasagna tonight and thought to double the recipe on a whim. My homemade sour-dough bread, too. You could use an extra hot meal, couldn't you?"

I stepped aside to let her through, trying to mentally calculate how many carbs were in one small slice of lasagna. The scent of the meal warmed the house. So much for a healthy cauliflower rice bowl. "That was kind of you. Thank you."

"Would you like to keep this warm in the oven?" She turned around, her dark hair perfectly smoothed back, not a hint of gray at the roots.

"Um, yeah. Sure." I rushed to put the oven on a low temperature.

"I just know how Josh and the boys love my lasagna. I thought he might appreciate a good meal, what with you having your hands so full with that bed and breakfast and all."

My gaze flitted to the half-grated head of cauliflower, no competition for the scents of sausage and cheese and fresh bread now filling the house. "I try...Isaac's not supposed to overdo the carbs, you know..."

But Josh would appreciate the meal. The first time I'd made lasagna, he'd gotten a funny look on his face after tasting it.

"What is it?" I had asked.

He'd shaken his head. "Nothing, it's great, Mags. I just never had...kale in my lasagna before."

"Spinach. I thought it would be good."

He hadn't said anything more, but I'd kept the spinach out of any future lasagnas. I was sure Denise had never added the vegetable to the Italian dish.

Denise whirled around after placing the pan in the oven and placed her hands on her hips, either ignoring my comment about the carbs or genuinely not hearing me. "Now, where are those boys?"

I shifted from one foot to the other. "My mom should be dropping them off any minute."

I'd been in the middle of setting up the Instagram contest, juggling a few last-minute reservations, and getting a price on fresh flowers for the New Year's Eve fundraiser when the bus dropped off the boys. Mom was going to the market and offered to take them for a few hours so I could finish out the day.

"You're welcome to wait so you can say hi. Do you want some tea or coffee?" I scurried toward my cauliflower, threw the rest of the head on the plate on top of the "rice" and the grater in the sink. I opened a drawer, retrieving the plastic wrap.

"I don't need anything to drink. Actually, I've been wanting to talk to you."

I pressed the plastic wrap around the edges of the plate. Little bits of cauliflower rice stuck to the wrap. "Oh?"

"Honey, I know it's not easy stepping in and being a new mother. You've done such a great job. But sweetie, I miss those boys so much." Wetness gathered at the edges of her eyes, and compassion filled me.

"I know you do." I spoke softly, unsure. "I've been teaching my mother and Lizzie about how to handle Isaac's diabetes. Maybe you could come over and be with the boys sometime and I could show you."

It was a leap for me. It was hard enough to trust my own mother with Isaac's care, but Denise loved the boys. She was the one who had diapered them and made sure they got to preschool on time. She spent those early years up at night with them, comforting them when they were crying for their mother. She deserved my trust.

There was no room for my insecurities.

She squeezed my arm. "Thank you. I know the family dynamics are unique, but I am their grandmother, and I think the boys miss Ray, too. He built them a swing in the backyard. We could have them stay over one night, let you and Josh have some alone time."

I cleared my throat. "Isaac's diagnosis is still new for us. Josh and I have decided to take things slow. Definitely no sleepovers yet, but we'll work something out. Maybe we could have dinner together sometime soon?"

Denise nodded. "Okay. Thank you, Maggie."

Out of the corner of my eye, I caught Mom's car pulling up our short drive. "Here they are now." We walked outside and the boys piled out of the car.

"Grammy!" Their chorus of joy echoed through the air.

I closed my eyes as she wrapped them both in one big hug. I needed to loosen the reins of control. I needed to face the realities of life...no matter how much they frightened.

I thought of the test below the bathroom sink and wondered if I had enough courage to face whatever it held.

For the hundredth time in the last two weeks, I reminded myself of God's strength.

Jesus, help me.

It wasn't much of a prayer. But it was all I had.

🦂 20 🦂

If only the hardest part of this doctor's visit was battling the traffic to get here.

I stepped out of the SUV and stretched, running through a mental list of questions I wanted to ask Isaac's doctor.

Not that I hadn't gone over them at least a dozen times in the nearly two-hour drive to get here. I sighed. Josh had insisted on seeing a doctor at the children's hospital. I didn't fault him for caring, but the drive grated on my nerves and I'd had to take Isaac out of school for half the day. The stress of it all was enough of an excuse to cause me to avoid taking the pregnancy test for one more day.

Again.

I opened the back door of the SUV for Isaac. Of course, if the long trip here was worth it, I'd drive all the way to West Quoddy Light for our son. So far, I wasn't convinced.

But who knew, perhaps today would change my mind.

Isaac placed his transformer toy on the seat and squinted up at me. "Am I going to get in trouble?"

"What? Why on earth would you think that, honey?"

"From the doctor."

I leaned against his seat, slid my hand into his. Dr. Lionel had been strict last time—not mean, of course, but firm in the importance of good habits to control Isaac's disease. But maybe she'd scared him? "Honey, Dr. Lionel is here to help you."

And yet, I couldn't pretend I hadn't felt the same fear tunneling through my own veins. When Dr. Lionel looked at Isaac's numbers, would she be able to tell all the times I'd failed as his pancreas? Would she be able to tell when we hadn't dosed him enough insulin or given too much? When I hadn't guessed the carbs right or had allowed my son a special treat? Perhaps I, too, was afraid of a failing grade.

"It's hard to eat good all the time." Isaac stared off into space, one cheek tightening in an adorable, but appropriately pitiful look.

I enveloped him in my arms. "I know, honey. I know. But you're doing such a good job."

"And Daddy helps."

I kissed him on the forehead, my heart softening tenfold at his words.

I wasn't privy to all of their father-son conversations, and neither did I feel like I had to know everything. But maybe I should give Josh more credit. He must have learned a thing or two about encouraging the boys over the years.

"I'm glad. He's a good daddy, isn't he? What does he say to make you feel better? Maybe we could remember that now."

Isaac shrugged. "He doesn't say anything. But he let me have extra pizza on Saturday for guys' night. That made me feel better."

I swallowed, fought to keep hold of myself. "Honey, I left you and Davey chicken nuggets and veggies on Saturday." I'd gone through the trouble of making a veggie platter that resembled a garden scene—a cucumber and broccoli tree, carrot caterpillars, red pepper flowers.

"I ate the chicken and vegetables too, Mommy."

"H-how much pizza did you have?"

Isaac seemed to sense that he'd said something wrong, for he clammed up quick, climbed down from the car. "Not much pizza. I passed my test, so I guess I did good."

I took his hand as we started toward the medical office building, confronting Josh in my head. He claimed to want to be on the same team, but how was that possible when I offered nut crackers and cheese while Josh dished out the fun of a greasy pepperoni pizza?

My phone rang from the small purse I carried. I released Isaac's hand to dig it out before opening the door of the building. The school's number flashed on the screen. Hopefully, they weren't giving me more grief about Isaac missing another day. "Hello?" I ushered Isaac into the warmth of the foyer and stepped off to the side where a large window overlooked the parking lot.

"Hello, Mrs. Acker?"

"Yes, this is Maggie Acker. Is everything okay? I know Isaac's missing more classes, but I've talked to his teachers and—"

"No, Mrs. Acker. This is Mr. Sedgwick. I'm not calling about Isaac."

A call from the principal. A slow, throbbing pain started at my temples, working its way downward and to the back of my neck, where all my stress sat in physical form—a ball of nerves that symbolized all the chaos of my life. Good thing I hadn't decided to take the pregnancy test that morning. Anymore life-rocking news would put me over the edge. "It's Davey? Is he okay? Is he sick?"

"No, he's not sick and he's not hurt. But he is sitting right here with me in the office." He cleared his throat, a foreshadowing of unpleasant news in the sound. "He was in a fight."

I paced before the window, pressed fingers to my pulsating temples. "What happened? Is he okay?" I couldn't believe someone would take issue with Davey. He was such a sweet-tempered child. Far from perfect, of course, and I supposed I *could* be a little biased being his mother and all, but who in the world would start a fight with him? With either of my sons, for that matter?

More silence, uncomfortably so.

"Mr. Sedgwick...what is it?"

"Davey hit a boy in his class. Matthew Nordic. I'm not sure if you're aware of any trouble between the two boys?"

I remembered Davey telling me Matt called Isaac a baby during gym class.

I told Matt to be quiet. I wanted to hit him, Mommy, but I knew I shouldn't.

Isaac and I had prayed for Matt, but we hadn't included Davey in the prayer. I could see that was a mistake now. Isaac and Davey were attached, connected. No doubt Davey was hurt by Isaac's diagnosis, albeit in different ways.

Why hadn't I realized that?

I slumped against the wall. "I know they've argued before. Last time it was about Isaac."

"Sounds similar this time as well, only it got quite out of hand. Matthew sustained a bloody nose."

"No, no, no." I pressed a hand to my forehead. "I can't believe this. I—I don't know what to say. We never condone violence as a way to work things out. Davey is the last person I'd expect—"

"Mrs. Acker, I didn't call to put any blame on you and your husband, believe me. I've talked to both boys separately, and I am about to talk to them together. It might be helpful if you could come down so we could work this out."

I dragged precious air into my lungs, trying to keep hold, trying to keep afloat. But the horrible feeling that I slid further and further out of control, down some long, winding, never-ending rabbit hole overtook me.

"I can't." My normally reserved voice came out tense and edgy. "I'm at a doctor's appointment with Isaac in Portland. Even if we finish in half an hour, which I'm sure we won't, I won't be back until late."

"What about your husband? I don't think we should delay this. We all need to be on the same page with the boys when it comes to fighting in school. They're young, and both with no previous discipline problems, so I'd like to stop this now before it has the potential to spiral further. Davey's never struck me as the kind of kid deserving of an in-school suspension."

Davey. In-school suspension. Before today, I'd never entertained those two phrases together.

"Mrs. Acker? Should I call your husband?"

Josh. That's right. Josh was in town, right at the high school. He could get another teacher to cover his class.

"No, I'll call him. I'm sure he'll be on his way as soon as possible."

I hung up the phone, felt Isaac tugging at my sleeve. "What is it, Mommy? Is Davey okay?"

"One second, honey." I pressed the phone to my ear, listened to its empty, hollow ring. No answer. I let out an exasperated groan and googled the phone number to the high school. Of course, Josh didn't keep his phone on in class.

"Mommy, was that my principal?"

"Isaac, I said wait please."

Again, the phone rang and rang against my ear. I wanted to climb through the virtual waves and demand that someone answer. It was the high school, after all. How could they not have someone available to answer the phone at all times? Maybe we'd have to do a fundraiser for the high school administration office as well, I thought bitterly.

"Mommy—"

"Not now, Isaac," I said sharply.

Isaac pulled back in surprise, his eyes wide. I rarely raised my voice and no doubt it surprised him as much as it did me.

"Honey, I'm sorry. Davey's okay. I just need to get a hold of

Daddy." I was only one person. I could only handle one problem at a time, and not even that, it seemed.

I hung up the phone, looked around as if the answer to my dilemma would be written on the walls. Nothing. I dialed Josh once more and left a harried voice mail, not bothering to keep the frustration out of my voice. I hung up the phone, leaned into the wall, dragging in deep breaths.

It was simple. As much as I wanted to rush back and solve the problem with Davey, I couldn't. I was needed here. That was that. Josh would call me back soon, then he would go to Davey.

I pushed myself off the wall, a new idea forming. In another moment, I was again listening to that wretched ringing in my ear, but this time, there was an answer.

I should have known a girl could always count on her mom. At least, a mom like mine.

"Mom, thank God."

"What's the matter? Aren't you at Isaac's appointment?"

I quickly rehashed the dilemma with Davey, ending with a request that she go to the school in my stead.

"I don't know, honey. I don't think that's what Mr. Sedgwick had in mind. Is it my place?"

My bottom lip trembled. "Davey must be scared, is all. He's never been to the principal's office, and he's in big trouble."

"He hit the other boy, is that right?"

"Yes, but the kid is practically a demon child the way he makes fun of—" I caught myself at Isaac's probing gaze. The boys could be entirely too perceptive when they wanted.

"Okay, okay. Honey, I'm on your side. Don't you forget that."

The knot in my chest eased. Is that all I needed to hear? That someone stood with me and for me when it seemed the entire rest of the world was dead set against every good plan I made for myself and my family? "Thank you. Does that mean you'll go?"

"No."

So much for a girl being able to count on her mom.

"But I will drive to the high school to get Josh. Lizzie's here. I'm sure she won't mind finishing the room prep for check-in."

"You're a lifesaver."

"Let me know if you hear anything."

"I'll try the school one more time before we head to the doctor's." I hung up and dialed the high school again, but still didn't receive an answer. I shoved the phone in my purse, trying to restrain my negative thoughts.

"Are you mad, Mommy?"

I grabbed Isaac's hand and pushed through the door to the stairwell. Better to get out my pent-up energy by climbing the stairs instead of taking the elevator. "Mommy is a little upset. But I'm sorry I yelled at you. That wasn't right."

"I forgive you."

I looked at him, his sweet green eyes studying me with concern. I wilted. Before I opened the door to the second floor, I knelt in front of him. "I don't deserve you, kiddo." I gave him a kiss on the cheek and he wrinkled his nose.

"Is Davey in trouble?"

"I'm afraid he is."

"Because of me?"

"No, honey. We can only make our own choices, right? People might say stuff to make us angry—"

"Like me when you were on the phone?"

All the wind rushed out of me. Could I be any more defeated this day? "Yes, although I wasn't angry with you, I was angry at the circumstances. But I still made a poor choice to speak to you how I did. I should have chosen differently. We always have a choice in how we respond to other people, even the ones that make us super, duper angry—which you, by the way, did not."

"Like Matt Nordic?"

I looked down at my son, who seemed to understand the entire situation more perfectly than I could have guessed. "Yes. Like Matt Nordic."

I opened the door to Dr. Lionel's office. Twenty minutes later, we sat in an examination room with still no word from my husband or mother. I tapped my booted foot lightly on the linoleum and forced a smile when Dr. Lionel knocked before coming into the room. I put my phone away, tried to force the questions I'd rehearsed toward the front of my mind.

"How are you feeling, Isaac?" Dr. Lionel asked as she performed a basic examination.

"Pretty good."

"Are you getting used to all the testing?"

"I don't like it, but I do it."

She smiled. "I think that sums up most of the children I see who come in here." She turned to me. "And how are you feeling, Mom? Any areas of concern?"

I thought of the scary Thanksgiving episode, the extra pizza Josh had given Isaac on Saturday night. "I guess what we struggle with most are special occasions and holidays. My family's big, so almost every weekend there's something going on. We try to make the sugar-free treats, but it doesn't always cut out the carbs." Especially with mother-in-laws bringing over lasagna and sourdough bread.

Dr. Lionel nodded, her glasses falling toward the end of her nose. "It's not an easy task by any stretch of the imagination. His A1C looks decent. Not incredible, but under control. The problem, of course, comes with too many fluctuations. Did you bring his log book?"

I went to my purse, fumbled amidst my wallet, keys, and phone. I'd place it in there this morning, hadn't I?

I dumped the contents of my purse onto my lap. No log book. I groaned. "I—I could have sworn I tucked it right in here. I can't believe I forgot it." How had I forgotten such important information? Had it fallen out in the car? I'd been so intent on asking questions, on being on top of it all. Now, Dr. Lionel wouldn't believe that we'd been as meticulous as we had in recording Isaac's activities, food, and numbers.

Except of course the pizza. I didn't recall seeing that in Saturday's log book.

"Believe me, Dr. Lionel, we've been recording every test, every food, every activity. It's becoming a habit."

She raised an eyebrow in a way that made me feel like a second-grader who was telling her teacher that the dog ate her homework. It seemed every day I slid deeper and deeper down a rabbit hole of insecurity.

I grit my teeth, but my bottom lip trembled. "We've been doing everything we can, the best we can."

The woman nodded. "What correlations are you seeing? What do Isaac's best days look like?"

My phone rang, and I jumped, looking down to see Josh's name on the call. I looked apologetically at the doctor. "I am so sorry. I've been waiting for this call for an hour. Isaac's twin had an...incident at school."

Dr. Lionel let out a sigh, gestured to the phone.

I swiped the screen. "Josh?"

"Mags, your mom just got to the high school. The phone lines were down. I'm heading to the boys' school right now."

"Thank God. I'm in with Dr. Lionel, so I have to go. The principal will fill you in."

"Okay, I'll talk to you later."

"Bye."

I hung up, turning to Dr. Lionel. "I'm sorry."

The doctor nodded, but a niggling, nagging feeling of being judged settled over me throughout her next several questions. The weight of it all threatened to crush me, for Dr. Lionel's condemnation echoed alongside my own.

I was failing. I'd lost my patience with Isaac, I'd forgotten his log book, Davey was fighting in school, my husband was going behind my back sneaking Isaac extra pizza, and I was fairly certain Dr. Lionel had a personal vendetta against me.

I thought I'd improved as a mother since that day I'd forgotten to pick the boys up at school, since Denise had rushed in to save the day, but no. I couldn't even face the fact that I might very well be pregnant without the threat of consuming failure.

I vowed that if Josh felt so adamant about Isaac seeing Dr. Lionel, then he could find a way to take him next time. The woman had the bedside manners of a feral cat.

At the end of the appointment, the doctor tapped on her iPad. "I'd like to see Isaac in another month, with his log book. Do you have any other questions?"

"Yes, I was wondering if you might be able to write us a prescription for a CGM. I think we're ready to try one."

The corners of her mouth turned downward. "I'm not against it, though I usually recommend my patients handle their diabetes without one for at least six months to get used to the flow of things. CGMs aren't perfect. They fail, and families and children should always be comfortable with the old-fashioned way of treating in case they have to fall back to it."

I felt as if I had pricked Isaac's finger and tested his sugar at least a thousand times over the course of the last couple of months. "We'd like to try, if you approve."

"There's lots of benefits to CGMs, though there are some cons as well. The sensor can be more painful to insert, it can cause skin irritation, there can be data gaps. They can fall off unexpectedly. They can also generate a lot of information that can be intimidating. If you decide on a pump, you need to check that it doesn't run out of insulin. They have a habit of running out at inconvenient times."

Isaac's eyes widened as he looked at Dr. Lionel, then me. I could have throttled the woman for scaring him out of something

I was certain would improve our quality of life. "I'm well aware of the challenges. I've read a lot on the subject matter."

"Well, it's your choice ultimately," Dr. Lionel's tone indicated she thought I was making the *wrong* choice. "I think another couple of months without one would be the better option. Have you given any thought to which one you'd like to try? Or which one your insurance might cover?"

I didn't hesitate, and Dr. Lionel scribbled a few prescriptions for all the materials. "I'll also fax over refills for his other supplies so you have them on hand."

I stood, prescriptions clutched tight in my hand, ready to flee the room. "Thank you so much, Dr. Lionel."

"We'll see you in the New Year, then."

The doctor left, and Isaac hopped off the examination table. He gestured for me to bend to his level. He wrapped his arms around my neck, and I sank into him. "She's scary."

I tried to hide a smile. I wanted to reassure him that I felt the same way but pressed my lips closed. We needed to get Josh's opinion first. "I think we should talk to your dad about that, okay? You and me together."

Josh might think Dr. Lionel was the best pediatric endocrinologist in the state, but if Isaac didn't feel comfortable with her, surely Josh would agree to seeing a doctor closer to home. We'd sort it out, and soon.

After we figured out what was going on with Davey.

❧ 21 ☙

Josh forced his foot off the gas as he entered the school zone. *Calm down*, he told himself. Davey would be fine. Josh would talk to him, make sure his son understood he couldn't go around hitting people.

Even if he was just defending his brother.

Even if the other kid did have it coming.

Even if, deep down, he was proud of Davey for sticking up for his brother.

The boys had been through hell in the short time of their lives. Was it so bad to know they had one another's backs through thick and thin? Maybe the next time one of the other kids thought about making fun of Isaac for a disease he had no control over, they'd think twice because of what Davey had done today.

Josh shoved aside the harsh thoughts as he pulled into a parking spot. No need to air his opinions in front of Mr. Sedgwick. They probably weren't what Davey needed to hear, either. He bunched his fists and released them several times, attempting to get his head on straight before he walked into that office.

He opened the car door and walked to the entrance. He wished Maggie hadn't called her mom. The phone lines had come back on a minute after he'd been summoned to the office. Sue Becker, longtime secretary of the high school and proud member of Aunt Pris's quilting club, had probably heard his entire conversation with Hannah.

And why did Maggie have to run to her mom every time there was a problem? Calling on Josie or Lizzie would have been preferable. Why couldn't she have reached out to *his* mom, who had nothing but time on her hands, who missed the boys terribly, and who wasn't busy running a bed and breakfast during the mad rush of the holiday season?

He rang the buzzer at the entrance of the school.

"Hello?"

"Josh Acker, here. I have an appointment with Mr. Sedgwick."

The secretary unlocked the door, and he walked into the foyer. It had been too long since he'd entered the doors of this school. At one time, when the boys were in pre-school, he'd been here every day. Dropping the twins off or picking them up. Having conferences with their teachers, seeing a school musical. Not without some shame, he realized how much he'd handed off to Maggie these last seventeen months. He thought it had been best. They all loved one another. The boys could have a committed, active mother in their lives and he could be the breadwinner, like he was supposed to be all along.

But now, entering the building and feeling like a foreigner, he wondered if he'd handled things all wrong. His son was sitting in the principal's office, after all. In trying to provide for his family, had the hands-off fathering approach done more harm than good? Had he again failed the people he loved most?

The secretary lifted her head when he entered the office. "Mr. Acker, great to see you." She pointed to a clipboard. "If you would put your John Hancock on this sign-in sheet, Mr. Sedgwick will be right with you."

Josh signed the sheet and cleared his throat, surprised how

suddenly nervous he was, as if he were the one being called down to the principal's office. Well, he had been, hadn't he?

He took a seat while the secretary called the principal. His feet tapped the floor.

The door with the principal's name stenciled on it opened. "Mr. Acker?"

Josh stood and gripped the man's hand.

"I'm Brian Sedgwick. Come on in."

Josh followed the man into his simple office. No Davey. His son must be back in class.

Mr. Sedgwick closed the door and sat behind his desk, gesturing Josh to do likewise on the opposite side. "I'm not sure how much your wife told you about what happened today."

"Enough to say I'm more than a little surprised." He crossed one ankle over a knee and leaned forward. "This isn't like Davey. He's never tried to hurt another child in his life."

Mr. Sedgwick's mouth tightened. The harsh fluorescent lights of his office showed off his balding forehead. "I agree. That's why I am not going to push for any extreme disciplinary measures. But of course, we can't simply ignore his actions."

"Of course," Josh agreed.

"I've talked to both of the boys and realize there was quite a bit of provoking on Matthew's side. But hitting...well, it can't come to that. I wanted to talk to you and Mrs. Acker, see if we can come to some sort of consensus on how to proceed. I like to get on board with the parents to help the child."

Help the child.

Memories of another time, years ago, sitting in another office alongside Trisha, came back to him. The rehabilitation counselor speaking to him and his wife.

Our goal is to help Trisha on this journey...

They'd failed. He failed.

He couldn't fail when it came to his son. When it came to either of his sons.

Mr. Sedgwick leaned back. "I'm sure Isaac's diagnosis has come with many trials. It's important to know we want to help in any way we can. I understand Mrs. Acker is coming in to give Isaac and Davey's class a presentation at the end of the week. I think that's a great start."

The man's kind tone pulled Josh back to the present. He relaxed his shoulders. The principal wasn't the enemy. Even this troublemaking kid Matthew wasn't the enemy.

Who was, then?

For a minute he found himself getting angry at God, angry at Isaac's diagnosis which had made their lives beyond difficult. Before, any troubles had seemed normal and manageable. Now, the diabetes stuck its nose in every area of their lives—from mealtimes, to bedtimes, to middle-of-the-night times, to family outings and get-togethers, to school. To his marriage. His kids' education. Everything.

Josh drew in a deep breath and tried to rein himself in, to think logically. "If he was one of my high school students, I would have both kids do some sort of community service together. I don't know what to do for Davey, though. My own kid."

"I can understand your frustration." Mr. Sedgwick tented his fingers beneath his chin. "I like the idea of the boys joining together to help others. Maybe spending some time together away from their peers will help them reconcile their differences. Has Davey talked to you and your wife about how he's feeling surrounding Isaac's diagnosis?"

"With all due respect, Mr. Sedgwick, I don't think it takes a rocket scientist to figure out what's bothering my son. His twin brother, the closest person to him on earth, the friend always by his side, is sick. He can't eat the same foods, even exercise affects his levels. Our world now revolves around finger pricks and insulin shots."

Mr. Sedgwick shifted in his seat. "It must be a challenge for all of you."

"Yeah. I know we should be grateful. I mean, kids are getting diagnosed with cancer and much more life-threatening diseases every day. They're in car accidents and disabled for the rest of their lives. At least diabetes is manageable."

"Aren't there support groups for things like this? Have you ever considered attending?"

Josh shook his head. "Maggie is active on several online groups. They help her. She's trying to get Isaac involved in an in-person one so he can meet other kids with type one. But honestly, I don't have much time these days."

It wasn't a cop out. He was paying two mortgages and needed to keep working on the house so they could move in and get rid of the other one. He was starting a new job that would give him more hours and hopefully more money. Not to mention the crush of Christmas. A support group? Even if he wanted to squeeze it in, he didn't see how it was humanly possible.

Besides, they weren't here to talk about him. They were here to help his son.

"I respect your recommendation, Mr. Sedgwick, and I will consider it. But let's keep this about Davey today?"

The principal held out his hands. "I understand. Matthew seems to know that his remarks were painful and that he shouldn't have said them. Davey appears to understand that he shouldn't have lost his temper and hit Matthew. It sounds great on the surface, but I couldn't be certain they weren't telling me what I wanted to hear. Still, if they can both make a change, I think we've made progress. I suppose time will tell. The novelty of Isaac's diagnosis is new to his peers. After a while it will wear off, I'm sure. How's Isaac dealing with it all? I haven't had him down here to talk about it."

"He's a trooper. I sometimes wonder if he's handling it better than everyone else."

"Or just being quieter about it."

It was a harmless comment, really, but it gave Josh pause. Was

Mr. Sedgwick right? What was his quiet child thinking? He remembered himself as a younger kid. Once he hit late middle school and early high school, he'd realized he didn't want to follow his father's footsteps into law school. But he hadn't said anything until after graduation. So many years of silence and quiet, so many years of pretending his father's expectations didn't bother him when they bothered him a great deal.

He sighed. "You might be right. I should probably be talking to him more." He couldn't leave everything to Maggie. He thought he'd been doing his share of the work by making the money for his family, by giving Maggie a home of her own. How stupid. They all needed so much more than his paychecks.

"Why don't we keep in touch, Mr. Acker? Is it okay if I give you a call in another week or so and see how both Davey and Isaac are doing? If you think I can help in any way, please don't hesitate to contact me, either. In the meantime, I'll plan on sitting in on Mrs. Acker's presentation to Ms. Lindrooth's class."

Asking to keep in touch was a kind and gracious offer. One he would have let Maggie handle in the past. But not today. No matter how many priorities he had, he vowed his sons would be at the top of the list.

"Thank you," Josh said, meaning it. He shook the principal's hand. "I can tell you care about these kids. That means a lot."

"I do. Sometimes I feel vastly outnumbered—there's only one of me and so many students, but I try to support them how I can. As far as coordinating something with Davey and Matt, I'll see how Matt's folks feel about it. Perhaps you'd like to see if your wife has any ideas?"

He smiled. Apparently, Mr. Sedgwick knew Maggie could be counted on for her creative ideas. If not fundraising for the school, then community service opportunities.

"Will do."

"We're about to dismiss the kids. Do you want to have Becky call Davey down?"

"That'd be great."

He shook the man's hand. Mr. Sedgwick led Josh out the door and spoke to the secretary. A few minutes later, Josh met Davey in the foyer of the school. The boy's small shoulders hunched beneath the weight of his superhero backpack.

Josh stuck his hands in the pockets of his pants. "Hey, sport. Rough day, huh?"

The boy's bottom lip trembled and he nodded. Josh wrapped an arm over Davey's shoulder and led him out the door. "Come on."

Davey didn't say anything as they drove out of the parking lot. In truth, Josh was at a loss for words as well. Without thinking too much, he ended up in front of Uncle Willy's Candy Shoppe. Davey's eyes widened from where he sat in the backseat. "Why are we here?"

"Because I think we both need a little candy and a little grace right now."

"What's grace?"

"When you get what you don't deserve."

The bottom lip that Davey had tucked into his mouth came loose, quivering and trembling with sobs.

"I shouldn't have hit Matt, but I couldn't stop. He made me so mad. He called Isaac a baby and a wimp. He said his grandmother had diabetes and died from it, and if Isaac didn't start exercising he would die, too." Tears flowed down the boy's face and Josh popped out of the driver's seat to climb into the backseat with him. He pulled his son into a tight hug, pressed his face to his hair that smelled of sweat and a lingering hint of watermelon from the Fresh Monster shampoo Maggie bought.

"Isaac is not going to die. You hear me? Your mom and I and his doctors are taking the best care of him. It sounds like Matt's grandmother had a different type of diabetes than Isaac and that she didn't do a good job taking care of herself. That is *not* going to happen to your brother. I promise. Do you understand me?"

"Really, really?"

"One-hundred percent really. People are going to say mean things sometimes. Sometimes it's because they don't understand and sometimes it's because they're being mean or sometimes they are hurt that their grandmother is gone. You can't go around hitting people when they make you angry, son. It's not going to solve anything."

Davey looked out the window. "Well, Matt *did* stop saying mean things about Isaac after I gave him a bloody nose."

Josh squelched the smirk itching at the corner of his lips. "I'm sure he did. But we need to solve things peacefully. It's harder that way sometimes, isn't it?"

His son nodded.

Josh wracked his brain, reaching for an example to share, something meaningful. "You know, when I was in high school I got in a big fight with a kid, too."

"You did? Did you give him a bloody nose?"

Josh nodded. "And a black eye."

"What did the kid do to you to make you so mad?"

"He was picking on me. Grammy and Grampy gave me an expensive car as a birthday present."

"And they didn't like that?"

"They thought I was spoiled because of it."

And maybe he had been. It hadn't been the wisest parenting move Josh now realized, but Brad Ingham had had it out for him since the third grade. When Brad put a cardboard sign covering the license plate of his new BMW that labeled Josh a profane and derogatory name—and bent his license plate cover doing it—Josh had let loose.

"Did he stop making fun of you after that?" Davey asked.

"Not entirely. Although I think he did back off a little."

"So fighting is good sometimes?"

Josh sighed. This was a loaded question. "I've wrestled with this question a lot, Davey."

"You have?"

He nodded, heard muffled voices as a mother with three girls climbed the stairs to the candy store. "You know, son, I think it's good to want to stand up for those who are weaker than us. It's also good to seek justice—you know, making what's wrong right. But we also have to love mercy and grace as much as we love justice. We need a balance."

Davey shook his head, eyebrows scrunched. *Epic fail*. Josh raked a hand through his hair. He was supposed to be a teacher— why was he trying to be Aristotle?

He fought off the urge to tell his son never mind, that what they both needed right now was some candy. He swallowed down the words that would brush off this hard conversation.

Man, parenting was tough. If anyone knew that, of course it was him, but his boys were getting older. They needed him *and* Maggie.

He began slowly. "I'm betting when Matt made fun of Isaac, you could only think about making him be quiet and hurting him. And when Brad Ingham made fun of me in high school, that's all I thought about, too. But we need to train ourselves to stop and think about a more peaceful way to stand up for others. Does that make sense?" Had he totally botched the lesson?

Davey bit his bottom lip, nodded slightly. "I think so."

One more try. He couldn't leave Davey like this, or himself for that matter. "Do you remember when Peter chopped off an ear of one of the guys who came to arrest Jesus?"

Davey smiled. "Yeah, that was cool," he said, as if he'd witnessed it firsthand.

"I don't know. Jesus didn't think it was cool. He told Peter to put his sword away. In not so many words, He told Peter to trust in God's ways instead of his own. It's hard for us tough guys, but do you know what's even tougher?"

"What?"

"Not using our fists. Using our brains and our hearts to stick up for those we love. Following God's way of peace instead of our own. Do you think you can try to do that with me?"

Davey looked deep into Josh's eyes, nodded. "I didn't like going to the principal's office. I don't want to be a bad kid."

"You made a mistake. But you have the power to choose if it happens again, or not. Ask God to help you, and He will. And let me tell you, buddy, no matter what, I am always going to be here for you to talk these things out. Hear me?"

Davey flung his arms around Josh's neck.

"Now, let's go get some candy. We'll get some of those chocolate caramels Mommy likes and the sugar-free chocolates Isaac's crazy about, too."

He walked up the steps to the candy store with Davey, hoping and praying he'd said something to help his son. He'd make these type of conversations a more regular part of their relationship. He couldn't leave everything to Maggie.

22

I ran a glue stick over a picture of a pancreas and pasted it onto the poster board. Beside me, Isaac colored in the bubble letters I'd printed at the top. *What is Type 1 Diabetes?*

"How's that, Mommy?"

"It looks great. I think your class is going to like our presentation."

I hoped so, at least. I hoped we could answer the silent questions from Isaac's classmates, that we could bridge the gap Isaac felt between him and his peers.

Josh had filled me in on the meeting with Mr. Sedgwick last night, and I'd filled him in on our appointment with Dr. Lionel.

Why was it that whenever we seemed on the same page, some new challenge reared its head? Denise calling last night to invite us over for Christmas Eve hadn't helped. I'd planned on us going to Orchard House after church. In the end, we'd invited Josh's parents to join us. I'd thought that had been a fine compromise until Josh made an offhand comment about always spending the holidays with my family.

I hadn't responded. We'd all been on edge from the day. Both of us were tired and anxious.

When Josh came home from school today, he was nearly chipper, and I hadn't asked him if he'd given any more thought to Isaac's doctor. Josh took Davey to the new house and Isaac and I stayed behind to work on the presentation.

"Do I have to get up in front of my class tomorrow?" Isaac clutched a red crayon, the point down to a nub.

I sat beside him. "Honey, I thought you were excited about this."

He shrugged. "I don't like talking in front of everybody."

"Okay." Isaac talking had been a big part of our plan. I didn't think our presentation would be as effective coming only from me. "Don't you think your friends will want to hear what you have to say?"

Another shrug. Well, I wasn't going to push him. I continued gluing in silence, and he grabbed a green crayon out of the Crayola box, continued coloring. After a couple of minutes, he placed the crayon on the table. "Can I have a snack?"

I'd given both boys apple slices and let them have a piece of the candy Josh and Davey had brought home from Uncle Willy's the day before. "Supper's soon." The cauliflower rice was already prepped. "Davey and Daddy will be back any minute."

"I wish I got to go to the house."

I studied my son, sensing his irritability. "I thought you were excited to work on the poster. It looks great."

"I want to go to the house too, sometimes." His whiny voice put me on alert. Crankiness was a sign his sugars could be off.

I went for his kit. "Let me test you, sweetie."

He stood up beside his chair. "I don't want to!"

I raised my eyebrows. "I know, but we need to make sure you're feeling okay."

"I feel fine!" He threw down his green crayon and stomped off upstairs.

I stood there, stunned. Isaac never yelled, much less at me. I thought to shout up to him, to tell him to get back downstairs and to watch his tone, but instead, I slumped against the counter.

His sugars were off. They had to be. I glanced at the poster, the slight coloring marks out of the lines where Isaac had been working.

Or maybe, like all of us, he'd had enough.

I closed my eyes and prayed for wisdom. Wisdom for diabetes and my marriage and Davey fighting and unopened pregnancy boxes. After a minute, I dragged myself upstairs, without the meter. I didn't want Isaac to feel I was sneaking up on him to attack him with a lancet.

At the open door of his bedroom, I peered in. I froze at the sight of him facedown on the carpet of his bedroom. "Isaac!" I rushed toward him, certain he'd collapsed, but as soon as I got there I saw he was fully conscious.

He wiped his face on the sleeve of his shirt, pounded a fist on the carpet repeatedly. "I hate my diabetes!"

My bottom lip trembled and that familiar emotion forecasting tears climbed my throat. I tried to tamp it down. Snuff it out. Put it away. For Isaac. For my family. I'd gotten so good at showing no emotion in front of the kids, and yet where had it gotten us?

I attempted to think of words that would soothe, but they all fell short. It simply wasn't fair. None of it.

I laid down alongside my son, stomach flat to the floor, and draped an arm around his sobbing body. A sob rumbled up my throat. I allowed it to come forth, the release overpowering. "I hate diabetes, too. Honey, more than anything I wish I could take it away." A tear spilled down my face and I clutched Isaac, both of us sobbing together on the carpet.

We stayed that way for a long while, crying and holding one another, my heart grieving and groaning for my son. Finally, Isaac rolled onto his side. "Don't cry, Mommy."

I wiped at my tear-stricken face and smiled through my tears, my breaths hiccuping on themselves. "I'm okay, honey. Are you?"

He nodded. "Do you think we should test my sugar now?"

I brought him close. "Oh, honey. How do you feel?"

"I feel better. I'll talk in front of my class tomorrow if you want."

I ran a hand through his hair. "I want you to do what you want to do, okay? This is all for you, and I don't want to make you uncomfortable in any way. Whatever you want to do, I'm on board with it."

He squinted his eyes. "Ice cream for dinner?"

I laughed, tickled his foot. "I mean as far as the class presentation, wise guy."

I clutched him tight, the release from the crying lightening my heart. "Thank you, kiddo."

"For what?"

"For letting me cry with you."

23

"**O**ur bodies are made up of millions of cells. Cells need energy so we can do things like grow, walk, and think." I looked out at Isaac's class, which included Davey. In the back, Ms. Lindroth and Mr. Sedgwick sat on small students' chairs. "What are some of your favorite things to do that you need energy for?"

A slew of hands went up. Isaac called on a small brunette in the front row with a pink headband.

"Play piano."

"Your fingers certainly need energy for that." I smiled.

Isaac pointed at a boy in the third row. "Matt."

I studied the child, a freckle-faced boy who appeared to listen to our presentation intently. Was this the boy Davey had hit? "Playing basketball."

"That's right." I turned to the poster. "The energy you have every day comes from the food you eat. Our food is broken down into something called glucose." I pointed to the picture of the pancreas. "We all have a pancreas, which has a very important job when it comes to glucose. When the glucose is released into the bloodstream, our pancreas releases insulin which is almost like a special key that helps the glucose be used for energy."

A girl in the second row waved her hand wildly. I smiled. "Yes?"

"I have a diary that has a lock on it. You need a key to get inside."

I nodded. "And that key is super important to you, I bet. You can't unlock your diary without it, is that right?"

"Right."

"That's kind of how our pancreas works. It gives us the key to our energy. It's super important." I looked at Isaac. "Do you want to tell them about your pancreas, honey?"

Isaac nodded, solemn. "My pancreas doesn't work. The key is missing in mine. That's why I need shots and why I need to test my sugar."

"Isaac has something called type 1 diabetes. It's an autoimmune disease that kids sometimes get. He couldn't have done anything to prevent it."

The boy named Matt waved his hand.

"Yes, Matt?"

"My grandmother had diabetes from having too much sugar."

I was glad he brought that up. "I'm sorry about your grandmother, Matt. It sounds like she had type 2 diabetes. That's actually a lot different from type 1. In type 2 diabetes, the pancreas gets tired. The key is still there, but it's broken and doesn't always work well." I gave the boy a small smile, then turned to the rest of the class.

We spoke about the types of food that were good for Isaac, and the kinds that he could have with more careful monitoring. We spoke about his testing and his shots, counting carbs, how he needed to go to the nurse before lunch and how it might be helpful for him to have a friend to look out for him on the way.

"And I'm getting a new monitor today," Isaac volunteered. "It sticks in me all the time so I can know what my sugar levels are."

After Isaac told Josh how he felt about Dr. Lionel, we'd had a long conversation. In the end, we agreed that seeing the original endocrinologist Dr. Green referred us to was the best course of action. We had an appointment with Dr. Cannon that afternoon on a cancellation. The new doctor was going to show us how to place Isaac's CGM.

"A needle is stuck in you all the time?" the girl with the pink headband asked.

Isaac nodded. "But it might be better than pricking my finger all the time."

"That's cool!" said a boy with a Hulk t-shirt. "Can you show us after you get it?"

A smile tugged at the corners of Isaac's mouth. "Sure."

Davey grinned at his twin. "I told you he's not a baby. He's braver than Iron Man."

My heart near melted, but I thought it best to direct the conversation in another direction. "Does anyone have any questions for me or Isaac?"

The kid in the Hulk shirt raised his hand. "Can I walk you down to the nurse tomorrow, Isaac?"

Isaac looked at Ms. Lindrooth.

"I think that would be fine, Jason." Ms. Lindrooth approached the front of the class. "Let's thank Isaac and Mrs. Acker for helping us understand type 1 diabetes, shall we?"

The class burst into applause and Isaac beamed. Suddenly, his eyebrows shot up. "Mom! We can't forget to pass out the cookies!"

※

JOSH CLUTCHED MAGGIE'S HAND AS DR. CANNON PRESSED A button that would attach the CGM to Isaac's upper thigh. It made a bit of a loud noise, and Isaac jumped. Josh placed his hand on Isaac's shoulder and winked at his son, who tried to wink back but ended up blinking two eyes.

Maggie squeezed Josh's hand and they shared a smile.

Dr. Cannon placed the transmitter onto the CGM. It would wirelessly send Isaac's glucose readings to their phones. "How does that feel, Isaac?"

"Kind of weird."

"You'll be used to it in no time." Dr. Cannon pointed to Josh's phone. "Mom and Dad, you've plugged in the number that was on the CGM?"

Josh nodded alongside his wife.

"The monitor is going to need a warm-up period of about two hours. I would go ahead and test Isaac manually tonight until the monitor starts doing its work."

Maggie let out a wobbly, emotional breath that caused Josh to suck in his own emotion.

"Once you're all comfortable with the monitor, I can help you with the pump. Or, if you'd like, Gabrielle can help you."

"Thank you so much." Maggie looked up at Josh, her eyes shining. In that moment, she looked more beautiful to him than ever.

He placed his arm around her, squeezed tight. A victory tune strummed inside. They were moving forward, conquering this disease that had thrown them the worst of curveballs.

And they were doing it together.

❧ 24 ❧

I leaned back in my chair and soaked in the sights and scents of Christmas day—the mistletoe hung overhead, the cranberries and pinecones intertwined with greenery, the tree adorned in gold and silver trimmings, the bows and crinkled wrapping paper at our feet, and the lingering scents of Christmas dinner.

Josh slid his hand into mine and my gaze caught the shimmering tennis bracelet on my wrist—a gift I'd found under the tree that morning. When I'd first unwrapped it, I had bit back the demand that he take it back.

I had shaken my head. "Josh...you shouldn't have."

"I couldn't help myself." He'd clasped it around my wrist, and I had to admit it was terribly pretty.

"But the—" I stopped myself. The house, I'd wanted to say. Isaac's medical bills. His CGM and insulin pump. The possible baby. I should have told Josh my suspicions by now. Should have worked up the courage to take the pregnancy test. Not taking it didn't actually change whether I was pregnant or not.

But I couldn't bring myself to bring up any of my protests, not on Christmas morning, not when a look of pure adoration wreathed his face. The last thing I wanted was to ruin Christmas by sounding ungrateful.

The toolbox full of hand tools I'd given him seemed small by comparison. Yet, he'd grown animated, his face glowing. He was happy. Truly happy, for the first time in a while. He couldn't stop talking about his new job or the home he worked on for us. He'd even taken both Davey and Isaac to the house the day before yesterday, had them handing tiles to him for the backsplash in the kitchen.

I looked at Isaac, tearing open a LEGO set from my Mom. He'd adjusted to the CGM like a champ. Though it wasn't without challenges, it felt almost like a new life. No more constant testing and finger pricks. I could check his nighttime levels by glancing at my phone instead of sneaking into his room with a headlamp and lancet. Once we paired the CGM with a pump, Isaac could have snacks during the day that included something besides nuts and cheese.

Today, as I carefully monitored my son's intake of carbs and sugar, I breathed a bit easier, knowing his machine would sound an alarm if his sugars were falling too fast or rising too high.

"What's this?" Lizzie opened a present from Amie, exclaiming over the intricate table lamp adorned with leaf patterns. "Oh, Amie, it's perfect. And I need a lamp for my desk. It reminds me of the woods."

Amie grinned. "I thought it was a good fit for you."

Lizzie gave her a hug. "I love it. Thank you."

Bronson dug for the next present under the tree, coming out with a slim package adorned in intricate gold ribbon. "To Josh and Maggie. Love, All of Us."

I took the gift, my eyebrows scrunched. "What's this? It sounds like some rule-breaking."

With our family so large, we usually drew names for one another and set a strict price limit. I'd pulled Josie's name and gifted her a beautiful set of pens and a handmade Italian journal inspired by Monet's garden.

"Not really. The two people who chose your names decided to combine forces. Actually, you'll see that the gift has an ulterior motive."

We tore open the red gift wrap with care, revealing a light-weight cardboard envelope. On the front was pictured a Victorian bed and breakfast that rivaled the elegance of our own Orchard House. Beneath the image read *Two-Night Vacation Getaway at the Mulburn Inn, Bethlehem, NH.*

"Oh, guys...this is so incredibly sweet, but I'm pretty sure it exceeds the price limit for our gift. In fact, I'm positive it does."

"And so now I will reveal my ulterior motive." Mom smiled. "There's a vintage bedspread that looks perfect for our Frost Room at a store close to the inn. But I don't have time to go and check it out, and it's something one of us needs to see in person. I trust your instincts, Maggie."

"But two nights...the boys...Josh is starting his new job soon." I glanced at my husband, who nodded agreement.

"We've arranged everything for this coming week." Josie sat beside Amos, who was having belly time on the floor. "Josh and the boys are on vacation. We're all going to pitch in to make sure your little guys are busy. It'll be fun."

"But what if..." I allowed my gaze to fall to Isaac, who played on the floor with Davey. "And what about the concert? We still have tons to plan." I looked at Lizzie for confirmation.

Lizzie leaned over and squeezed my knee. "I have it under control, Mags. You've given us a great head start. When you come back, you can pitch the story to the newspapers and shout it out on social media. That's probably the most help you can offer. You've coached me and mom extensively on Isaac's diabetes. We've got this. Go. Enjoy yourselves."

While the thought of getting away was tempting, the thought of leaving Isaac caused a knot in my stomach. I grasped for more excuses. "Aunt Pris, I'm sure your quilting club could whip up a quilt for Mom. Why this one?"

Aunt Pris shook her head. "We're busy working on something for the fundraiser. Wait until you see it. But Hannah showed me the quilt for the Frost Room, and I agree. It's lovely."

I hooked Josh with a frantic gaze. "I—I don't think we should. I'm sorry, guys. This was beyond generous. If you can't get a refund, perhaps Josie and Tripp should use it. Or Mom, you and Aunt Pris could go. You could see the quilt for yourself that way."

Josh cocked his head at me, his gaze searching mine, something that almost looked like hurt in those green pools. "He'll be fine, Mags. Have a little faith, honey," he whispered. "This will be good for us."

I closed my eyes. Was that my problem? Lack of faith? And yet, I knew how unexpected life could be. Josh did, too. This wasn't about faith, it was about responsibility. We'd only been living with Isaac's diagnosis for three months. Was it irresponsible to leave him for two days?

"I—I need to think about it."

"I've been reading up on type 1 diabetes ever since we spoke at the bookshop story time. I think I understand the basics, Mags," Josie said. "And Mom and Lizzie know how to test his sugars and give him the shots. You'd just need to coach us a bit on his fancy new gadget. And if I understand correctly, you will have constant access to his levels from your phone, no matter that you're three hours away."

I bit my lip, sensed Isaac staring at me, weighing the conversation. Hadn't I been one of the biggest proponents of not letting diabetes define who he was, of not letting it control his life? But what did my actions of fear say to him? Surely, they spoke louder than any words I'd used to instill courage.

I looked to Josh again. His eyes pleaded with me. "We could really use this, Mags."

I dragged in a deep breath. "I—I suppose it might be nice to get away together."

The grin on Josh's handsome face was my reward. Josie clapped her hands. Mom smiled.

"That settles it, then." Mom looked at Davey and Isaac. "You boys okay with staying at Orchard House for a couple nights on your vacation?"

"Yay!" They jumped up and down.

"Well, they can hang out with us during the day, too. Amos would love it," Josie said.

"And we can have a wrestling match with Uncle Tripp?" Davey asked.

Tripp puffed up his chest. "If you think both of you can take Tripp the Titan Terror."

Visions of Isaac's CGM getting dislodged popped into my head. "Oh, Tripp, I don't think—" I started, but Josh put a hand on my arm.

I looked at him, the words dying on my lips. He slid his fingers into mine, pulled me close. "He's playing around, Mags. I'd trust Tripp with my life."

I had thought so at one time, too. In fact, there had been a time when I wouldn't have thought twice about placing my sons' lives in the hands of anyone in this room.

But that was before. When life had been mostly smooth. Not always easy, of course, but resilient and pliable.

Now that I knew the truth of how tender and breakable we each were, I couldn't think of our lives as anything but completely and hopelessly fragile.

❦

MY HANDS SHOOK AS I WASHED THEM IN THE BATHROOM SINK. I glanced at the timer on my phone, perched at the edge of the sink. Thirty more seconds. I dragged in a quivering breath, forcing my gaze away from the pregnancy test, and sat on the closed toilet seat. Its chill raced up my legs. I tapped my feet nervously on the floor.

The timer on my phone sounded, and I shut it off. I picked up the test.

Two pink lines stared back at me.

I released a surprised gasp, staring harder, certain it was a mistake. How many times had I taken such a test, praying for two pink lines such as the ones in front of me? From somewhere deep within me, excitement stirred, but all too soon, it was replaced by fear.

Black spots came in and out of focus. I concentrated on breathing deep, hauling breaths straight to my core.

This was it. I was really pregnant. Soon, I would be completely responsible for a tiny, helpless life. How in the world could I be all it needed? How could I be the best possible mom to Davey and Isaac with another tiny human in my care? How could I care for a crying infant in the middle of the night while monitoring Isaac's blood sugar? I was already in over my head. The new house. The B&B. Yet, I'd wanted a baby so badly.

Now, I feared a baby was just another person in my life that I would be at risk of failing.

25

I ushered Davey into the senior center and adjusted my pocketbook over my shoulder. The idea of Matt and Davey visiting the center together for their community service was a suggestion from Lizzie during a fundraiser planning session. I kicked myself for not thinking of it earlier. With the holidays, a lot of the older people were lonely if their families lived far away. There was nothing like a young face to brighten a room.

Those were my sunshiny thoughts before I talked to Rachelle Nordic. Matt's mother wasn't rude exactly, but neither was she all over the idea. I'd told her we weren't tied to the senior center idea, that she could feel free to volunteer other suggestions. But the woman hadn't. Instead, in somewhat of a huff, she had agreed to the senior center and found an excuse to get off the phone.

I couldn't help but think that maybe the apple didn't fall far from the tree. Maybe Matt's unkind words were simply a product of his mother's bad example.

Now, here we were. For better or worse.

We stepped into the foyer and I smiled at an older woman with glamorous silver hair in a glittery red top sitting at a desk. "Hello. I'm Maggie Acker and this is my son, Davey. We might be a little early, but we're here to read some stories. There's another boy and his mom coming as well."

"Oh yes. I'm Dot. We know Matt and Rachelle well. Rachelle's mom used to be a regular here. It's so nice to see them again, and it's wonderful that they brought friends."

I returned the smile, trying not to show surprise. Was that the reason for Rachelle's hesitancy on the phone? Perhaps she wasn't being difficult. Perhaps this place was painful for her.

I searched the room, saw the young boy I recognized from Isaac's class presentation. Beside him stood a woman with mousy brown hair, looking a bit forlorn.

Davey tugged on my hand. "Mommy, do we have to do this? Can I come back when Matt's not here? *Please?*"

Though I wouldn't admit it for the world, I felt the same way. Sometimes people just didn't get along. And maybe they shouldn't be forced. Truthfully, it bothered me more than a little to hear what Matt had said regarding Isaac. The fact that Matt had put those fears in the twins' heads made me angry.

Yet, Matt had seemed receptive during the presentation. Perhaps this was a new beginning.

I pushed aside my fears and spoke to Davey as much as to myself. "I think this is a reasonable compromise, honey. You're not being made to stay after school. This is helping people. Who knows? Maybe you'll get to know Matt a little better. It's harder to fight with someone we've worked with toward a common goal. Does that make sense?" The words were something Mom would say, and I tried to believe them myself.

Davey's slow nod showed his reluctance. I breathed out a long sigh, throwing my shoulders back. Pasting on a smile, I forged ahead toward Matt and his mother, holding out my hand. "Hello, I'm Maggie."

Rachelle stuck out her hand. One corner of her mouth lifted slightly.

"It's nice to meet you. Thanks for coming." I pointed to the front desk. "I spoke to Dot. I didn't realize you had such a history with this place or I wouldn't have suggested it. I'm so sorry."

Rachelle shrugged. "No worries. You didn't know. It's been a couple years since my mom died."

Something hitched inside me, and I absentmindedly placed a hand over the spot where my babe grew. "We lost my father last year. I don't know that the pain will ever go away."

Rachelle nodded, her mouth tight. "It doesn't. It changes, I suppose, maybe dulls at times. But I don't think it will ever go away."

I didn't know what to say. Briefly, I thought of Josh and Trisha. Did it still hurt for my husband to think of her? Of their times together, of her death? I suppose I'd been naïve to assume the pain would go away with time and a new marriage. As much as I might hate to admit it, Rachelle was right. There was more to it than that.

Davey gripped the book he held in his hand. *The Night Before Christmas*. It was one he read very well, probably because he had nearly memorized it. "What book did you bring?" he asked Matt.

Matt showed him a book with a cartoon kid playing basketball titled *Basketball Break*. "I don't like reading in front of people."

"Really? I don't mind. I can go first if you want," Davey offered.

"Okay."

Davey glanced at me, then back at Matt. "I'm sorry about hitting you. I got angry. But my dad told me it's tougher not to use my fists. So I'm going to try."

I stared at my son, his fingers tight around the book, his gaze downcast. Josh had told him that? Suddenly, all I could think about was getting away with him for a couple days, alone, rekindling what we had once shared not long ago. I would tell him about the baby, and Josh would be over the moon. If I could only do it all without worrying about Isaac....

"I'm sorry, too," Matt said. "I think I get it now."

It was enough. The boys, at least for the moment, had called a truce. Perhaps facing the somewhat intimidating prospect of reading to a bunch of elderly people had cemented peace. Whatever the reason, I was grateful. I shared a smile with Rachelle, and the animosity I felt earlier loosened its grip.

An elderly woman with wrinkled dark skin came toward us. "You must be Matt and David. I'm Cora." She squinted her eyes at Davey and then at me. "Aren't you Priscilla's family?"

"Yes. She's my great-aunt."

"Oh, how lovely to meet you! I'm part of the quilting club. Wait until you see what we have in store for the high school fundraiser."

"I've heard only good things. I can't wait."

Cora turned back to the boys. "We're setting up in the event room, boys. Our guests are very excited to have you read to us." She led them to the room where a group of about eight seniors, a couple in wheelchairs, sat in a semi-circle. Two chairs stood at the front beside a small, simple artificial tree decorated in red and gold. The woman led us to the chairs. Matt clung to his mother's hand, but reluctantly crept toward the seat.

Cora clapped her hands. "We have some special guests here to read us their favorite books this afternoon." She gestured to Davey. "Some of you know Priscilla Martin. This is her great-nephew. And this is Matt, Michaela Wharton's grandson."

A few murmurs sprinkled through the crowd at the mention of Matt's deceased grandmother, then soft smiles came like a wave through the group. "They are in first grade at Camden-Rockport Elementary. It's so nice of you boys to take some time on your vacation to come down. Now, which one of you is going to go first?"

Davey raised his hand. As he started the story filled with familiar, well-loved words of sugarplums dancing and clatter's arising, my heart threatened to burst. A few tender smiles from those in the crowd spoke of their genuine enjoyment. No doubt they had read the story to their own children. I hoped it brought back sweet memories.

For the first time, I thought of the babe growing in my womb with fondness instead of fear. Within me grew a precious little human. Another child to share stories with, to love and cuddle, to sit on the floor and play with, to watch grow. This babe was a gift. How horrible that I had let fear steal that truth from me.

When Davey finished, the room broke into applause and Cora praised Davey on what a fine job he did. She then turned to Matt. "Now Matt's going to read us one of his favorite stories about basketball." A gentleman with a Vietnam veteran baseball cap in the front clapped his hands and cheered. Laughter rippled through the room.

Matt started a bit unsure but did well for the first few pages. When he got stuck on a word, Rachelle bent over to help him. After he finished, everyone clapped. Cora stood beside them. "Good job, you two."

Matt leaned over to Davey. "I'm glad it's over."

Some of the folks came up to thank them, including the older man with the black-and yellow veteran's hat. "Now what made you two fine fellows decide to come here today?"

"We got in a fight," Davey volunteered.

I winced, shared a nervous glance with Rachelle. I hadn't thought to explain to Davey how it wouldn't be tactful to tell the seniors this was a sort of disciplinary action.

Davey continued. "At first I didn't want to come here. But now that I did, it was pretty fun. I think next time we should bring Isaac. Can we, Mommy?"

I tussled his hair. "I think that can be arranged."

"And maybe Matt can come, too?"

Matt nodded. "I used to like coming here to visit Nana. And they have Jolly Ranchers in the candy dish at the front. She used to sneak me a bunch of them." He stared at the gray and blue carpet of the floor. "She died from diabetes and I didn't want that to happen to Isaac."

Rachelle knelt beside her son. "Remember how we talked about how Grandma didn't take care of her diabetes? She ate whatever she wanted and didn't want to go to the doctors. Isaac's parents are taking good care of him and he knows what he needs to do."

Matt shrugged. "I guess some days he won't be able to play basketball with us because it's not good for him?"

I nodded. "Some days, yes. But most of the time he'll be playing right alongside you guys." At first it had been hard to encourage Isaac to exercise, but I was slowly learning that it was actually an important part of his health.

"Does that make him sad?" Matt asked Davey.

Davey scuffed the rug with the bottom of his sneaker. "Sometimes. But being called names makes him sadder. And it makes me angry."

"I won't call him names anymore," Matt said.

Rachelle squeezed Matt's shoulder. "Good."

Cora invited us to stay for hot chocolate before bidding us goodbye. Impulsively, I squeezed Rachelle's arm before we left. "Thank you for this. It's been a blessing to me as much as it has for the boys, I think."

Rachelle nodded. "Me too. I should've come back here a long time ago. In the weirdest way, I'm almost grateful Matt got into trouble. We've had some good conversations about his grandmother's death. I hadn't realized how much it still bothered him until the past two weeks. It was a blessing in disguise. A big disguise."

"We should have coffee sometime," I said. "It would be great to get to know you better."

Rachelle wrinkled her nose. "You don't remember me, do you?"

I blinked. "No, I'm sorry..."

Rachelle shrugged. "It's okay. You were always too busy with your friends to notice someone like me."

I searched my brain, briefly remembered a younger version of Rachelle. A pregnancy that'd been covered up in high school. "Wait...were we in a biology class together, freshman year, maybe? You loaned me about a dozen pencils?"

"That was me."

I shook my head. "Rachelle, I'm so sorry. I'm horrible with names and faces...and yes, I suppose I was a bit wrapped up in myself during high school. But I'd like to think that's changed."

Had it? I thought about the last few months, how overwhelmed I'd been with everything, how I'd struggled to find time for coffee breaks with my husband. Perhaps I was still wrapped up in myself.

"I'm sure. But aren't you one of those super-involved PTO moms? I hate to be blunt, but I'm not sure we have much in common."

Wow, that *was* blunt. And yet something within me couldn't leave things like this. "And yet, we both have known the loss of someone dear to us recently."

I didn't want to push Rachelle, but I also didn't know if I could sleep that night knowing Matt's mother thought of me as a rude snob. Despite what I told myself, I did care what others thought of me. Perhaps too much. With shame, I recalled the many likes on my recent Instagram posts surrounding Buddy the Elf, the validation I felt from people thinking me clever for the amount of time I took positioning a doll. What a measly way to measure my worth. More important was how I measured up with Rachelle, a real person who I had hurt in the past.

I swallowed hard, pushed every last bit of pride aside. I couldn't control the past, but I could decide my actions now. "I promise I won't try to convince you to join the PTO or get you to organize fundraisers...unless you want to, of course."

Rachelle smiled. "Yeah, sure then. I guess if you want to,

coffee would be great. It might be fun to catch up on the last eight years or so." We exchanged cell phone numbers and bid one another goodbye.

I draped an arm across Davey's shoulders as I lead him to the car. "I think God showed us both something we needed to see today."

"What?"

"He gave us a glimpse into another person's story."

Davey pressed his small lips together. "You know what, Mommy? I think I might like Matt. And we both like basketball. We could play together sometime. We have a hoop."

"That sounds like a plan."

I drove home, my heart light. Maybe we were turning a new page. Maybe our happily-ever-after was right around the corner.

❧ 26 ❧

As Josh and I drove away from the Orchard House and toward New Hampshire, I leaned back against the truck's headrest. I forced breaths in through my nose and out through my mouth.

This was it.

We wouldn't worry about Isaac. I'd tell Josh about the baby as soon as we placed our suitcase on the floor of our room at the Mulburn Inn. In the spring, our house would sell for higher than the asking price, and all would be perfect. A happy ending tied in a neat little bow.

I sighed as we turned onto Hope Street. I focused on how in love Josh and I were at the beginning, then almost laughed out loud at the absurdity of it all.

I sounded like an old woman. My marriage was still new. How hard was it to remember my stomach fluttering at the sight of Josh picking me up for a date at the house I'd grown up? How hard was it to remember the first taste of his lips on mine, and the way we'd danced beneath the moonlight to the slow tune of Ed Sheeran's *Perfect* on a steamy July night?

The thing was, it wasn't hard to remember. Even now, the

memories nearly made me giddy with thoughts of an entire three days away with my husband.

No, it wasn't the memories that were hard—it was the troubles that had come since the memories. The many bumps life had thrown at us, the circumstances beyond our control.

Josh slid his hand into mine, and I squeezed the roughened calluses of his skin. The boys were fine. This time away was a gift, a blessing.

"Feeling okay?" Josh asked.

I smiled, anticipating the look on his face when I told him about the baby. I studied his handsome profile, the crisp collared edges of his polo shirt.

I'd been surprised on our honeymoon when he'd sought out the iron and began meticulously ironing his clothes. Even his t-shirts, he pressed with religious fervor. Such a contrast to Dad, who would tug out whatever button-up shirt was closest to him in the closet.

Josh's ironing had become something soothing to me over the last year. In these past crazy months and sleep-deprived days, it had been a constant.

"Does it bother you that I throw my clothes in the dryer to 'iron' them?" I asked.

"What?" He glanced at me, laughed. "No, Mags. Of course not. Why would you ask that?"

I settled into the warm seat, wriggled my toes in my snow boots. "Just wondering. You have such an order about you when it comes to that stuff. It hit me that maybe it bothers you that I don't care if my jeans aren't ironed."

"I have never seen you present yourself as anything less than elegant."

I rolled my eyes, but couldn't resist a laugh. It felt good. Real good. "The boys will be okay, won't they?"

I needed to hear it from him. One more time.

He squeezed my leg. "The boys are in good hands. The best. I promise."

"Thank you."

His hand returned to the steering wheel as we headed west toward northern New Hampshire.

I slid my boots off to sit cross-legged on the passenger seat. "I know we need this. It will be nice. No cooking, no dishes, no laundry. Being pampered with meals, sleeping in—"

"Not to mention all the incredibly hot sex we're going to have, right?"

I laughed. "That definitely sounds like it should be part of the plan."

"Okay, just want to make sure it was in there because, heaven forbid, we stray from a plan," he joked. Although the comment hit a raw nerve somewhere deep within me, I tried to let it go.

He drummed his fingers on the steering wheel. "I researched some restaurants for tonight. But we can think about that when we get there. Three hours alone in the car with you is a pretty great thing, too."

I tuned the radio to a station playing 80s music and started singing along to Tom Petty's *Free Falling*. As we drove farther from the ocean and farther into the mountains, the white landscape and frosted tree branches dominated the view out my window.

I gnawed my bottom lip, tried not to let the change in landscape bother me, but it all shouted how far we travelled from home. How long would it take to get back to the kids if something horrible *did* happen?

"You're worrying again."

"How on earth do you know that?"

"I can read you like a book. One I have a wonderful time reading, I might add." Josh gave me a wickedly dashing grin followed by a once-over. "You stick your tongue in your cheek when you're worried."

"I do not!"

He laughed. "Yeah, you do."

"Well, I suggest you keep your eyes on the road and leave my worrying to me."

He slid his right hand to my shoulder. "I know what will help relieve some of that stress you have knotting those shoulders. A massage, maybe a romantic bubble bath. Our room has a Jacuzzi."

I rolled my eyes. "You only have one thing on your mind, and it's not my knotted shoulders."

He sobered. "Is it wrong that I want to make love to my wife like we haven't been able to do since our honeymoon? We've been through a lot this past year. I don't want to lose us in the midst of it."

Hadn't I been thinking that? How could I argue? And I loved that Josh loved me, wanted me.

"I'm sorry. You're right. I'm looking forward to this trip as much as you are. All of it." I laid my head on his arm and snuggled up to him as much as I could while he was driving. "So, tell me how the house is coming. From what I saw yesterday, it looks beautiful. I can hardly wait to set up and decorate."

He shifted in his seat. "What do you think about putting the current house up for sale after the New Year?"

I lifted my head off his arm, pressed my lips together to keep from overreacting. "But where would we live? We can't move into the new property without an occupancy permit."

Josh kept his eyes on the road. "Well, I was thinking if the house sold that we might be able to move into the bed and breakfast. We'd have to ask your mom and aunt, of course. And while I don't know how much Josie might have told you, she and Tripp put an offer on a house. The apartment above the book shop might be free sooner than we think."

I blinked and reached for my phone in the side pocket of the door. "What? This is huge. How could she not tell me? I could have sworn Tripp would want to start from scratch and build, but I'm happy for them." I tapped out Josie's number.

"Mags, can that wait? Please? We're having a conversation."

I forced my hands to put the phone down. "Yeah—yeah, sure."

He flung up a hand. "Forget it. I can tell you're already miles away from me again."

"Josh, don't be silly. I'm right here. I had no idea Josie and Tripp were considering buying a house. I wanted to congratulate her, but you're right—it can wait. Back to house talk."

"So what do you think?"

"About selling so soon?"

"Yeah."

I stretched a cramp from my calf. "I don't want to take advantage of my mom or Aunt Pris. I suppose if we paid her some rent, I'd feel better. We don't know if the house will sell quickly or not. January through March are generally slow months for real estate, aren't they? I don't know, maybe we should wait until the spring to put it up for sale. Are you nervous about money?"

His knuckles turned white on the steering wheel. "Not nervous, exactly. But I don't want to overextend ourselves more than we need to. It'd be nice to have some cash for the new house."

If only he hadn't jumped full in on buying it in the first place. While I couldn't deny a part of me already loved the house, there had been better ways to go about this entire process. Josh joked about me being a stickler for plans? Well, this was why. If he had bothered to talk to me about the house first, we probably wouldn't be in this predicament.

Now though, it was too late. And the last thing I wanted was to start arguing over it. What was done was done.

"Maybe we could rent something small for a few months?" I suggested. "And if Josie and Tripp move out, we could take the apartment? But their process could take months as well. I don't want to feel like we're pushing them out."

Josh nodded, stared at a billowing mound of clouds in the distance. "That sounds reasonable."

My chest swelled. There. We'd had an amiable conversation and made a decision. "So you want to put it up after the first?"

"I think so."

"Okay, it's settled. I'll find a realtor, start getting things cleaned up and packed away when we get back."

"Whoa, whoa. That all sounds great, but let's not think of any logistics for the next few days, okay? We're only talking."

I sighed, trying not to buck against the sentiment. Things didn't get done by talking. We needed plans, action. "How about a compromise? We start planning on the three-hour drive back?"

He grinned. "Deal."

We pulled into a rest stop so I could use the bathroom and then settled in the car again. I hummed softly along with the music as we chatted about how well Isaac's CGM was working, how much we liked his new doctor, and how Josh looked forward to working with Tripp.

"As long as I pass the construction supervisor test, I'll be good. Funny. I thought my studying days were behind me."

"You'll do great. You're a teacher. Besides, you know what you're talking about."

"In essence, I suppose. But the building codes are a mile long. I haven't been in the industry long enough to know them all."

"Josh, you've got this. And if you don't, you'll take it again. I'm sure the class will help."

"Tripp sounds as sure as you do. But the salary he promised depends on obtaining the license."

Hmm, I had missed that piece of information, I guess. "So, you take it until you pass. You are the smartest guy I know. I believe in you." I looked at the mountains looming ahead. "Bethlehem...that's on the other side of the White Mountains, right? We're not going through them, are we?"

"Of course we are."

"Oh, no. Not this time of year. The weather's too unpredictable."

"Maggie, you're worrying for nothing. I checked the weather. It's a few fair-weather clouds. It will take an extra hour-and-a-half, maybe two, to go all the way around."

Something about the ominous mountains and what Josh called "fair-weather" clouds didn't sit right in my gut. Nevertheless, I pushed aside my trepidation. "Okay."

I trust you.

✣ 27 ✣

This was *not* in the forecast.

Josh made a conscious effort to loosen his jaw as he gripped the steering wheel and drove through the heavy snow around a daunting curve of the Kancamagus Highway. Though he hesitated to take his eyes off the road, one quick glance showed Maggie gripping the handle on the side of the door and practically squeezing her eyes shut. Didn't she trust him?

"It's okay, Mags. Just a passing squall. We'll be out of it in no time." He pointed to the brightening sky as they made their way up a large mountain and rounded yet another curve. "See? Almost out."

"Watch out!" She screamed and gripped his arm, causing him to overcorrect and veer into the middle of the road at the sight of a burly-looking man in camouflage.

Josh bit back a curse and maneuvered the truck onto the proper side of the road. The guy had no right walking this pass in such dangerous weather and wearing clothes that made him blend into the landscape.

As if to test Josh's anger, the man stuck his thumb out. Josh huffed, continued onward.

Maggie sat up straighter. "Josh." She craned her neck around to look at the man.

"Can you believe that guy? In camo, no less!"

"He was looking for a ride."

"Oh, come on, Maggie. What if he's crazy? What if he has a gun and shoots me and does God knows what to you?"

She threw up her hands. "'Have a little faith, Mags.' Isn't that what you told me about this trip? Well what, I might ask, do you want me to have faith in? Faith that life's going to work out well because I want it to, that all will be hunky dory? What about faith in humanity, Josh? How can you sit in front of a classroom of high-schoolers and be so cynical?"

"I'm not cynical. I'm realistic. What's the guy doing in the middle of the road anyhow? He's probably on drugs or drunk out of his mind."

"He was not in the middle of the road. *You* weren't looking at the road."

Silence ate up the space between them. Why was she so unreasonable? Trisha would have never demanded he stop for a hitchhiker.

He winced. He tried not to compare Maggie with his first wife, knew it was detrimental to his marriage. Usually, when he found himself comparing them, Maggie won on every count. Only this time, when he couldn't get past his bafflement, did he concede a win to his first wife.

Surely, he wasn't in the wrong.

"I'm not turning around."

"Fine, then." But she crossed her arms over her chest, lifting a barricade between them.

He drove another mile, keeping his eyes focused on the road and the hint of clear sky up ahead.

"What about doing good and serving the needy and strangers, helping those it's in our power to help?"

So this argument wasn't going to dissipate as quickly as the storm.

"What about using the brains God's given us? What about a man protecting his family and his wife from potential harm? Look, why don't we call the police and let them know the guy's out here?"

"There's no town for miles. He was probably a hiker who veered off a trail. Now he's caught in a storm. He could be cold and tired."

"There are rangers around. Someone will find him. You know, we didn't all grow up in the great Amos Martin's home. Not everyone thinks it normal to have strangers sleeping on their couches every night. We all have gifts, Maggie. And maybe reaching out to strange men who look ready to take down a moose isn't one of mine."

He pushed the gas pedal harder to steer the truck up another hill, could feel his wife simmering and stewing beside him. Honestly, though, what did she want him to do? Stop for every hitchhiker? The traveler seemed capable enough to take on the elements, big and decked out in his hunting gear. A guy didn't hike in the White Mountains in December without being prepared. A smart one didn't, anyway. And if he was that stupid, well....

He breathed deep. It wasn't the guy he was mad at, though the hitchhiker had no right walking in the road in the middle of a storm.

It was Maggie.

Maybe this trip wasn't a good idea. He'd thought it could help them reconnect, turn a new page, but maybe there were no new pages. Maybe the rest of their book contained nothing but emptiness.

He wasn't going to turn around.

I leaned against the passenger side door and rubbed my forehead, tried to calm myself but failed to grasp anything beyond my anger. The bracelet Josh gave me for Christmas clattered on the side window and suddenly it constricted so much that I had the irrational urge to unclasp it and fling it far from my body.

Josh's words about my dad pinched a scarred nerve deep inside. I thought he'd admired my dad and my family. Turns out, he thought us foolish simpletons.

We saw things differently. I knew that. Despite our shared faith, we disagreed on many a political issue. We disagreed on the boys and on the leniency of Isaac's diet. We disagreed on doctors and the logic of ironing t-shirts. And now, we disagreed on the hitchhiker Josh had nearly mowed down with his truck.

In reality, it was one more piece of evidence in a long line, but for some reason it had the power to push me over the edge. Maybe we should turn around. Drive past the hitchhiker once more if that's what Josh wanted to do, but this time drive all the way back home.

My phone dinged and I picked it up from where I'd left it in the side of the door. Josh's mom. A picture.

I tapped into it. The picture opened up, Davey and Isaac in big movie cinema seats, Josh's father between them, a large bucket of popcorn in his lap. Underneath, Denise had written, "Seeing the new LEGO movie! They're excited and doing great!"

I sat up. We'd been gone less than three hours. The boys were supposed to be with my family. How…

"The boys are with your parents." I scrolled to Mom's name on my phone and dialed.

"Yeah. My mom asked about taking them for a few hours. I talked to Hannah while we were at the bathroom stop."

Something inside me threatened to boil over, to consume me alive. I put the phone down. "Why didn't you tell me that?"

He waved a hand in the air in frustration. "Cause I knew you'd overreact, that's why."

"I haven't coached Denise on the CGM. How do they know how to handle everything? And why did they wait the second we're out of town to plan something like this?"

"They miss the boys, Mags. You're like Nazi Mom sometimes, you know? It's hard for them to get near them. It's not like my mom wasn't a nurse for forty-five years. Isaac will be fine."

My chest rose and fell. Flashes of the picture and that big bucket of popcorn consumed me along with Josh's words. *Nazi Mom?* I was trying to be the best mother I could. I loved those boys as if I'd carried them nine months myself. Why couldn't he see that?

I thought of our babe, growing in my womb at this moment. I'd been so excited to tell Josh, now I doubted how the two of us could properly raise a child from birth to adulthood when we couldn't even manage a two-night trip away.

Had we gotten caught up in a summer romance that had little power to last? Like Josie, had I been grieving Dad's death so hard I hadn't seen reality when accepting Josh's marriage proposal? Had he been so desperate for a mother for his sons that he'd chosen the first willing woman for the job?

"I don't think I want to go on this trip with you right now," I whispered. "Will you please take me home?"

I felt the weight of his gaze, but fixed my own solidly ahead, unwavering in my decision.

"Mags, come on. You can't be serious. We have the next three days. We're going to be there in less than an hour."

"I don't want to take this road with you right now." The weight of my words, and the meaning behind them, hung thick in the cab of the truck.

"I'm sorry. I shouldn't have said you were a Nazi Mom. I didn't mean it. Please, let's forget about the last fifteen minutes."

I refused to answer. Our problems were real. They weren't

going away, and despite all of his offers of counseling and morning coffee dates, Josh wanted to sweep them aside.

Suddenly, I felt every fiber within me collapse, as if the strength to forge ahead with this trip, with my marriage, was an insurmountable task. Like hiking Mount Washington in December. Plain hard. And maybe not worth it.

Josh drove another half a mile before veering onto a dirt pull-off and turning around. He looked both ways before turning in the opposite direction we'd come.

"We're not going home." He gripped the wheel, determination firm in his tone.

"I mean it, Josh. I don't want to take this trip anymore." *Not with you.* My unspoken words were no doubt plain enough.

"We're taking this trip." I'd never heard his voice so firm, so decisive. Not even when we'd disagreed over what endocrinologist to see for Isaac. Not even on that horrible Thanksgiving day when I'd been tempted to dose Isaac insulin without testing him first. "We're taking this trip, but first we're going to pick up your blasted hitchhiker."

"What? *Now* you want to be generous? *Now* you want to play the good guy?" I turned toward him, my hackles raised, ready for a fight. "Because that's what you're so good at doing, isn't it? Playing the good guy when things get tough. Help the hitchhiker when your wife is mad at you. Let your mom take the kids when I'm out of town. Give Isaac extra pizza when he gives you those puppy-dog eyes."

He shook his head, glanced at me as if I'd lost my mind. "I just want peace—is that too much to ask?"

"This trip was a mistake."

"We're not going home. Not like this. We finally have time to be alone together, to talk things out. We need to take it, Maggie."

"I'm not up to it. I can't—I need to cool off."

He ran a hand through his hair. "We should have gone for counseling weeks ago when I first brought it up."

"And when would we have done that? When you were teaching or gaining construction experience or building your dream house? When you were leaving me alone to take care of the boys?"

He was quiet for a minute, his jaw clenched, his foot pressing harder on the pedal. "Everything I've done, I've done for you. For you and our family. I love that you love my boys the way you do."

A sharp sting tore at my insides. A searing pain. Like the sharp talons of an eagle hooking into the core of my spirit, shredding it to pieces. "*Our* boys, Josh. Our boys. If you still can't think of it like that—then I'm not sure we're going to make it."

"Maybe we're not."

The words sharpened the pain, and I leaned toward the passenger door, wanting to get as far away from him as possible.

I'd thought there was no hole we couldn't climb out of if we climbed together. But what if we'd both lost the motivation to climb?

He dragged in a heavy breath, and I felt the car slow, felt my husband sober. "I'm asking you for a few days, Maggie. A few days. If you can't give me that—if you can't give our marriage that —then...maybe we need some time apart. Some time to rethink things."

Rethink things...like the last year and a half?

As much as I was angry, as much as I wanted to get away from him in that moment, the weight of his words struck me. Scared the daylights out of me. Is that what I truly wanted? For Josh to not be in my life? To not sleep beside him for all the rest of my days?

And yet, what right did he have to threaten me with ultimatums when he'd been the one to prove largely unavailable the last several months?

And what about the boys? What about our baby?

Outside, the snow whirled around the car, great big mounds of white rock and dirt on either side of us, billowing higher and higher into mountains.

The truck slowed. "Is that...?" Josh pulled to the side and turned the truck around.

I craned my neck, gasping at the lump of camouflaged clothes on the side of the road, fast covered in snow. "No...no, please, Lord, no."

We should have stopped. Josh should have listened to me.

Now, from the dire looks of things, we were too late.

✣ 28 ✣

Josh pushed open the truck door and planted one boot firmly in the snow as he pulled on his jacket. *God be with him.*

He should have stopped. He'd thought the guy was a threat, and now...had he aided in his demise?

He rushed over to the large mound of camouflage. The man lay on his side, knees curled upward. Ice clung to his bushy eyebrows and eyelashes. His lips held a bluish tint, though his cheeks still held color.

Josh pressed a foot against his back, wondered if the guy indeed was drunk, if that's why he'd been weaving in the middle of the road.

"Hey, buddy. You okay?"

Maggie hopped toward them as she pulled on one boot. "Is he...is he alive?"

Josh knelt beside the man. "I don't know." He felt for a pulse beneath the man's beard, found it there, faint but sure. This close, he looked more Maggie's age than Josh's. "He's alive. And he's breathing." He shook the guy's shoulder. "Sir, can you hear me?"

The man groaned but didn't move.

"We have to call for help." Maggie took out her phone. "No service."

"We're twenty miles from help, anyway. He needs heat and warmth. Now."

She put her phone away. "Then let's get him in the truck. I'll keep trying to call on the way."

Josh nodded. "Sir, if you can hear me, we're going to take you someplace safe." He lifted the man's torso, but it proved to be deadweight.

Without warning, the guy swatted an arm at him. "Not dead. Just want to be left alone."

Josh sat back, blinked. He looked at Maggie, whose brow scrunched beneath her white knit hat. He shook his head, at a loss how to proceed.

Maggie bit her lip, knelt beside them and placed a tender hand on the man's arm. "Sir, we want to help you."

"Don't need no help, ma'am."

"Buddy, I almost hit you a half hour ago. We saw you hitchhiking. Don't tell me you weren't looking for help."

The guy breathed deep. "That was you?" He looked to the sky, and let out a humorless laugh, addressing what appeared to be the falling snow. "You got me good, didn't you?"

The guy was cracking up.

Maggie scooted forward. "We all need help at one time or another. My dad—he died more than a year ago—he said asking for help was one of the strongest things a person could do."

The man shifted slightly, so he was more on his back than on his side. "Not sure how I feel about that one. I was kind of thinking God's help was to let me die right here."

Josh's gaze met Maggie's, something in them connecting in that moment. He wasn't sure what it was, or if he imagined it, but it was something. The pain exuding from the man, the way they could both relate. The humanity of it, swollen and festering.

They'd just been experiencing it in their little truck, wrapped up in only the small bubble of their life, their problems. But here, plain enough, was evidence that others walked the same road. Maybe not the same story, but the same heart struggles.

"What's your name?" Maggie asked. She'd always had a way of breaking through to the wounded. She'd been one of the first to break through to him, after all. He'd forgotten that about her. Or maybe he'd taken it for granted these last several months.

"Eric," the man said, quietly.

"Eric, can we give you a lift? Set you up somewhere? Maybe you should see a doctor."

The man rolled to a sitting position. "I suppose I could use a ride to somewhere that has a hot shower and a hot meal."

It took both Josh and Maggie to help the man to his feet. The massive guy trembled beneath Josh's support. In a few minutes' time, they had him in the passenger's seat of the truck, his gear beside Maggie where she squeezed into one of the small back seats of the cab.

"My clothes are a mess. I hate to make a spectacle of your truck."

"Nah, don't worry about that," Josh said. "We have two six-year-old boys. If we were scared of a little mess, we'd have been goners by now."

They settled back into the truck, the heat a welcome embrace from the biting cold of the air. Beside him, the man's teeth chattered. Josh turned up the heat.

Maggie cleared her throat. "So, what are you doing way out here?"

"Hiking the Appalachian Trail."

"Hate to break it to you, man, but you're quite a bit off the Appalachian Trail." A good eighty miles off.

"I know." The weight of the words seemed enough to break the man. He didn't offer more information.

"The Appalachian Trail, huh?" Maggie said. "That's a big deal, isn't it? My sister Lizzie loves to hike. She always talks about hiking the trail one day. Don't only one in four hikers complete it?"

Josh glanced in the rear-view mirror at his wife, grateful for her constant jabbering but a little bewildered by her abrupt change in attitude. She'd been so mad at him. Was this simply a show for their unexpected guest? Or perhaps he'd redeemed himself in her eyes by turning around to pick up the hitchhiker?

"Yeah...yeah, I think I heard that." Josh continued driving back in their original direction, toward Lincoln.

The man—Eric—cleared his voice. "That's right."

"Are you warming up at all? We have some extra clothes in the back. I'm not sure how wet your things are..."

"I'm okay, ma'am. It's right toasty in this truck and I appreciate the ride, so I don't need to go bothering you with anything else. I'll be warm in no time, I'm sure."

"Okay, if you're sure. So, how'd you get so far off track?"

For a moment, the only sound came from the snow hitting the windshield, the wipers swishing back and forth, and the hum of the heat circulating through the vents. Josh opened his mouth to assure the man he didn't have to share any information he felt uncomfortable with, but Maggie beat him to it. "Forget it. I'm too curious for my own good sometimes."

Josh's fingers itched to turn down the heat, but he forced them to stay on the steering wheel. Unfortunately, as their guest thawed, he also let off an unmistakable stench. From the smell of it, the man hadn't bathed in some time.

Maggie wiggled out of her own jacket in the back, and he caught himself trying not to stare in the rear-view mirror, trying to keep his eyes on the road. She was beautiful.

When had he stopped telling her that? When had he stopped noticing? For that matter, when had he stopped noticing everything special about her, from everything she did for the boys and for him, to all the spectacular work she did to help her family's bed and breakfast business? The way an endearing little snort came out of her when she laughed. How she insisted on scooping out the large cookie chunks in their cookies n' cream ice cream for him. How her favorite place to snuggle was in the crook of his arm. She was the type of woman who didn't know what it was to do something halfway. Why then, was she giving up on their relationship so easily?

Or was he the one who was giving up? He'd thought he was working to give her everything she deserved, but maybe what she needed he hadn't wanted to give. Maybe he'd been scared to give it, scared he'd drive her away as he had Trisha.

The thought didn't sit well with him.

Eric cleared his throat. "I was almost at the end."

"Of the trail. Is that what you mean?"

"Yes, ma'am. I'd traveled the entire thing from Georgia, started five months ago. Started too late in the year, but back then I didn't care. Only here I was in New Hampshire, nearing Maine, getting closer and closer to my destination, and yet not one foot closer to what I'd been looking for."

Josh swallowed, a part of him uncomfortable with the man's words, but also incredibly curious. "What were you looking for?"

He heard the man shift in his seat. "Can't rightly say. Something to latch onto, I guess. A reason to keep going. Hope."

"Hope?" Maggie asked.

What a hazy thing to look for on the Appalachian Trail. It was something he could picture Maggie's father looking for—something big and intangible in the midst of nature. Something philosophical or theological.

The violent chattering of the man's teeth had dissipated to a slight quiver. "When I started, all my hope had been drained out. As empty and dry as the Grand Canyon. I started this journey to try to regain it. Guess I thought I'd find it by the time I got to the top of Mount Katahdin, but here I was, almost two-thousand miles into my journey and no closer to my destination."

He dragged in a breath, as if he needed the energy to keep

talking. Maggie handed him an unopened water bottle and he gulped the water like he hadn't had any in days. "Thanks." He swiped a sleeve across his mouth. "I took a detour. A big one. I don't really know why. Sometimes I think God was telling me to, sometimes I think I was half hallucinating to think I should go east. Sometimes I think it was my own sentimentality. My wife... she used to visit Conway as a girl, talked about going there all the time."

More silence, but it was a sacred sort, as if speaking would ruin everything the man said.

"I thought maybe going there would help me find what I was looking for."

"Your hope," Maggie whispered.

"My hope," he agreed.

"Your wife...she died." Maggie appeared to have no hesitation in impeding on the man's history, and yet he had opened up in a way Josh hadn't expected.

"A horrible, freak accident. She was washing windows on a ladder. Five months pregnant. She fell...I lost them both six months before I started on the Trail."

A small sound came from Maggie, and Josh blinked back his emotion, all of it hitting a bit too close to home.

"I'm so, so sorry," he said, the weight of his wife's gaze on him.

"I can't imagine how horrible that must have been." A moment of silence, and then, "Josh lost his first wife in an accident, too."

Josh tightened his grip on the steering wheel. "There's no way we can compare what Eric went through to what Trisha did."

"I only meant—"

"Maggie, his wife died trying to clean windows. Mine died trying to get her next fix. It's not the same at all, and I can't offer him any advice or platitudes of wisdom, because if you can't tell, I've got nothing. Nothing."

His hands began to shake on the wheel and he immediately

regretted the words that had flowed from his mouth, in front of a mere stranger no less. "I—I'm sorry for your loss, Eric."

It's what everyone said, right? It was the right thing to say, the socially acceptable thing. To pretend he understood what it felt like for Eric to lose his wife was ludicrous. Why Maggie had pushed him into the conversation didn't make sense. He had no wisdom. He had no inspiring and hope-filled words. He wasn't like Maggie's father, or his, who was never at a loss for something to say—law school had seen to that. He was Josh. That's it.

But that, it seemed, was never enough for his wife.

29

I stared at my husband's profile, disbelieving how rude he'd been in front of Eric. And just when the man had started opening up to us.

I hadn't meant to imply that Josh had advice for Eric, only that he might be able to understand and relate to him.

I tried to think of something to say to make Eric feel less uncomfortable, but found myself at a loss.

"Pain is pain, I'm thinking." The big man adjusted himself awkwardly in the passenger seat. "Hurt is hurt. There's no need to compare. Sounds like the kind of hurt your first wife put you through is a heck of a lot different than the one mine put me through. But it's no matter. They're both real."

Josh didn't say anything, kept his eyes straight on the road.

The need to fill in for his lack spurred my words. "What'd you do for work before taking your trip, Eric?"

"Pastor."

"A pastor who's angry at God, huh?"

"Josh," I snapped. Seriously, what was with him?

"That's why I figured it was time to take a sabbatical. Besides, I was a pastor who never quite fit into the church. Not in the nice, neat way my congregants wanted me to, anyway. I was too radical for them, I guess. But I knew one thing was certain—I might not fit in with the church, but I always fit in with Jesus."

I turned in my seat again. "I think my dad felt the same way. But he stayed with the church because he was certain that's what God wanted."

Eric nodded. "Love God and love His people, including all the messiness that goes along with it. That's for sure. But after Selina, my wife, died, I needed time away. Time alone with the Lord to pray and grieve. And search. Only I haven't found what I've been looking for. Not yet." He looked out the window, sighed. "I'll go back to my flock, I suppose, if that's where the Lord's leading. But first, I have to find my hope. I can't go back there pretending to have my faith all perfect. I don't, and I'm done pretending. You know what it's like to feel as if you're putting on a show for people? Like you have to have all your ducks in a row and you're everybody's hero?"

I stared at the car console as Eric's words seared my spirit. Hadn't I just been doing what he spoke of? Putting on a show. And I'd been mad at my husband for not playing along. What would Eric have thought if he'd witnessed my little tantrum in the truck not thirty minutes before? While it might be good manners not to drag this stranger into our personal mess, me thinking I was above Josh just because I could hide the ugly from a stranger didn't make me a better person—it only made me more deceitful.

I licked my lips, wishing to shrink deep into myself. "Yes," I whispered. "I do."

He continued. "Back there on that cold road, watching car after car pass me and ignore me, I felt like a nobody. Like nobody cared. And would you believe that gave me relief? If that ain't the craziest thing you ever heard, I don't know what is."

I leaned forward. "Why'd you feel like that?"

"I suppose because, even though I walked miles of lonely trails to get here, for the first time, I was alone. Alone in the sense that

I didn't know where I was going or how I was going to get there when or if I did. And I started talking to God like I used to. Before I got too caught up in the ministry. Listening, too." He gulped more water. "I didn't realize it, but I'd been blaming myself for Selina's death. The babe's, too. She'd been asking me to wash those windows for weeks, and I'd found excuse after excuse to do something else. Build the baby crib, put in extra hours on my sermon, visit an elderly member of my congregation. An elder's meeting, then a mission's meeting. And then...I came home and there she was, on the ground beside the ladder, her neck all bent out of sorts."

I covered my mouth with my hand.

Eric sniffed, tears shining in his eyes, the ice on his bushy eyebrows long-ago thawed to droplets of water. "I couldn't be her hero. I hadn't been. I let her down, and I have to live with that fact every day for the rest of my life." He cleared his throat. "When I was walking back there, I said to God, 'One more car. I'll raise my thumb for one more car and then if they don't stop, I'm going to sit down and be done with it all.' But you know what Jesus said to me when I was laying on the side of that road, giving up and waiting to die? He reminded me that He'd already done all the hard work. That all I need to do is walk in His ways with His strength, but that I can't go around being anyone's hero. That's His job." Eric shrugged. "I was ready to die in peace accepting that fact. I thought maybe I'd finally found what I'd been looking for, my hope. Thought maybe I just had to die to get there."

"I hope we didn't ruin your plans." Josh said.

I couldn't tell if the man's bold preaching was getting to him.

Eric let out a hearty laugh. "You know...I admit, at first I thought you did. I was ready to meet Selina and my babe at the gates of glory, spend the rest of our days hangin' with Jesus. But something tells me that you were His plan. That one more car I told God I'd stick my thumb out for? That was your truck. After you about hit me, I figured I had my answer. I'm not sure I would have gotten up off the side of that road for anyone else. But since it was you two, I figured God was telling me something. He was telling me to live."

Huh. Maybe God was really using us. Or using Eric—I wasn't sure which. "We should get you to a hospital to have you checked out." I picked up my phone, but as before, no bars lit the screen.

"Oh, ma'am, that's mighty nice of you, but I'm not sure any self-respecting hospital will want me in their emergency room stinking like I do. You folks are fine enough putting up with me. Would you mind dropping me off at the nearest hotel so I can get washed up?"

Sunlight peered out from behind the clouds in front of us. An idea brewed within me. I caught Josh's gaze in the rear-view mirror, jerked my head toward Eric. He sighed. Then he nodded.

Something softened inside of me in that moment, for quite suddenly I felt the very thing Eric had been looking for all these months. Maybe it was Eric's words, his story, or the fact that God had used us. Maybe it was the fact that by some miracle Josh knew without words what was on my heart, that he didn't shut me down.

"Eric, how about a nice room at a beautiful bed and breakfast not far from here?"

"Well, I don't see as I have the money to swing a fancy joint like that."

I shook my head, hoped I'd truly read Josh right. "It's already paid for."

⚜

They dropped Eric off at the Mulburn Inn and insisted on picking him up in another hour or so to take him to get checked out. Though he wasn't overly comfortable with it, Maggie wouldn't hear otherwise.

Josh couldn't say he minded. Though part of him resented

giving up his room and his plans to the hitchhiker, another part of him felt okay with it. More than okay, maybe. He liked the guy. And if it wasn't for Eric, he and Maggie might be back home, going their separate ways.

Did he believe that? He wasn't sure. But he did know that now they were at least *in* their destination town. Spending time with Eric wasn't the worst thing. Maybe Maggie was right—it felt good to help a stranger. They'd take him to the hospital, maybe grab something to eat, and then they'd still have plenty of time with just the two of them.

Once back in the truck, Josh started it, blew warm air into his hands.

"Thank you." Maggie sat with her hands folded in her lap, stared at the many windows of the Mulburn Inn ahead of them, where Eric stayed in the room that had been intended for them. A room with a Jacuzzi.

Ah, well. "I'm glad we were able to help him."

The corner of her mouth closest to him—the corner he'd kissed on their date while sitting on those two chairs on the wharf —lifted. "Me too."

"Honey, I'm sorry about what I said. About everything. I don't want to argue with you. But sometimes...it's like I can't win, you know?"

"What are you winning, Josh?"

"This marriage," he whispered.

She opened her mouth, something like understanding overtaking her features. "You didn't lose at your marriage with Trisha."

He tried to keep in a snort. "I'm not sure what you call it when your wife loves drugs more than you and kills herself in a car accident—and almost kills your kids, too, but it sure isn't winning." He grasped for her hand. "Maggie, I don't wish I was in that marriage anymore for all the world. But it still haunts me. Every day. And when I fail you, I guess I get scared about what it could mean for us. For the boys."

She was quiet for a long time before her bottom lip started to tremble. "You're right."

His throat squeezed tight. It was hard for him to confess these things. He had to admit a part of him wanted Maggie to assure him that he wasn't failing her, that she was ready to stick with him through the thick and thin. But all he could remember were her words before they picked up Eric. She'd demanded he take her home. She'd claimed she didn't want to take this road with him. With their marriage.

Was this the end? Was this what he feared all along?

She sniffed. Tears pooled at the corners of her long eyelashes and he tamped down the urge to wipe them away.

"You're right because..." Her voice wavered, so vulnerable—so like anything he'd ever seen from his wife. "Because I was ready to run away from you. We had an entire three days to talk and I was ready to leave. To go back to the boys and the bed and breakfast and the fundraiser for Lizzie. Everything except work on our marriage. I can see why you're scared of me leaving, and I'm so, so sorry."

The last sentence merged with broken sobs and he reached for her, pulled her close.

Emotion clogged his own throat. "What Eric said about not being able to be a hero...that struck something within me. I couldn't save Trisha. No matter how much I loved her, supported her, no matter how many AA meetings I took her to, no matter how many times I searched the house for drugs. I guess I thought if I worked hard enough to give you everything you wanted or needed that I would save us the way I couldn't save my first marriage. Is that totally messed up?"

She buried her face in the crook of his neck. "Yes, that's messed up."

He tried not to let the words sting.

"But not anymore than me trying to be a hero by micromanaging every aspect of the boys' lives. By feeling I have to control everything. I was trying to be the perfect mother, to make up for Trisha. For you. For the boys. For myself, maybe." Maggie pulled her hand from his, clasped her small fingers together. "But it's like I'll never win in my head, either. She gave you those precious boys...and ever since that day I forgot to pick them up at school and your mom had to step in, I feel like I'm coming up short. Over and over again. I wish I had seen the signs of diabetes in Isaac. I wish I could have somehow prevented it all from happening."

His heart nearly broke in two at her words, at the pale, trembling lips speaking them. He had no idea the depth of her insecurities. Or how Trisha played into it at all.

He reached out a hand, stroked her cheek. "Mags...your blood—your womb—none of it is what makes you a great mother. It's your love. Honey, you love those boys more actively than Trisha ever did. You are their mom, through and through. There is no one—no one—who could do a better job."

As he spoke, the truth of the words settled deep. There *was* no one better for the boys than Maggie. He could admit that there'd been moments this past year-and-a-half that he hadn't trusted her with the boys. He'd trusted Trisha, after all, and she'd proven that trust misplaced.

But now, assuring Maggie of her worth as a mother made him realize how, despite the struggles they shared the last several months, trust was not an issue. Over and over again, he placed the boys in her hands. There was no one he found more faithful. There was no one who cared about Davey and Isaac more than their mother. Maggie.

A sob trembled up his wife's body, shaking his own arms around her. He'd never seen her so bereft, so broken.

"I'm sorry, Mags. I didn't realize...I should have realized. I had my priorities screwed up. Things will be different from now on, I promise."

"I'm sorry, too. I have been a Nazi Mom. I have been insecure when it came to your mother. I haven't trusted you or anyone with the boys. I haven't even trusted myself. I definitely haven't trusted God. All along I've been blaming you for not putting in the work of our family when I haven't been facing how I've been doing exactly what I've accused you of." She leaned further into him, and he couldn't imagine feeling anything better. "How are a couple of messed up parents like us supposed to nurture and grow two young boys?"

He pulled her onto his lap, nuzzled his nose in her hair. "With a lot of grace, I think. With doing what Eric said—trusting God for strength. Leaning on one another."

She blew out a long breath. "Instead of fighting with one another. I don't know, maybe we do need counseling."

"Or maybe we need to start listening to each other. Let's start these next few days, okay?"

"Few days? I'm afraid we've given up our room."

"Maybe we find a hotel, then. I saw another inn up the street. It doesn't have to be fancy, as long as I'm with you."

She smiled. "I like the sound of that."

❧ 30 ❧

I curled my fingers around Josh's as we walked into the hospital. We'd gotten a room at an adorable inn down the street. The smallest, least-expensive room available—one with no Jacuzzi—but one I hoped would prove a perfect escape for us to talk things through, to reconnect, and throw ourselves at the feet of God.

Together.

I dragged in a deep breath, prayed this wasn't like all our other truces. Prayed that we could cling to the truths the last couple hours revealed, that we could explore them deeper and ground ourselves in a commitment to our marriage.

I'd wanted to deny that anything could shake our marriage. I wanted to vow that I was in this for the long haul, that I'd walk through fire for our marriage. But our argument in the truck had proven my intentions. I'd wanted to run. Run back to my to-do list instead of choosing the hard task of working on my marriage.

I could tell myself tons of things that would make me feel as if I were doing the better job in our marriage, but in the end, I wasn't the one willing to put in the work.

I thought of the parable Jesus told of a man who asked both

his sons to work in the vineyard. One had said yes, but did not go. The other said no, but had changed his mind and went. I saw myself now as the son who had vowed to show up, but hadn't. I vowed to fix my marriage all too often, failing to recognize that in many ways, I was the one who had broken it in the first place.

Marriage was work. The vows I'd taken seventeen months ago didn't keep my marriage secure—rather, it was my continual choice to keep those vows. And sometimes, I wouldn't feel like it. That's when I needed to remember how impossible it was to rely on myself alone to save everything.

It didn't matter that I'd had stars in my eyes at the time of our wedding, that I hadn't been able to fathom any real struggle. I'd been naïve. But now was the time to work for the sake of my marriage, for the sake of my family.

"You two don't have to come in with me. I feel silly getting checked out to begin with." Eric almost looked like a new man in clean clothes and with the dirt scraped from his skin. He certainly smelled a whole lot better.

"We wouldn't feel right leaving you otherwise," Josh said. "You were passed out cold when we found you. At least get the go-ahead from someone who knows what they're talking about before continuing your journey."

Eric pulled open the glass door, held it for both Maggie and Josh. "I wish I could repay you two somehow."

I glanced at Josh. "We're the ones who should be thanking you."

Eric cocked his head and stared at us before shrugging and heading to the desk.

"Can I help you?" A pleasant looking woman with a mass of curly red hair smiled at Eric. He stepped forward, going on to explain some of what happened on the road.

The woman's eyes lit up. "You're hiking the Appalachian Trail? I've always wanted to do that."

I glanced down at the woman's name badge, my gaze snagging

on the four letters. No. Surely, I was reading too much into things. Fanciful thinking was all. But that name....

Hope.

I hid a smile as Josh and I sat in a corner of the waiting room. Eric filled out paperwork, then was led into the back. The pulse and thread of people coming in and out—some calm, some anxious, caused me to contemplate and pray in silence. So many people in this world, each with their own story and moments of pain and struggle.

Those who were hurt came to the emergency room. For the last several months, I too had found myself broken. Lost, and alone. But I hadn't sought help—from Josh or from God.

For the most part, I'd trudged on, depending ultimately on myself. But depending on myself alone set my whole world on a precarious cliff. I wasn't enough to stop myself from slipping off the edge and dragging those I loved down with me.

Nearly two hours later, Eric emerged from the back of the room, hospital bracelet hanging on his wrist and a wide grin on his face. "I'm healthy as a horse. Doc said I likely went into shock with the cold, but says he doesn't see any evidence of it as far as he can tell. I'm free to go."

I stood beside Josh. "That's great."

A burst of wind came through the door along with a frantic elderly woman. She held a large bag with trembling hands and wore a knitted cap. "My grandson was brought in by ambulance with my daughter. I'm here to see him."

Hope spoke to the woman in soothing tones, then directed her to sit while she searched for news. As soon as she sat, a floodgate of tears opened up.

Eric shifted his large frame from one foot to the other, his gaze settling on the woman and then coming back to Maggie and Josh. "I—I don't know how to thank you for all you've done for me. I can't explain it, but it was more than just picking me up from the side of the Kancamagus. I hadn't realized it, but I hadn't only struggled over my faith in God, I'd lost faith in humanity. I'd grown hard and bitter, run away from my calling." His gaze went back to the crying woman, so small on the seat, her booted feet barely touching the ground. "I can't explain it, but I think I'm supposed to stay here. I'm sorry you waited so long. You gave up your room for me...I don't know if I'll ever be able to repay you."

Josh shook his head, placed a firm hand on the large man's shoulder. "No repayment necessary. I'm glad you found what you were looking for."

Eric looked at the crying woman again. "I think I did."

We exchanged phone numbers and Eric assured us he'd be out of the room in the morning so we could enjoy our remaining night. As we left, I glimpsed him approaching the elderly woman in his humble way, talking to her in gentle tones.

"Do you think he really found what he's looking for?" Josh opened the passenger door for me.

I smiled. "Yes. Yes, I think he has."

His grin showed we understood one another. "You hungry?"

I nodded. "Starving."

We drove into the darkness. When Josh reached for my hand, I welcomed it. There was no use fearing the intangible. I had to trust God to stay with us though our angel in disguise was now gone.

❦

THE SIMPLE ITALIAN RESTAURANT WAS EXACTLY WHAT THE doctor ordered. Josh leaned back and stared at the empty pizza pan before them, napkins crumbled beside their plates. They'd called the boys before coming in to eat. Hannah assured them everything was under control, that they'd had a wonderful time at Josh's parents but were tuckered out and nearly ready for bed. After checking Isaac's blood sugars via their phone apps, they settled down for a quiet dinner.

He reached across the table to grasp his wife's fingers, the small diamond solitaire catching on the light of the candle. He'd given Trisha a ring with three diamonds, big and flashy. She wouldn't have settled for anything less. Besides, he'd been young and single. At the time, he'd had plenty of money in the bank.

By the time Maggie came into his life, his savings had been all but depleted trying to keep up with the boys' care and the mortgage on a modest teacher's income. He'd been embarrassed by offering the single solitaire, and yet he could still remember her precious reaction that hot summer night when he'd proposed.

They'd taken a walk down the rocky shoreline of Camden Hills State Park where the beautiful mountains met the harbor. They perched on one of the ledges, the waves not much but a gentle whisper near their feet. He remembered the weight of the ring in his pocket, how it was comfortable there after the last couple of weeks of waiting for the right moment. Sitting there with Maggie, the sun shining on her hair and illuminating her clear skin, his life was about to change.

She'd leaned against him. He'd taken her small hand in his, but words had failed.

She squeezed his hand. "I don't think I've ever thanked you for all you and your father did these last few months to help Mom with the details of the will and sorting through the insurance and stuff. You've been a tremendous comfort to her. I only wish I knew how to thank you."

"I could tell you how."

She shook her head and smiled but didn't play into his opening.

"The waves are quiet here." She closed her eyes, tilted her face to the sun.

He studied the gentle curve of her chin and her face, her high cheekbones and pert nose. The last few months had been a hurricane of Maggie. When he wasn't with her—when he was teaching or running the boys to his parents or to daycare—he was thinking about Maggie. What was she doing? Did she feel the same way about him? How it would feel to wake up beside her every morning, to go to sleep beside her every night?

He stared out at the calm water, the reflection of the sun caressing the surface. "It makes me realize how big the world is. How right now, in this moment, you are the closest person to me." He met her brown-eyed gaze and it snagged something deep within him. "And I'm the closest person to you. And I'm realizing how I want it to be that way. Always."

"Oh, Josh." Those sweet eyes searched his, back and forth, softening, as if he were the only other person in the world. "I feel the same way. I've never felt about anyone the way I feel about you."

He eased the ring from his pocket, hoped she didn't think it too small and simple, but rather a reminder of the meager love he offered. Meager, but brighter than the diamond solitaire shining brilliantly in the sun. "I love you, Maggie Martin. Will you marry me?"

Doubt passed like a shadow over her face. If he were honest, he'd expected her to jump into his arms and kiss him. But it was obvious. He'd failed to meet her expectations. It was all he could do to keep from shoving the ring back into his pocket...or throwing it into the ocean.

She licked her lips, her breaths heavy, her eyes on the solitaire. "I love you so much, Josh. But this isn't about just you and me. Are you sure I'm the right woman to mother your boys?"

"Mags, how can you not be the mother they deserve? They absolutely adore you. But you're right. You wouldn't just be marrying me, you'd be marrying my boys, too. If you don't see that in your future, then I get it." The corner of his mouth tightened. "Okay, I wouldn't. But I'd try to be understanding as I sobbed myself to sleep every night."

She laughed.

He sobered. "But if they're too much..."

She clasped her hand over his. "There is nothing I want more than you and your boys. I love you all so much."

His heart ricocheted beneath his ribcage as he lowered his lips to hers, tasting the hope of their future, deepening and cementing his intentions with each gentle probe of his mouth. Finally, he pulled away. "Is that a yes?"

She grinned up at him. "It's a yes."

Now, at the restaurant, her past smile dissolved into the pensive look before him. "You're miles away, Josh. What are you thinking?"

"About the day I asked you to marry me."

"Regrets?"

He pressed his fingers into hers. "Are you kidding?"

She shifted in her seat, clearly uncomfortable. "You ever wonder what might have happened if Trisha didn't die? If she got help or if she never became addicted in the first place?"

He wanted to lie. It would be easier for both of them. But he couldn't. She deserved so much more than untruths.

"I used to. A lot. The weeks and months after her death were filled with about a dozen-a-day 'what if's.' Then when I met you, after the boys were growing up so fast and life without Trisha was normal, it was hard to imagine what life *with* her would be like. I guess time does that, you know?"

She nodded.

"When I married you, Maggie, you were the light at the end of a very broken road. Like everything led me to you. Only I forgot that I came with my own brokenness. I was fighting to give you what I didn't give Trisha. I guess we're both still competing with her in our own ways."

"You never told me what happened to her. Not exactly."

He rubbed a hand over his face as his spirit bucked at the thought of going to that place. He'd told himself countless times it wasn't in Maggie's best interest. It wasn't in his, either. But if they were going to start down a new road with one another, perhaps it began here—with the bumpy, dirt one he came from.

"Trisha had back surgery after a car accident. We'd been married only a few months, but she needed the surgery. After that, the doctor prescribed pain meds. A couple of weeks later, she was still in a lot of pain. They couldn't find anything wrong but they kept prescribing the opioids. I tried to talk to her, convince her to get some help. I'd wake up at night to her sobs. She was in pain, though I don't think any of us realized it was emotional as much as it was physical.

"We went on two years like that, searching for answers, but finding none. When her doctor cut her off, she turned to other things—alcohol, street drugs. I couldn't keep up with it all and didn't know how she knew where to find the stuff. Two times she admitted needing help. We went to counseling and rehab and AA meetings. I thought we were making progress. When she got pregnant, she did so well. Stayed away from it all. I guess she found something else to live for. For a little bit, anyway. It was soon apparent she was severely depressed. I didn't love the idea of her being on antidepressants while pregnant, but I was also scared of what she'd do without help. She took them, and we seemed to find some sort of peace."

He closed his eyes, hating to go back, but pushing forward because he sensed this was the way to healing. "After the boys were born...well, twins are a lot for anyone. I took some time off to focus on our family. The boys were both colicky. Trisha had postpartum depression. Then her sister died. The doctor prescribed more pills. I was in over my head."

He dragged in a deep breath. "I had parent-teacher conferences at the school one night. By that time, it was normal for me to check the house for Trisha's hiding spots—under the mattress, under the refrigerator, the back of the toilet. I hadn't found anything for weeks. I thought she was okay. Not great, but okay. I left for the school. When I got home, the car wasn't there. We often used car rides to put the boys to sleep. But another hour passed, and I started to worry. When a police cruiser pulled into the driveway, I thought my life had ended. And it nearly had. She hadn't even buckled the boys into their car seats. She'd been so high when she hit that tree—had been driving so fast, that it was nothing short of a miracle that the firefighters pulled our boys out alive."

Emotion burned the back of his throat, and he couldn't continue. What more was there to say?

Maggie came around the table to sit in the booth beside him. She clung to his arm, buried her face in his shoulder. "Josh, I'm so sorry. I mean, I knew some of it, but...well, I didn't understand how hard it must have been."

He stroked her hair, thankful for the dim lighting of the restaurant which gave them privacy. "I wanted to pretend it wasn't a part of my history. But it is, and I guess that makes it a part of yours, too."

Maggie bit her lip before speaking. "I love every part of you, Josh. The good, the bad...the unpleasant. Because it all makes you the man you are today." She laid her hand on his face until he looked at her. "I don't need you to be enough for me by doing anything. You already are."

Something in his chest eased around her words. That may have been the most precious thing she ever said to him.

He kissed her softly, nudged her cheek with his nose. "Thank you."

She picked up the empty wrapper of a paper straw on the table, folding it accordion style. "I guess I've kind of had the same problem. Competing with Trisha, competing with your mom. I know I shouldn't feel threatened, that it's selfish of me, but it's like the boys have had three moms—Trisha, your mom, and now me. If I can't be the best one, where does that leave me? Where does that leave us?"

He pulled her close. "You are what's best for the boys, Mags.

There is no competition. But my parents love the boys, just like your family does. They would never do anything to hurt them."

She sniffed. "I know. Each of us brings something good to their lives. The bed and breakfast runs smoothly because we all pull together and work as a team. Our marriage should be more like that, but I haven't acted like it at all. I've acted like the wellness of the family is all my responsibility. I'm supposed to be the organized one, the sunshine maker. But it's hard sometimes, Josh. It's so hard."

He pulled her close. "You are not responsible for our happiness. Life can be hard and gritty. It can royally stink sometimes. I don't need you to pretend. I don't need a fake wife that pastes on a smile for me when she's hurting. Maybe if we can both learn to let go a bit and cling to one another instead of our own plans, we'll start to get somewhere."

She sat quiet for a moment against him. "Josh, I'm pregnant."

His fingers stilled against her arm. He couldn't have heard right. "What?" He gently shifted away from her so he could look into her eyes.

She gave him a small, unsure smile. "We're going to have a baby."

Excitement built within him like a wave tunneling onto the shore. "You're serious? You and me...a baby?"

She nodded her head. "It's a good thing, right? I'm terrified Josh. Please tell me it's a good thing."

He crushed her to him. "It's an amazing thing, Mags." He kissed the top of her head, caught an older couple staring at them from across the room. He grinned. Pointed to Maggie, then himself. "We're going to have a baby!"

The man let out a cheer, which started a small round of applause around the restaurant.

After it died down, Josh asked a slew of questions—when did she find out? How did she feel? When did she think the baby was due? She answered each one, the truth of her news anchoring in his spirit.

"I can't wait to tell Davey and Isaac they're going to be big brothers."

"It will be a lot." Maggie bit her lip.

"I'm going to be here for you, Mags. For all of our kids. I promise. Will you let me? Will you allow me to help shoulder the load?"

"Yes. I'll definitely work on that."

They were quiet another moment, taking in the ambiance of the dim lighting and candles around the restaurant.

"I'm scared," Maggie whispered. "What if we go back home and nothing changes?"

"That's not going to happen. And we have the rest of this trip to plan out how we're not going to let it happen."

She snuggled into him. "Plans, huh? You know I'm always up for a good plan."

❧ 31 ❧

The alarm on my phone jolted me out of one of the best sleeps I'd had in months.

Josh and I had talked into the night, had fallen into bed alongside one another, consumed with a passion born of our newfound commitment.

I scooped up my phone, my nerve endings coming to life at the alarm signaling Isaac's blood sugar was off. One-thirty in the morning. I looked at the numbers. Low. Very low.

With shaky fingers, I dialed my mom's cell phone.

Beside me, Josh rolled toward me. "What is it?"

"Isaac's low. His alarm went off." Hollow rings sounded in my ear.

Mom answered on the third ring. "Honey, what's the matter?"

"Isaac's alarm went off. He's low."

I heard Mom rushing around. The creak of bedsprings, the whine of a door. "I gave him some juice an hour ago. I'm going to him."

"Test him first."

"I'm in his room. I'm putting you on speaker."

I heard her talking to Isaac in soft, soothing tones. "Is he responding?" I tried to keep my tone calm.

"Barely." The fear in my mother's voice was enough to send me off the bed, pulling on clothes.

"He's low. Sixty."

Josh put a hand on my arm. "Talk her through this, Mags. He can't wait until we get there. He needs you now, guiding your mom."

I nodded, knew he was right. "Give him three glucose tabs."

"Okay." The tremor in Mom's voice came through the phone and my body grew hot with adrenaline.

"Grandma? Is Isaac okay?"

Davey.

"He needs some sugar," I heard my mother say. "Do you think you can wake up Aunt Lizzie and ask her to get him some juice?"

Good idea. Mom shouldn't be alone, and Davey needed a job.

"Mom? How is he?"

"Isaac, baby. Can you chew these?"

A groan. Isaac mumbling, saying his fingers tingled. The click of a light.

"He doesn't look good, Maggie. Oh—Isaac!"

My knees weakened. "Mom—Mom, what is it? Answer me!"

Lizzie's voice on the line. "Mags, I'm calling an ambulance. We think he might be having a seizure."

"Yes, do it. We're leaving now."

I kept them on the phone as I filled Josh in, swallowing down my tears and wishing with all that was within me that we could snap our fingers and be with Isaac.

We dressed, threw our things into the suitcase, and raced out of the room. Once in the truck, I listened to my mom broadcast every step of the EMT's coming upstairs to get Isaac, Mom climbing in the back of the ambulance.

"I want Mommy." The words weren't loud, but they were intelligible. They nearly broke me in two. Tears slid from the corners of my eyes as Josh drove as fast as was possibly safe down the dark New Hampshire roads.

"Put him on, Mom."

"Okay, here he is."

"Isaac, baby. We're on our way home, okay?" A small sound. "The doctors are going to take good care of you. Mommy and Daddy love you so much."

I started praying, my words pouring out from a desperate heart. I begged God to comfort Isaac, to wrap His capable arms around our little boy and help him not be afraid. I recited Isaiah 41 to him, promising him—and myself—that God was with us, that He would strengthen us and help us now, in our time of need.

"We're at the hospital. I'll call you as soon as I know anything, okay, honey?"

"Thanks, Mom."

I hung up and grasped for Josh's hand as he sped through the night. I shook my head, more tears gathering at the corners of my eyes. "I feel so helpless. I don't know what to do."

Josh squeezed my hand, and I leaned into him. "We pray the whole way. Trust that God will protect Isaac while we can't."

I sucked in a deep breath, felt a sense of comfort at Josh's words. "Okay."

He started praying then, and though he'd prayed with me before, this time I sank into his voice as he poured himself out to our Creator, his words echoing my own sentiments.

After a while, he grew silent, and I took over, falling back to small bits of memorized scripture when I ran out of words. Silence took up most of the car ride, each of us in our own thoughts, praying silently. I spoke to Mom a couple of times, and she assured us that Isaac was awake and coherent, that they were treating him for his sugar low, but that they planned a CAT scan and an EEG to rule out the possibility that the seizure he'd had was unrelated to his diabetes. Not likely, but something the doctors said was standard procedure.

I hated that we were so far away, that Isaac had to endure the pokes and prods of doctors and nurses without us by his side. I sank into the seat, closed my eyes, pictured myself placing our vulnerable boy into the large, secure hands of the Creator.

Over and over, with Josh's hand in mine, we lifted him toward God, knowing that some parents did this same thing and didn't receive their longed-for answer. But here, not only clutching the hand of God, but clinging to one another, I felt an otherworldly peace. There was nowhere else to turn. No one else I'd rather run to. No one I could trust more.

We drove into the hospital parking lot just as fingers of pink climbed the dawn sky. We raced into the emergency room. I clutched Josh's hand like a lifeline.

When we finally saw our son, I couldn't contain my sob. I told myself I needed to be strong for Isaac, I needed to be strong for everyone. Yet, I couldn't anymore. I couldn't, and for once, I was okay with it.

I kissed Isaac's warm cheeks, pushed his hair back from his head. "How are you, honey?"

He clung to me as if he'd never let go. Josh came by our side and wrapped us both in his arms.

I turned to my mom. "Any more news?"

"They said he had a slight fever when he came in. They think he's fighting off some sort of virus, that's why his sugar dropped so rapidly. I'm so sorry. I can't believe this happened. I feel terrible." She worried her bottom lip between her teeth, her face lined with the depth of creases I hadn't seen since Dad died.

I threw my arms around her. "It's okay. I know. We couldn't have handled anything better if we'd been here. It's so unpredictable sometimes." I looked at Josh.

Though I'd have felt better if I'd been here for Isaac, he would have still likely landed in the ER. If we hadn't gone to New Hampshire, if we hadn't traveled on the Kancamagus, then we'd have never met Eric and had the privilege to help him. He wouldn't have helped us. Josh and I wouldn't have had some important conversations. I hugged my mother tighter, a sudden peace—almost a knowing—coming over me. "He's going to be okay."

A short time later, they rolled Isaac away for his CAT scan.

"He's such a brave little boy." Mom stared at the space where his bed had been. "He handles it so well. He wanted you both, of course, but after he was conscious, he kept telling me he was fine, like he was more worried about me than himself. He's amazing, you guys. You all have gone through so much, but he's such a special boy to be able to put up with it the way he does."

"He sure is." Josh cleared his throat. "I'm going to step out. I'll be back in a bit. I have my cell."

I squeezed his hand, noting his sudden agitation. "Okay, honey." Maybe he simply needed some space. After I made sure my mom was okay, I'd go check on him.

I watched Josh walk out of the room until it was only me and my mom behind the curtain.

"We've had a rough last few hours," I explained. "Though yours certainly haven't been any easier."

Mom looked after Josh and twirled the wedding band she still wore around her left ring finger. "He's a good man. He loves you and those boys so much."

I nodded. "He does. Though we've struggled these last few months, I think we're finding our way."

"You will, honey. You will." Her tone echoed of far-off thoughts and while half my heart was with Isaac, I couldn't help but notice how uncharacteristically distraught my mother appeared.

"Is something wrong, Mom?"

She shook her head. "I suppose with everything that happened...I was so scared for Isaac. I haven't felt that alone in a long time. Being here, in the hospital...I've been missing your Dad all over again, I guess."

That's right. This very emergency room was where Dad had died, where Mom found out her other half had moved on to eternity without her. "I'm sorry."

Mom blinked. "Enough of that. I am well and fine. Isaac's the one we need to focus on."

I wrapped my arms around her. "I'm so thankful for you, Mom." Together, we huddled and prayed for my son. Life was unpredictable. It didn't always make sense and sometimes it was plain unfair and tough. But I'd spent too much of the last year focusing on what I didn't have. It was time to take stock in what I did—plenty of blessings through and through.

𝕊 3 2 𝕊

J osh gripped the pew in front of him, his forehead pressed against his hands. The quiet of the hospital chapel enveloped him in a cocoon of sacred space. He didn't know why he knelt here, the unforgiving surface hard against his knees. He'd prayed for three hours with Maggie on the ride back to the Maine coast. He shouldn't feel such an excessive thirst for this quiet, holy space, but he did.

He should get back to the ER. Isaac would return from the CAT scan soon. Hopefully they'd have results and be cleared to go home. Together.

An overwhelming feeling of gratitude rushed through him at all he possessed. He thought of Maggie and their conversation the past couple days. Of him wanting to be the hero, wanting to prove it by giving her stuff she didn't care about. Like bracelets and houses, when all she wanted was more of him. He'd left her to wade through the bulk of Isaac's diagnosis. Yes, he'd offered help —mostly when it was convenient. And she had shunned that help too often.

But that was going to change. *They* were going to change.

He'd seen how capable she'd been in guiding her mom last night. What would he have done without her?

He might as well ask what he would have done without half his heart, because that's what living without her would be.

God, I've messed up. Help me through this.

He hadn't felt this close to his Creator in a long time. He supposed pleading with the Lord for his son's safety during the last several hours had done that. But as close as he felt, something still hitched inside his spirit, stopping him from receiving the full blessing that was in this place of communion.

He groaned, knowing what he must do. He'd sensed it for too long now, had known his unforgiveness held him back. Trisha had given him two of his most precious gifts on earth, but she'd taken so much from him as well—the most notable being his confidence that he was enough for his family.

He stepped into the pain for a moment, allowing all of the hurtful memories surrounding Trisha to surge forth. The distrust, the horror, the betrayal. He realized that a small part of him believed her also responsible for Isaac's diabetes. If she had taken better care of herself before and during the twins' pregnancy, would his son suffer from an incurable autoimmune disease?

He'd never know. But he did know one thing. Holding onto these bitter feelings and nurturing them wasn't getting him or his family anywhere. It wasn't changing anything for the better. God wanted him to forgive. When it was hard, when it seemed near impossible. And yet, God also didn't expect him to do it alone.

Give me your strength, Jesus.

Eric had said he'd felt weak. That he needed to depend on a strength not of this world. Maybe Josh did, too.

It'd been a long time since he'd saturated himself in the very essence of God. But now, soaking in that grace and holy peace, he felt a mounting within him, a power not his own. Forgiveness was a decision before it was an emotion, and in that place, he felt the invisible Spirit stepping in and prodding him forward. Much as a parent might prod a child toward what is best.

"I forgive you, Trisha," he whispered into the blessed quiet. "And I forgive myself for not being able to save you. Thank you for giving me our boys. I'm letting you go now. Really and truly this time."

He released a wobbly breath, a lightness filling him. The authenticity of his words saturated, chains clattered from their hold on his spirit. Freedom.

"God, thank you." All he could feel was gratitude, pure and unabashed thankfulness. In that moment, he knew what Maggie had known back in the ER—that Isaac was going to be okay. That they were getting a second—or maybe it was a third or a fourth— chance. That mercy upon mercy had been given to them.

A warm hand landed on his shoulder, and he straightened.

"I thought I'd find you here." Maggie slid her arm around him, and he turned to her, burying his face in her waist, hugging her, letting foreign tears wet her shirt.

"Honey, he's okay. The doctors confirmed it's a virus that messed with his sugars. My mom said his stomach was off yester-day. But no epilepsy. He feels much better."

Josh nodded. "That's a relief."

She knelt beside him on the kneeler of the pew. "I love you, Josh. We're going to be okay, too."

He ran a finger down her cheek, brought her lips to his. He sank into her, the kiss meaning so much more with all the battle of prayer behind them, and the good news about their son. When they parted, he smoothed her hair from her face, the dim light of the chapel glistening in her eyes.

"We're going to be more than okay, Mags. I know it. There's bound to be hard times, but honey, it's nothing compared to what it'd be without you by my side. I never want to know what that's like, Maggie. Can we start over together?"

She smiled. "There's nothing I'd like more."

Then she kissed him, and he knew the gentle reassurance she intended in the gesture. He sunk deeper into the kiss, into the feeling that something new was beginning for them. Something that felt a whole lot like hope.

❦ 33 ❦

A generous crowd gathered in the large barn of Orchard House. I held the microphone, poised to speak, as Isaac fished out one of the raffle tickets in the large jar on the table to select the winner of our Instagram giveaway. He pulled out one ticket and held it proudly up to me. I smiled at the name on the ticket.

Perfect.

The concert had been beyond successful. Lizzie's new song evoked wild applause and requests for an encore, which my shy sister did indeed provide. She was most definitely coming out of her shell.

From the look of everything—and with the help of the gorgeous quilt Aunt Pris's quilting club had crafted—we'd raised enough money to get the art and music departments through another semester.

"Rachelle Nordic is the winner of our Instagram giveaway!" I searched the crowd, doubtful Rachelle was here but hoping my new friend might be present. "Rachelle has won a two-night stay in our Hawthorne Room. Congratulations, Rachelle!"

From the middle of the crowd came a woman in a black dress.

She beamed as she climbed the stairs. I presented her with the winner's voucher. "This is awesome," she whispered.

"I hope you enjoy. And we're still up for coffee soon, right?"

"You betcha."

I thanked everyone for coming, reported the amount we'd brought in with the auctions and the tickets to the concert. Cheers erupted and Lizzie and her band played one last song before the midnight countdown.

I descended the stairs and entered Josh's waiting arms.

"You did great, honey."

"Thanks. You did great last night yourself."

He pretended to stretch and preen. "Glad to know I still got some talent in the bedroom."

I slapped his chest. "With Isaac, you goose. Helping nurse that low blood sugar like a champ."

He tapped my nose. "And you did great letting me handle it and getting some sleep."

I smiled. "I'm not so sure you were worried about my beauty sleep. If you were, you wouldn't have woken me up like you did after Isaac was settled."

He nuzzled his nose in my neck. "Better watch out or I'll do it again, Mrs. Acker."

"I hope so, Mr. Acker."

I soaked in the moment, as Amie announced that we would begin the midnight countdown in one minute. Davey and Isaac jumped up and down with excitement at the anticipation of the New Year. Beside the boys, Josie and Trip and Amos, Lizzie, August and Amie, Bronson and a couple of his friends, Mom, Aunt Pris, and Ed Colton all gathered to end the year and begin a new season.

Might Mr. Colton sneak a kiss to Aunt Pris? Now wouldn't that be a memorable surprise?

A new year full of surprises. One I determined to give over to God before it started.

My first step had been earlier that night by agreeing to let Josh's parents take the kids next Saturday. And when Josh had told me news of a potential house buyer through a private sale agreement his father could arrange, I hadn't panicked—I'd accepted it as the beginning of the new. We'd find a place to live, even if it was in a camper on our new house lot. We would get through the messy because we would get through it together.

Josh's phone dinged and he looked at it and grinned. "Eric." He turned his phone to me. It was a picture of him and Hope in the waiting room of the ER, party hats on, a Christmas tree in the background. It read, "Just accepted a job as the hospital chaplain. Plan to finish hiking the trail in the spring—possibly with some company. Happy New Year!"

"Wow." I stared at my husband's handsome profile. "That's definitely something."

"I guess it's good we stopped for him."

I raised my eyebrows. "After some convincing, I might add."

He pulled me toward him as the countdown began. "We make a great team, Mrs. Acker. What do you say we keep teaming up for the rest of our lives?"

I placed my hand on our unborn child, and Josh covered my fingers with his.

I turned my hand so our fingers wound together. "I like the sound of being on the same team as you. Forever and always."

"Forever and always," he repeated, sealing it with a kiss that ended the year and signaled the beginning of forever.

NOTE TO READER

Dear Reader,

One of the reasons I love reading and telling stories is because of the precious gift they often leave us—the gift of empathy. Before writing *Where Hope Begins*, I understood very little about type one diabetes. In interviewing mothers and caregivers of children with type one, I began to glimpse the all-encompassing task of handling this disease. My respect for the children and parents who live with type one day-in and day-out has grown a hundred-fold. If that was the only blessing that came from this book, (which it definitely wasn't!) it would have been worth it to write.

In this story, the Orchard House bookshop features the products of Narratology. This is a true-to-life store with a beautiful mission. If you'd like to learn more, visit www.narratology.gives

If you enjoyed *Where Hope Begins*, I would be so very humbled and appreciative if you might leave a review on Goodreads or wherever you purchased this book (even a few words is helpful!).

I am beyond excited to introduce you to Book 3 in The Orchard House Bed and Breakfast Series, *Where Love Grows*, releasing fall of 2021. I hope you enjoy the following sample from Lizzie and Asher's story!

P.S. Be sure to join my newsletter and get a free short story! Visit www.heidichiavaroli.com

Where Love Grows
(Coming Fall, 2021)

PROLOGUE

Twenty Months Earlier

Asher Hill opened the email, adrenaline rushing to his limbs in the same way it did when he was heli-skiing or bungee jumping or placing first in a triathlon. His eyes skimmed the numbers in the report, landing on the bold one at the bottom of the page.

He jumped out of his chair with a hearty, primal shout of victory and pumped the air with his fist. The door of his office burst open. His best friend and president of Paramount Sports stood at the threshold. "Sales numbers that good, eh boss?"

"Yeah, buddy. Man, it feels good to be on top."

"We'll be saying the same thing at the top of El Cap by the end of the weekend." Lucas pocketed his phone. "Checked with the tech team, and they're all set to film. I'm heading out. See you tomorrow, bright and early."

"Sure thing."

"Don't work too late—the missus won't be happy." Lucas chuckled at his joke and closed the office door.

Alone, Asher leaned back in his chair and smiled. Hiring the new director of marketing had been a good choice, after all. Another few months like this and Asher would hand out hefty bonuses to his team.

He closed his eyes, and imagined climbing over the last ledge of the Dawn Wall in Yosemite. The rush. The scent of pure, fresh air. The feeling that nothing was impossible.

Though he'd never free-climbed the mountain, victory rushed through his blood already. Those sales numbers were just a fore-taste of the success to come this weekend.

Asher's phone rang, her name lighting up the screen. The fact that those five letters didn't make him apprehensive or urge him to run away was both foreign and strange.

He picked up. "*Mon cheri*," he said, low and seductive, already anticipating their time together that night—the scent of her long blond hair and the softness of her honey skin. How her laughter reminded him of a bubbling brook, or the sound of the first bite into a crisp apple.

"Asher Hill, I don't care if you are one of *Forbes 30 Under 30*. I don't care if you are the hottest guy I've ever dated...Asher, you do not stand a girl up—you do not stand *me* up—for dinner."

He looked at the display clock on his laptop and cursed. "El, I'm on my way right now. Just tying some things up at the office."

"You're always tying things up at the office."

He sensed what she doesn't say heavy beneath her words. *When are you going to tie things up with us?*

He shivered at the thought of marriage. "Give me twenty minutes."

"Tonight was supposed to be about us. What if you fall off the top of that horrid mountain and I never see you again?"

"Free climbing, Elise. It doesn't mean we don't use protective gear, we just don't use special gear to help us ascend. I'm not stupid. I'll be home safe and sound and into your waiting arms by Sunday night."

"Okay, but hurry over now. I want every last minute I can with you." Her voice turned husky. It stirred desire within him. "I promise I'll make it worth your while, especially if you leave your phone at the door."

"Oh, really?" He played into the game. "And how would that be? The hottest guy you ever dated deserves some details, don't you think?"

She giggled, and he thought of that bubbling brook again. Could this be the woman he was meant to be with forever?

"I'll see you soon, Mr. Forbes."

Asher hung up the phone while loosening his tie. He slid his laptop in his briefcase and walked out the door of his office. He passed down a long hallway, each room now empty, and into the reception area where a large professional picture of him hang gliding was suspended above the desk. *Asher Hill Takes on the World*, the *Sports Illustrated* headline read. The magazine had interviewed him about his hobby-turned-multi-million-dollar business.

On a normal night, he would stay a few minutes and enjoy the quiet heartbeat of the company he built, but Elise's words propelled him out the glass double doors.

He pushed the button to the elevator. It opened to reveal a grungy-looking fellow closing a guitar case. There was a music agency on the floor above Paramount run by a family friend of his parents.

Asher whistled long and low after getting a glimpse of the guitar. "That a Gibson?"

"Sure is, and it just got me an agent."

"Sweet. Congrats, man."

Asher's gaze dwelt on the guitar case. Someday soon he'd pick up his guitar. When things settled down, when he could be sure the company he'd worked to build could survive without his constant supervision.

He said goodbye to the guitar man as his phone rang out from his pocket.

His lawyer. Asher groaned. The man didn't call to make small talk.

"Ted, what's up?" He pushed open the door and entered the busy city streets of Los Angeles, vibrant and hopeful. As full of opportunity as it was of culture and diversity, greasy food and nightclubs.

He passed a man in ragged clothing with a cardboard sign asking for handouts and Asher dug into his wallet for one of the coffee shop gift cards he kept for such a purpose. He may have grown up privileged, but he always gave to the less fortunate. Life handed out hard turns, and he often wondered if he'd be where he was today if he wasn't raised in the home of his childhood. If he hadn't had the privilege of going to the best schools and getting a lesson on any sport he'd taken to at the moment. If his parents hadn't been so obsessively encouraging.

Thinking of his family reminded him of the deep-sea fishing trip he promised his younger brother Ricky the month before. Asher made a mental note to scour the internet tonight for a boat to take them out on the water. Tonight, after his time with Elise.

Ted's voice brought him back to reality. "Nothing good, sorry to tell you. You remember that lawsuit I told you about?"

Asher searched for a cab. The sky spat rain. The air smelled of wet pavement. "The guy with the prosthetic who claimed we fired him because he was handicapped when, in fact, he was smoking pot on our time?"

"That's the one. Well, I hate to say it, but it sounds like he actually has a leg to stand on. No pun intended."

Seeing a vendor selling flowers, he decided to get Elise a bunch to make up for his tardiness. He craned his neck to peer around the slight turn in the road. It was clear. "We spoke to the manager. Seemed straightforward to me. What's the issue?"

He pressed his phone to his ear and began to jog lightly across the street as the sky opened up.

Not until he was halfway across did he realize his mistake.

Elise hated flowers. She was allergic and would much rather have something tiny and sparkly, something that adorned the third finger of her left hand. She'd told him so last week.

He hesitated for a split second, thinking to turn around, hearing Ted's voice drone in his ear about a disability act and the guy with the prosthetic. He heard a horn and turned. Too late, he saw a car glossier than that Gibson guitar careening toward him. He tried to move, but for once, his body failed him. All he could see was the hood of the car, the Mustang logo in between the sting of raindrops. A scream overpowered the murky air, foreign and so filled with primal fear it couldn't belong to him.

And then, everything went black.

CHAPTER ONE

Present Day

I t wasn't the glossy black truck that first caught my attention. Nor was it the incredibly handsome face or the muscled arm that grabbed the coffee from the donut shop's drive-thru window. It wasn't even the fact that he may very well pay for my coffee again.

No, it was the gentle curve of the guitar case sitting in the back of the cab that attracted my notice. The window was clean, free of any stickers or adornments, and I could make out the cased neck of the instrument. I imagined those strong fingers on wood and strings, wondered what kind of music the mystery man played, if he leaned more toward rock or jazz, contemporary or country.

The girl at the drive-thru window handed the mystery man some napkins.

Seven Fridays in a row I had found myself behind the man with the guitar at exactly 7:48 a.m. in the donut shop drive-thru. The third week, I noted he wore no ring on the left hand that grabbed the coffee. By the fifth week, I had conjured up all sorts of exciting careers and hobbies for him—was he a park ranger somewhere in the White Mountains? Did he hike for fun, like I did? Perhaps he played in a band on the weekends. Perhaps he did charity work on the side—he was certainly generous paying for my coffee every week.

The rational part of me believed he must pay for the coffee of whoever was behind him each and every day. The irrational part thought that perhaps—despite the odds—this was *him*. The guy meant for me.

Not that it mattered, for I would never get up the nerve to talk to him. My younger sister Amie had been in the drive-thru line with me last week, had apparently seen "love" written all over my face, and promptly urged me to jot my phone number on a piece of paper so she could run up and hand it to him.

I'd been mortified.

"Come on, Lizzie. If he doesn't call you, it's not like you have to see him again. There are other coffee shops around town, you know." She scribbled my number on a torn corner of notebook paper.

"Amie, no." I said the words low, but with as much ferocity as I had ever mustered. Only because I'd come close to tears had she given up on the idea. But days later she continued to ask me about what she dubbed "Mission Mr. Coffee."

"The man of your dreams could be five steps away, and you're doing nothing about it!"

I now contemplated my dramatic sister's advice.

Five steps.

Not so far away, unless you're in a drive-thru line. I snuggled into the beat-up seat of my Honda Accord, the comfortable boundaries of metal and glass between me and Mr. Coffee. Surely it was illegal to get out of one's car in a drive-thru line, anyway? And if he wanted to introduce himself, wouldn't he have given *his* number to the girl at the window to pass on to me?

Not to mention that I would never consider pulling an audacious move like my sister suggested.

I studied the man in his side-mirror. Beard neatly trimmed and skin tanned, I could picture him hiking the White Mountains or Camden Hills State Park. Maybe even with me by his side.

He smiled at the girl in the drive-thru window, and I shrunk farther into my seat. My face heated as I pulled up to the window, the scent of coffee wafting from the building into my car.

"Woohee, he's a cutie, isn't he?" the girl at the window said, staring after the truck.

"Um, yeah." My hands shook as I fumbled for my cash. "How much do I owe you again?"

"It's paid for."

I couldn't hide my smile as I thanked the girl, took my coffee, and drove away, thinking what a beautiful, promising Friday it would most certainly be. I would go make music with my students. Tomorrow, I'd get in a good hike and spend plenty of time in the garden. And I'd do it all while savoring the possibility that maybe one day, Mr. Coffee would indeed pass his number back to me in the drive-thru line.

❀

IF THERE WAS A TIME TO BE LIKE MY SISTERS, IT WAS NOW.

I opened my mouth, pushed forth words that jumbled on my tongue. "But Mr. Snizek, I don't understand. I thought my working as a volunteer this past spring would help the music program survive at least another year. After our New Year's Eve fundraiser..."

The older man with a slight paunch looked around the small music room where I had taught for the last year. I followed his gaze, took in the piano where I'd instructed students. The guitars standing at attention along the wall. The cases cradling brass. The drum set, which attracted many a preteen boy.

"I'm afraid it's not my decision. It's the board's. Apparently, keeping the program is too much money, even with you volunteering your time. They want to give the kids a good start in learning a language, or perhaps begin a career and computer class."

"But the kids...they need music."

"I'm sorry, Lizzie. Maybe we can plan an after-school music program in the fall for students who'd want to participate. We could charge a small fee to make it work, and that way, you'd actually get paid."

I swallowed down more protests. If I were Josie, I might argue with the principal. If I were Maggie, I might plan another fundraiser on the spot. But I was not like either of my smart, outspoken older sisters.

In truth, working for free wasn't working. I had school loans to pay. I had dreams to achieve. Dreams that required money.

But the kids...my family...they'd worked so hard on the fundraiser. I hadn't summoned the courage to tell them we didn't raise enough money for both the music and art programs, or that I volunteered my part-time hours to finish out the second semester, living off the small amount I earned from the family bed and breakfast.

Now, though, it seemed my career hinged on the hazy potential of an after-school music program. It could be a blessing to a few kids who loved music and whose parents would lay down the money, but not a way to make a living.

"I understand," I whispered, even though I really didn't.

❦

"IT'S OKAY, LIZZIE. YOU'LL FIND SOMETHING." MY BROTHER Bronson shoveled a heaping fork full of blueberry pancakes bathed in maple syrup into his mouth.

"You could apply to other schools." Amie sipped her coffee. Her blond hair piled neat on her head, makeup done to perfection, despite the fact it was Saturday morning.

"I looked. No one's hiring a music teacher within seventy-five miles."

Josie dribbled syrup on her pancakes. Nine-month-old Amos sat on one knee, eyeing the pooling syrup with interest. "Would another fundraiser help?"

I blew out a long breath. "The music program can't live off fundraisers."

Across the open floor plan and from the nearby kitchen, Mom carefully arranged two pancakes on a plate and sifted confectioner's sugar on top. She placed two sprigs of lavender on the side, did the same with another plate, walked over, and handed both to me. "For the Neilsons."

I breathed deep, preparing to greet our guests. The first few months after the bed and breakfast opened, Mom served the food. I'd been so scared of dropping a plate of culinary perfection or speaking to so many strangers at once. Only seeing Mom completely overwhelmed in the kitchen one morning had prompted me to offer to serve the food.

Our method saved Mom's sanity, and so I continued. I took one table at a time, focusing on a singular task before planning my next move. Whatever it took to get through the breakfast rush.

I licked my lips and walked through the butler's pantry that separated the kitchen and our living quarters from the main living area of Aunt Pris's Victorian home. We'd turned the old house into Mom's dream—The Orchard House Bed and Breakfast, complete with author-themed guest rooms and a five-course breakfast. Pride filled me at the thought of all we'd done, and all we continued to do.

Two plates in hand, I pushed open the door of the pantry with my shoulder, finding the middle-aged couple at a table-for-two near the fireplace. I forced a grin. "How was the coffee cake?"

Mr. Neilson patted his stomach. "I dare say you've managed to ruin every breakfast for the rest of my life. We sure are spoiled here."

I placed the two plates on the laced paper placemats and cleared away the fruit dishes and coffee cake plates. "We're glad you're enjoying your stay."

"Pardon, dear? I couldn't hear you." Mrs. Neilson leaned closer to me.

I forced my shoulders back, pretended I was outspoken Josie or graceful Maggie or endearing Amie. Any of my three, outgoing sisters. I projected my voice. "We're glad you're enjoying your stay. Can I get you anything else?"

"Perhaps more coffee?"

"Absolutely."

I scurried back to the kitchen, making brief eye contact with the other couples at the tables out of my peripheral vision and giving them a slight nod of acknowledgement.

"The Marsdens just sat down," I told Mom upon entering the kitchen.

Mom glanced at the orders our guests had indicated the previous day, tacked neatly to the refrigerator. "They both want the Eggs Benedict."

I checked the bacon crisping in the oven. "Almost done."

Mom whisked melted butter and egg yolks together for her Hollandaise sauce. "Hey, Lizzie...we can talk about this after breakfast, but with spring upon us, not to mention solid bookings, I could pay you a bit more. Perhaps we can do some flowers along the landscaping to spruce up the place? If you wanted, that is."

My heart near burst at her words. "Really? I would love to help with that. But I don't want you to pay me more. This place is still new. Let's let it sail for a year before you start giving raises."

"Not a raise so much as more hours. If you're doing more work around here, it's only right you're paid for it."

I kissed my mom on the cheek, grateful for her efforts. "That sounds great. Let's talk later, okay?"

"I'm out." Bronson rinsed his dishes in the sink before loading them in the dishwasher. "Wish me luck with the kid I'm tutoring this morning. He's a doozy."

Josie knocked the brim of Bronson's hat with a flick of her finger. "You weren't a star student yourself, if I remember. You'll relate to him just fine."

I tickled Amos's belly. "Need me to watch the bookshop today?"

"Can you stop by around lunch so I can feed this guy?"

"Sure thing."

My older sister studied me. "You feeling okay? You look a little pale."

"Never better," I brushed Josie off, hating the extra attention that an eight-year-old illness still managed to muster in my family.

I escaped to refill Mrs. Neilson's coffee. As much as serving strangers intimidated me, it was better than succumbing to the over-zealous concern of my family.

CHAPTER TWO

I *'m still me.*

    Asher Hill ground his teeth against the sentiment as he used his arms to propel himself out from under the hood of his truck.

I'm still me.

It was something his doctors reminded him about a lot. So did his therapists—all of them. Physical therapists, occupational therapists, recreational therapists, psychotherapists, even his family who *thought* they were therapists.

But he had trouble believing those people. All of them.

Because he wasn't really still the Asher Hill who had walked out of the offices of Paramount Sports the night of September 22nd, twenty months earlier. He was another version altogether. A version who couldn't bungee jump or run marathons or climb the Dawn Wall. Heck, he couldn't even go to the bathroom like he used to. If he was any type of version of Asher Hill anymore, it was a very different version. A flawed and broken version.

He pushed himself to a sitting position on his creeper seat and craned his neck towards his workbench, searching out the headlamp he'd forgotten to bring beneath the truck. He spotted it, right beside the radio that played *Don't Stop Believing*.

Yeah, right. Believe in what? Believe in who? Certainly not himself anymore.

No doubt about it. He'd taken his legs for granted. What used to be a quick jump up and walk over to a workbench to grab a forgotten tool was now a project and practice in patience. He backed himself up to his chair, locked the wheels of his creeper seat, placed his hands on the handles of his wheelchair and used his arms and abs to lift himself up and backward. His skinny legs dragged behind, and he raised them one by one onto the footrests.

Elise had tried to stick around. She'd made it three months after the accident. In the end, she blamed leaving on his poor attitude. She said *he* was the one who had pushed *her* away. Though he couldn't deny it, it didn't make the wedding invitation sitting on his low, custom-built kitchen counter any easier to bear.

Elise and Lucas.

Ouch.

Some best friend. Good thing Asher didn't have to see his face at the office anymore, day-in, day-out. Weekly virtual conference calls were so much easier than Monday through Friday in-person meetings.

After grabbing his headlamp and lowering himself back on the creeper seat with his tools on his chest, he shimmied beneath the engine. He placed a container beneath the oil pan before using his ratchet wrench to unscrew the drain plug. Oil streamed out.

He positioned his wrench to unscrew the filter but struggled to loosen it. Readjusting his grip, he thrust his muscle behind the tool. His oily hands slipped off the wrench. His knuckles smashed against the truck frame.

He cursed good and loud, shaking out his hand.

He could have simply gone to his mechanic, but he liked accomplishing what he could himself. He thought he did, anyway. Especially when it came to his truck—one of the only places where no one could see the brokenness of his body. He could smile at the kids making faces at him from the back of a school bus, sit at a crosswalk to allow an elderly lady to pass by, or buy a coffee for the car behind him. No one had to know.

Asher Hill takes on the world. Ha, what a joke.

He was far away from it all now, both in physical distance and physical ability. Far away from the family and the friends he'd grown up with. Far away from Elise and his corporate office.

He could still hear his mother's voice from their latest conversation.

Come home, honey. We'll give you your space. We promise.

But it wasn't so much about space. It was about navigating this new life away from pitying eyes. It was about finding his way. Alone.

Piano Man ended on the radio and the morning show DJ came on, announcing it was time for their *Connections* hour.

The DJ's voice rang through his garage, loud and clear. "We have Lizzie from Camden on the phone. Let's see if we can help her find her drive-thru dreamboat today. And if so, will it be a connection or a misconnection? Lizzie, why don't you go ahead and tell us about the man you're trying to find. Perhaps he's listening right now."

Asher positioned his wrench again, placed as much pressure against the tool as possible. Still, it didn't budge.

"Hey, Melanie. Thanks for giving me this chance. So, I've been going to the donut shop on the corner of Elm and Norwood Street for the last several Fridays and I happen to be behind this man in a truck. And every time he pays for my coffee."

Asher lowered his wrench, interested. He did go to that shop every morning, as it was right down the street from his house.

"Oooh, so we have a chivalrous hero providing a much-needed morning dose of caffeine. Consistently, too."

The woman on the phone laughed. "I'm sure he must do it for whoever is behind him, but I'd love to find him and thank him in person. Especially since I've been the one behind him for the last seven Fridays."

The DJ's sultry voice came out over the airwaves. "Coincidence? I hope not for your sake, Lizzie. Could you give us a description of the truck, or of this man so, if he's listening right now, he'll know we want to find him?"

"Well, he's in a black Chevy Silverado. He's pretty cute. I think he has a short beard." The woman on the phone giggled, and Asher rolled his eyes. If she only knew.

He wiped his oily hands on his shirt, raised his wrench again, twisted hard.

"Oh, and he has a guitar in the back cab of his truck. That really caught my eye because I play guitar, too. I like to write songs."

Again, his hand slipped and he banged the same knuckle, cursing up a blue streak as he pushed himself out from beneath the truck.

On the radio, the DJ put out a call for the handsome coffee shop man in the Chevy Silverado with a guitar in the back of his truck.

Asher wiped his hands on a rag, noted his bleeding knuckle. He thought of the woman on the radio, searching for him. She sounded nice enough. Maybe in his former life they could have dated. Maybe it would have turned into something. Or maybe not. What kind of a girl was desperate enough to call into a radio station about a man who bought coffee for her in a donut shop drive-thru?

He thought of the wedding invitation with Elise and Lucas's names in elegant script at the top. His knuckles burned. He looked with scorn at the dead weight of his useless legs.

He dug in the pocket of his wheelchair for his cell phone.

Better to set things straight for this girl now before he passed her at the coffee shop again.

❦

AFTER I FINISHED THE BREAKFAST RUSH WITH MOM, I ESCAPED to the gardens to weed. Later, after I cleaned the guest rooms, I'd head out for a hike. Maiden Cliff, probably. There was nothing like a dirt trail beneath my feet and a canopy of trees to inspire a song in my head. I grabbed up late-spring weeds by their roots and shook off the dirt, quietly singing the song I'd started writing last week.

My deepest song to date, I was trying to tap into some of my own insecurities and fears, to travel to places I hadn't yet taken my music. Perhaps the music would heal some of those old fears inside myself.

My hand found the scar at my neck, the spot where they'd taken out my thyroid when I was fifteen. In my head, I knew the cancer could come back at any time, to any part of my body, but in my heart I knew I'd been healed. That God had given me victory over the illness.

While I wanted to sink into that, my family—by means of their sweet attention—had rendered me weak. Everyone looked out for me, and while I loved them for it, I couldn't help but wish they'd throw their extra attentions around Amie or Bronson. Hover over someone else for once. I was strong. I felt it. If only what I knew inside showed on the outside.

It was one of the reasons I loved hiking. Alone in the woods, conquering mountain upon mountain, I proved myself tough, resilient. There, victory and healing sank deep in my bones. While my family sometimes inadvertently confirmed my weakness, the mountain trails confirmed my strength.

I chastised myself for the ungrateful thoughts, turning my attention back to my song. If there was any fear left within me— and I knew there was—the music always drowned it out, made me forget. Like the voice of a sweet friend, it called and assured.

I sank into the song, singing the first verse over and over to myself, hearing the melody and the tune playing on my guitar, trusting the next line to enter my mind in time.

"Lizzie!" The scream snapped me from my song and my work. I jumped up from where I'd knelt beside the raised herb beds, the scent of thyme and basil fresh in my nostrils.

Amie ran toward me, phone in hand.

"What's the matter? Is it Isaac?"

Maggie, my oldest sister, had a son who'd been diagnosed with type one diabetes last fall. He'd been doing well, but I still remembered the rough start, the hospital trips, the fickleness of the disease.

Amie shook her head, eyes wide. She smothered the phone in her sweater. "Don't be mad, okay?"

"What?"

"I—I called the radio station. You know how the morning show has a *Connections* hour?" The corners of her mouth inched up into a smile she tried hard to contain.

My breaths came fast and hard, my knees weakened. "Amie, no. What did you do?"

"It's only because I love you and I want to see you happy." She studied me, air in her cheeks. She let it out in one whoosh. "I pretended to be you. I told them about Mr. Coffee. Lizzie, he called in! He's on the phone right now and wants to speak with you."

"Amie, no. How could you?" If I was the type of person to see red, the brightest scarlet would have flashed before my eyes. Instead, I knew only betrayal. Horrible betrayal. And fear. I was no stranger to fear, but this...this was paralyzing. Tears pricked the back of my eyelids. I shook my head, wanting to deny the last thirty seconds. "No. I am not talking to him."

"Lizzie, he called in. If he wasn't interested, he could have ignored you. This could be your chance. The chance to meet the guy of your dreams! Take a risk for once."

Take a risk for once.

"I can't. You already pretended to be me. Why don't you keep it up? Maybe he's *your* dream guy."

She shook her head, held out the phone. "He's waiting, Lizzie."

I looked at the phone, the seconds ticking off, the red circle bright and inviting at the bottom. I should reach out and tap the button to end the call. Sever this nightmare and any chance I had with the handsome guy in the pickup.

A pickup with the potential for off-roading adventures and cozy camping trips. A guitar with the potential to play romantic love songs. Unbidden, an image of a crackling campfire and the handsome stranger strumming a guitar came to mind, effectively weakening my resolve.

I stared at the phone, my heart knocking hard against my ribcage.

Take a risk for once.

If I didn't take this call, would I forever wonder? I'd just been thinking how I was stronger and braver than others saw me. When the chance came, would I prove it, or would I slink away with my tail between my legs?

ACKNOWLEDGMENTS

A huge thank you to Becky Van Vleet and her daughter Liz Van Vleet for taking the time to answer my many questions surrounding type one diabetes and for sharing their experiences so openly with me. Becky, thank you for reading the manuscript through. Any mistakes contained within the book are my own.

Another thank you to Heather Tyler for answering yet more of my questions on what it's like to be a mother of a child with type one diabetes. Your insights were beyond helpful, Heather. Thank you!

To brainstorming and editor extraordinaire, Melissa Jagears, for your continued help and brilliant insight. I'm convinced this book would have fallen flat without your help, and I'm so grateful for you!

Thank you to my agent, Natasha Kern, for giving me confidence to start this series. Thank you to my critique partner, Sandra Ardoin, for pointing out some tough early truths, and to my mother, Donna Anuszczyk for her important last-minute edits.

Thank you to Doug and Louise Goettsche, who own our favorite inn, the exquisite and charming Cornerstone Victorian

Bed and Breakfast in Warrensburg, NY. Not only are Doug and Louise fabulous hosts, they were beyond generous in answering my many questions and sharing their experiences and stories with us. The Orchard House Bed and Breakfast (including Hannah's five-course breakfast) is modeled after the Cornerstone Victorian. I highly recommend a stay!

Thank you to my sons, James (who after a bout of boredom decided to give my dual timeline books a try and was actually impressed—yay!) and Noah, along with my husband Daniel for never getting sick of my story obsession. I love you all so much! Lastly, thank you to the Author of life for allowing me the privilege to create in this manner. May all glory go to You.

ABOUT THE AUTHOR

Heidi Chiavaroli (pronounced shev-uh-roli...sort of like *Chevrolet* and *ravioli* mushed together!) wrote her first story in third grade, titled *I'd Cross the Desert for Milk*. Years later, she revisited writing, using her two small boys' nap times to pursue what she thought at the time was a foolish dream.

Heidi's debut novel, *Freedom's Ring*, was a Carol Award winner and a Christy Award finalist, a *Romantic Times* Top Pick and a *Booklist* Top Ten Romance Debut. Her latest dual timeline novel, *The Orchard House*, is inspired by the lesser-known events in Louisa May Alcott's life and compelled her to create The Orchard House Bed and Breakfast series. Heidi makes her home in Massachusetts with her husband and two sons. Visit her online at heidichiavaroli.com